AFTER
OUR FALL

CRAIG L. HAYES
PURE LOGIC PUBLISHING
ENTERPRISE, UTAH

Copyright 2020 Craig L. Hayes

All rights reserved

ISBN-978-0-578-57185-0

Published by Pure Logic Publishing

PO Box 117-257 South 300 East

Enterprise, Utah 84725-0117

CraigLHayes.com

LIBRARY OF CONGRESS CATALOGING-IN-

PUBLICATION DATA

AFTER OUR FALL

ISBN-978-0-578-57185-0

Edited by Linda K. Hayes, Sharron Leavitt, Chris M. Allen

and Kelli Wolf

Book layout by Victoria Hart at Pink Kitty Creative

Printed in the United States of America

For more information visit: CraigLHayes.com

10 9 8 7 6 5 4 3 2

TABLE OF CONTENTS

Acknowledgments V

Dedication.. VII

Foreword IX

Preface XI

First Interview 17

Second Interview 39

Third Interview 57

Fourth Interview 79

Fifth Interview.....................................111

Sixth Interview 147

Seventh Interview 167

Eighth Interview 197

Ninth Interview................................... 207

Tenth Interview 251

Eleventh Interview............................... 257

Twelfth Interview................................ 275

Epilogue..321

ACKNOWLEGEMENTS

There are about 83,000 words in this book. I could use another 83,000 words and only begin to express my appreciation for those who gave of their time, skills, knowledge, and passion for this work. I think it only proper and right for me to tell each of them how much I value them.

Linda. You are the first in line to read and edit my work. You find the first batch of misspelled words and incorrect paragraph usage. Thank you for your help.

Sharron. Thank you for using your experience as a school newspaper editor and finding better words and phrases to replace my sometimes bland story lines. Thank you very much once again.

Christine. A very warm welcome goes to you as the newest member of the editing team. Thank you so very much for your time and the skills you applied to this work. Your experience and input as an English Teacher, journalism advisor, and creative writing teacher has been priceless.

Kelli. It took me what seemed like forever to get you on board due to the sheer magnitude and scope of this book.

Sorry if I drive you crazy for being so picky. I want you to know I deeply appreciate your input and dedication to making this the story that it is. Thank you.

Victoria. You always deliver a superior product in every book of mine you design. Thank you for your mad graphic skills.

My endless appreciation and deep gratitude goes out to each of you.

"My Editing Team" My wife Linda, my mother Sharron, my newly added secret weapon Chris, and Kelli, my dear friends, thank you for helping me make this very important project a timely reality for the sake of our Representative Republic.

Love,
Craig

DEDICATION

I dedicate this story to my daughter Sharron-Marie. Like her father, she is a history buff and stout originalist when it comes to our nation's Constitution. I am proud of your accomplishments including your work ethic, getting your college degree, and being a great wife to Evan. You have given your father four of the most wonderful little people on the planet as grandchildren.

My dearest babygirl, I wish I had spent more time with you as you were growing up. I take solace in the fact I have spent the last year within these pages with you while I wrote this book. Stay strong in your core beliefs as a Constitutional Conservative and always maintain your love of this most precious nation. I hope you will always remember your Dad loves you very deeply.

FOREWARD

Having or not having a formal education does not determine knowledge or the capacity to learn. When college was not in his future, Craig chose self education in numerous diverse subjects.

As roadblocks appeared, he found detours around them or built bridges over them. When visual challenges occurred, he increased the pace and urgency of his writings and studies while continuing to work and provide for his family. Quitting is just a word in the dictionary.

Through the years, and on a weekly basis, we have discussed and dissected many subjects. I approach these subjects with my beliefs and opinions. He often shares those beliefs but supports them with facts.

Religion and the love and pride for America have always been the priority subjects for Craig's research. He knows America is exceptional and is a gift and a blessing from a loving Heavenly Father and it must be treasured. His children were encouraged to study and memorize the Declaration of Independence and other founding documents with the hope they would develop an understanding and a desire to defend this amazing country and its purpose.

This is a story that serves as a lesson in American history. I experienced a transition from a review of past historical events to occurrences commencing with World War II that I lived through and are now included in my memories.

It is about hope, love, and renewal. When the Lord's children do not obey and defend His gifts and blessings, He, as a loving parent allows them to experience the consequences of disobedience. As dreadful as this will be, there will be the opportunity for those that survive to start anew.

Just as the Pilgrims sailed to the Promised Land with hope to live free and righteous lives, our posterity will have the opportunity to begin again.

Sharron Y. Leavitt

PREFACE

The final push and full frontal attack on our rights is being waged this very day.

Every empire collapses. There is no exception to this rule. Some of these empires last for decades, others last for centuries. None stay at the pinnacle of power and influence for a millennium. The one thing all empires have in common is after they collapse, they never return to their former power and glory. This grand experiment we call the United States of America is, as of this writing, 244 years old. Is the U.S.A. like all other empires or are we able to disprove history?

This story, which is in the form of 12 interviews, takes place some 10 years 'After Our Fall,' or the collapse of the American Empire.

Since the founding of America, there have been opposing forces at work determined to undermine, dismantle, and eventually destroy this nation. These malevolent forces have for the most part been frustrated in their designs for the first 140 years of our Republic. In the early 20th century the *Progressive Movement and Agenda* was unveiled. The *century long push* to implement their agenda was launched by true believers in this ideology. *It is important to recognize this agenda throughout this book.*

During the interviews depicted here, Sharron Emmatay, a Historical Librarian with the Department of History and Records is being given a brief history of this nation by the *un-named* interviewee/narrator. This history, behind our history, shows all who read this story how our nation had been manipulated and shaped throughout our history by people with self serving, evil intent.

There are many ways to describe evil. The desire by anyone to control another person's thoughts, actions, and future is evil. The destruction of liberty, free will, individualism, freedom, or any other actions depriving an individual of their God given sovereignty is evil. The political ideologies and agendas that seek to do these very things are all inherently evil. The names of these doctrines are *Progressivism, Socialism, Fascism, Marxism, and Communism.* I also include in this list almost all *monarchies.*

It would be easy to blame the *'fall or collapse'* of our nation on any or all of the aforementioned ideologies. I believe this would be intellectual laziness. The roots of these ideologies are evil but the true cause of our downfall is simply our embracing evil and wickedness.

After his inauguration, George Washington dedicated this nation to Jesus Christ. He knew if America stood firm and obedient in our Judeo-Christian values and kept God's Commandments, with exactness, no power on earth could conquer this land. Abraham Lincoln made this same statement some 80 years later.

This is a nation dedicated to the Lord, conceived in liberty, and founded on the belief that man is endowed with certain unalienable God-given rights. If we as a people truly believe this statement then turn our backs on our Creator to follow the *'Author of All Lies,'* the fate of this nation is all but sealed.

Even though governments are instituted among men to protect their rights, it is a fact of nature that government will try to infringe on those rights and liberties in order to exercise unrighteous dominion over man and enslave him to the State. This is why the freedom of the press is enshrined in our Bill of Rights. So critical to our nation's survival was a free press that it was placed in the first Amendment of our Constitution. The first obligation of a free press is to report the truth and be a guardian against government tyranny.

But what happens to a nation when the press or media is fully invested with an ideology?

The several decades leading up to our nation's fall showed how little regard the press had for their *First Amendment Rights and Responsibilities.* They had for the most part lost their way. They no longer understood their purposes for existing were to strengthen society and support the principles of a Constitutional Republic. This is done by reporting the news as facts *without bias.*

Without our Republic, there is no *Democracy.*

Unfortunately, the main stream media squandered their birthright and became the Democratic Party Press which was an ideologically driven media. Instead of the 'Media' being a guardian of America against the ideology of Karl Marx, they embraced and promoted all forms of tyrannical governance.

It is infuriating to witness the *Democratic Party Press* hide behind the 1st Amendment while at the same time working to destroy the Bill of Rights and our Constitution. They are privately owned companies and are free to do this very thing but this was not the purpose of a free press as it is written in the Bill of Rights. If a media company's C.E.O. has Marxist beliefs, he will give like minded individuals a platform to promote their beliefs in exclusion of truth.

So as we enter the year 2020, we can depend on the main stream media being the guiding force to direct the Democratic Party down the path of *Socialism.* From this point forward until the collapse of America, we can no longer depend on or believe the media for the truth. I cannot help but believe if the press had done its job, perhaps this nation might not have gone down the path of self destruction.

When this nation does collapse and spiral into total destruction, which will people blame for their woes? I believe they will blame the usual suspects such as the opposition party, the rich, evil corporations, and so on. Will anyone take even a small portion of the blame for our fall? I believe it is not in man's nature to accept blame for those things he feels are out of his control.

The cleansing of America will take place in the near future. Is America like every other empire found throughout history? The short answers are: yes and no.

As stated before, like all other empires, the fall or collapse of America is all but guaranteed. The difference between all other empires and America is once we fall, the survivors will repent and this nation will rise like the Phoenix from the ashes of destruction as a humbled nation. We will work to correct our prior errors and by doing so, we will become a righteous and powerful Republic again. The only question is will we repeat the cycle of greatness and destruction? Only time will tell.

As the year 2020 begins, I declare, here and now, the three most destructive forces that will destroy our Republic, the United States of America are: the *Progressive Ideology, the Democratic Party,* and the legacy/mainstream media {or as it should be called} the *'Democratic Party Press'.*

Chapter 8 describes the general conditions in our nation prior to its collapse. Taken one by one there is nothing obvious that jumps out at us that we can blame for what is coming. I tried to show the big picture regarding how leveraging the future of our children and generations yet to be born, with debt that can never be paid back, destroyed our present.

Chapter 9 is based on direct revelation given to Thomas *{last name withheld for the sake of privacy}* by an Angel of the Lord. I took very little artistic license with this chapter. I believed it needed to be presented in its purest form so everyone could determine how these events will or might affect them. This is by all means and definition a clear and resounding voice of warning.

Chapter 10 and 11 are self explanatory in their titles.

Chapter 12 was my favorite one to write. It is speculative in many ways but it is how I believe our nation should correct its course after the cleansing of America has ended. I think every person who is interested in politics has ideas regarding how they would solve our problems if given the chance to do so. I actually was able to put my thoughts and reasons on paper for all Americans to read and debate.

I hope the readers of this story enjoy the historical timeline, perspectives, and commentary. I also desire the reader to carefully consider what I am confident are future events. Now is the time for all of us to prepare. Before we know it, our future becomes our present.

THE FIRST INTERVIEW 1791-1860

The doorbell rang. As I arose from my chair and walked towards the door I remember thinking this might be a very interesting day. A tall and very attractive woman, silhouetted by the noonday sun stood in my doorway. She introduced herself as Sharron Emmatay. She had been sent to interview me by the Department of History and Records, an agency within our newly founded Federal Government. After further introductions and pleasantries, I invited her inside and after she introduced herself to my wife we proceeded into my study.

I took my seat as she requested and she began to set up her devices. She then set up her video recorder and backup voice recording equipment and adjusted the viewfinder of the video camera to ensure I was properly in the frame with room for movement. Next she checked the sound levels and light balance and then took a seat just to the side of the video camera. She pulled out her notebook and pen and prepared to begin the interview.

Years ago this type of activity from a government employee might have been under entirely different circumstances. This very likely would have been an interrogation instead of just an interview. There is a vast difference between the two. Had I been captured by the government at that time I would have been interrogated and likely punished for my activities and rebellion against what I knew was an unconstitutional government. Today, our new government wanted an accurate and detailed record of what had taken place prior to, during, and after the fall.

To lighten the mood and put us both at ease with this process, Sharron shared with me a little information about herself. She had worked for the Forestry Service prior to the fall. While in school she had concentrated much of her studies to American history, political science, and world history. She had some minor studies in economics but admitted her math skills were not the best. I told her she should be a politician because I never met one who knew anything about economics. A little laughter always puts people at ease and we were now ready to begin.

She asked me if I had any questions about this interview process. I did. My question was how extensive in details did she want this interview to be? She said the more detailed the better. I could begin anywhere I wished and work through the details of what and where I believed our nation had run off the tracks. She wanted details on how we fought our way back and my role in our return. Future generations would hopefully learn from my interview along with the many other interviews going on in the nation. This might help them from making the same mistakes over and over again. I also had concerns about this interview record being accomplished in one afternoon. She assured me that we had as much time and as many days that I felt we needed to make this an accurate and detailed record. These stated conditions were agreeable and we were ready to begin.

   Prior to the fall I had written several books on a few topics I found to be of great interest. I had also written over 100 short stories and essays on an even wider array of topics. All of that was done several years ago before everything in our nation and in the world was turned upside down. There are no words to describe the sadness I felt having witnessed the destruction of this nation as part of the fall. I will add my part of the truth as I lived it. It might be but a sliver of wood from a mighty Sequoia of truth but it will be what I know to be true.

   Sharron pushed the record button on each of her devices and waited for five seconds to begin. She introduced herself, the date of the interview, the topic of the interview and then introduced me. She had me spell my full name and date of birth. This was necessary for when the interview was complete; the entirety of it would be transcribed and published. Accuracy was very important. She examined her notebook reviewing potential questions she would ask of all the people she would interview. I was not the first to be interviewed and I would certainly not be the last.

   Sharron's first question set the tone for this entire process. It was an open ended, thought provoking query. She asked me when I believed our nation's downfall began. It was a loaded question based on knowledge and perspective. I paused for a moment to collect some thoughts on this question. I could begin by claiming many dates and events from our past as the beginning of our downfall. I asked her if we could do some background to her question and then answer her query in groups of time. She said she thought that would be great. I proposed to start from 1791 and move towards 1860 as our first block of time to discuss. She seemed pleased at the prospect of this being a history class, which is a topic she loves, and an interview all rolled into one.

I believe it is important for everyone to understand some past history. In 1775 there were three groups of people, or should I say, there were three competing beliefs concerning our continuing allegiance to the British Crown. The first idea and group of people wanted the status quo. They wanted to continue being subjects of King George. The second group and belief was that of an independent America. They wanted to take the greatest risk of all and have their own nation and form of governance. The third group would go along to get along. They had no real opinion either way. They would support whichever side won this struggle.

After more than eight years of war, we secured our liberty from the most powerful nation on earth at that time. We would be guided by the Articles of Confederation, a precursor to our current Constitution, from 1777 to 1789. Not wanting to replace one tyrant king with another tyrant government, the Articles of Confederation were crafted to be weak. In fact they were too weak to secure liberty and maintain it. Too much power and you have a dictatorship. Too little power and you have anarchy or close to it. A balance must be found between the two. Limiting government limits man's natural desire to rule over others.

   Circa 1787 our Founding Fathers called for a Constitutional Convention. The balancing act of creating a more perfect Union was about to begin. First and foremost everyone should know there is no such thing as a perfect government. The only exception to this would be if Jesus Christ were to reign as our King. In 1787 God had placed some of His most brilliant minds in our nation. They would use history to design a form of government that would inspire and be the envy of the world. As James Madison drew up the Constitution, it seemed perfect in many ways. Yet there were great concerns about this new government and how powerful it would be. This new Constitution described each branch of government and defined their roles, limitations, and responsibilities. Concern grew over there being no mention of individual rights. It was assumed by many at the convention that if you limit and define government power, you make plain the liberties of the individual. This was not acceptable to a portion of the Delegates.

   It was getting late in the Convention and the delegates were to vote on the new Constitution soon. If approved they would carry this document to their States for debate and a vote on whether to ratify it. The debate on individual rights being listed was about to be a deal breaker. At the last moment, a promise was made that if the delegates would vote for this Constitution in its current form, then the delegates would draw up Amendments to be debated and voted on later. Their next gathering would be for the sole purpose of describing individual rights. An accord had been reached and the convention was saved.

I had to pause for a moment and think about what I had just said. In today's politics, promises are made for political gain with the intent of breaking them and blaming others for having to do so. Our Founding Fathers were different from the politicians of today. They had honor and integrity. For the sake of liberty they had placed their lives, their fortunes, and their sacred honor on the altar of potential sacrifice for freedom and self determination.

True to their word, the delegates would meet later and add 10 Amendments to the new Constitution. They are known as the Bill of Rights. The States would ratify these Amendments and they would be the supreme law of the land. These Amendments defined the rights of man in no uncertain terms. The rights of the States were also defined. Mainly, these Amendments placed the new Federal Government in a box to only be opened when necessary. The individual was to be sovereign and supreme in all matters concerning governments. The government was established to defend and protect the individual and their rights. The government was not to rule over the individual or place him in servitude.

The writing was on the wall for all to see. Those Americans who sided with the British in the War of Independence could see their desire to return to a monarch ruling over them disappear. They knew in their year of 1791 everything had changed and would possibly never go back to how they fondly remembered it. Perhaps some of them thought if this experiment we call America were to fail, then maybe we could return to our Monarchy and have our positions of status and privileges of wealth returned to us. Time was now an ally for their desires.

Sharron had been taking notes the entire time I was speaking. When I paused for a moment she told me how sad it was that this history had not been taught to her and other students in school. No matter which grade she was in, the Founding Fathers and the history of creating this nation had not been taught with any love or respect. Her point made, she returned to taking notes.

I contemplated what she had said for a moment and began to speak. The plan had worked. It took many years to fully implement but in the end the goal had been achieved. What was this plan? It was very simple. Take over the education system by making it a government controlled system. Once this is accomplished remove our heritage from the schools. Slowly remove our founding documents from the education system and never, ever encourage the students to read them. Tell students what their rights are and add other so-called rights to the list.

Lie to our kids? Yes, lie to them and fill their heads with disinformation. They will grow up believing they have far more rights than those listed in the Bill of Rights but this does not matter. They will not look up the truth for themselves. They would rather believe a teacher or professor than put any real effort into not being useful pawns. Propaganda is a tool of war. Make no mistake, this was a war against our nation waged by traitors and carried out by generations of our children.

Another vital part of this plan was to diminish and demean our Founding Fathers. It is much easier to disregard the words and ideas of men and women we do not respect or hold in high esteem. Our Founding Fathers were not perfect. Nobody is. But every flaw and fault they had were to be used as weapons against them to destroy their legacy. In the end, not a kind word would be spoken of them nor would the slightest amount of gratitude be shown them for what they had established. In government run schools and classrooms the children would be taught *what* to think, *not how to think.*

1791, yes, the year was 1791 and this brave new experiment called the United States of America had just begun. Did the formal creation of our nation and our Constitution along with the Bill of Rights end all forms of injustice? No. Slavery was a subject of much debate and contention. The solution to that question would be relegated to the future. Had the delegates of the Constructional Convention really pushed hard to end slavery and indentured servitude the convention would have collapsed. We most likely would have had two nations instead of one. I believe the slave States would have formed their own nation at this point. What would the future have been from that point forward? Slavery would end, but not for another 75 years. The cost would be the lives and blood of some 600,000 to pay for this heinous sin.

It is 1800 and the exploration and expansion into the West were the focus for many Americans. While we were looking west and growing into our newly acquired territories, our old enemy from the East struck us. 1812 was the year Great Britain decided to attempt to place us under their rule one more time. Even though the outcome was the same as in 1784, this war was a reminder about how fragile liberty is and how we must always be on guard to protect it.

After the war it was back to the expansion and growth of our nation. Growth and expansion have evil brothers called *greed* and *corruption*. No one knows these evil brothers better than the American Indians. European nations may have laid claim on vast tracks of land in this nation but the American Indian Nations occupied the choicest real estate. We may have purchased the claims from the European nations, but it was our government who committed the theft, forced relocation to reservations, and starvation of our Native Tribes. The land was then sold for huge profits. This was not just a local problem. It was a full scale land grab and profiteering by the Federal Government.

After we purchased the Louisiana Territory from France in 1803, acquired Florida from Spain by way of a treaty in 1819, purchased the Oregon Territory from Great Britain in 1846, and fought the Mexican-American War form 1846-1848 and purchased Mexico's claims, we now had a nation that reached from the Atlantic Ocean to the Pacific Ocean. With a land mass of such great size there was a problem. It was almost empty. This territory is what we call the lower 48 or contiguous States. We needed to populate it with immigrants who wanted to be Americans.

After pausing for a moment to contemplate what had occurred during those 57 years, I began to speak again.

We had gone from a nation of 14 States in 1791 to acquiring all the land of the contiguous 48 States. In my 58 years, I have bought and sold many pieces of property. They would add up to about 5 acres in total land mass. Can you conceive of buying 1,000,000 square miles of land in what would be my lifespan? There was still more to buy in the future. This was truly remarkable for such a young nation to expand so rapidly.

Sharron then asked my opinion of *Manifest Destiny* and if there were any other events taking place from 1800-1860 that I felt were important for this interview.

I will start with Manifest Destiny. I have never liked the term Manifest Destiny. It always sounded to me like God had shown up in our nation's capitol and commanded a joint session of Congress and the President to push the boundaries of the nation west to the Pacific Ocean. Could the leaders of this nation been inspired to do this very thing? Of course it is possible. Do I believe the final outcome has been a great benefit on the whole? Yes I do, but I have a problem with the whole 'the ends justify the means thing.' Even if our leaders were inspired to push west, I am sure God did not tell them to treat our Native Americans inhumanely.

The United States of America is a highly favored land of promise. It is choice above all other areas on earth. This land is a special land with a special purpose in God's eternal plan. This land is to be a beacon to the rest of the world. It is to shine through the darkness of tyranny and illuminate the cause of liberty to all those who seek it.

Imagine what the world would be like today if there was no United States of America. That is enough of me on my soapbox for now.

I said, "Sharron, did you know the term Manifest Destiny was not even used until after 1848 when our expansion west had already been completed?" She remembered learning something about this in one of her history classes. I then continued speaking. At that time we had pushed our borders as far as possible and we needed to find a catch phrase or some form of terminology to justify our behavior. Regardless of how our ancestors justified their actions, we must be vigilant and never again let our expansionist desires override our humanity and moral compass.

I find the second question you asked to be even more interesting. I believe your question was, "What other events were taking place in America from 1800-1860 that I felt are important to this interview? Is this correct?" Sharron answered in the affirmative. Where to start and which subject to explore is the real question here. I think I would like to start this section on immigration. In 1791 there were 14 States in the Union with a population of less than five million living here. By 1850 there were 31 States in the Union with a population of around 50 million people living here. Increased birth rates and legal immigration made this massive jump in population possible.

There are many reasons cited for this massive increase in immigration. One answer may be found across the Atlantic Ocean. Much of Europe was in upheaval. France had their own revolution and then a return to a dictator named Napoleon thus causing another revolution. Other parts of Europe had famine, disease, pestilence, and wars. The prospect of a long healthy life in any European nation seemed hopeless. People were looking elsewhere in the world to start a new and hopefully better life. America was just such a nation.

The situations that afflict the human condition may be the catalyst to move people from one nation to another, but they are not the main reasons why people wanted to, and still want to come to America. Freedom and the ability to pursue one's own happiness were and still are the main reasons for immigration. The freedom and liberty the American people experience and have come to expect is a rarity in the history of the world.

All men are given freedom from God as a birthright. Governments insert themselves between God and man for control and power. Much of the world believed the monarchies would last forever. They too believed their existence was eternal. They scoffed at the new ideas America promoted such as: All men are created equal and endowed by their Creator with certain unalienable rights... life, liberty, and the pursuit of happiness. The very thought of royalty and peasants being equal was laughable.

Sorry, I digress in thought from time to time. Let me get back to my point.

Freedom. We took it for granted for so long that we did not recognize those in power and those who wished for power were chipping away at our liberty. I have to say that those who wished to enslave us were patient. Incremental changes were placed into our system without notice. It would take a drastic situation to bring their treachery to light. I had heard many times in my life the words of our Founding Fathers: Liberty once lost is never recovered. We would put this belief to the test in a most evidentiary way.

Next, I would like to talk about The Bill of Rights. Can we even begin to imagine what it must have been like in the early 19th century for those immigrants from nations ruled by monarchs to be able to say what you really thought about the government? You are now allowed to not only speak your mind on laws the politicians are proposing but you can speak out for and against the politicians themselves. There can be no punishment for doing so because our Bill of Rights empowers us, not the government. Such speech by these immigrants in their previous countries would have sent them to prison or to be tortured or put to death.

The freedom of expression as applied to literature and art is a two edged sword. What one person calls art another may call vulgar. This is the beauty of such an amendment. The freedom of expression is not truly free due to the possibility of community imposed standards. A continual balancing act is performed by those who wish to have no limits on expression and those who wish to censor. The courts have and will be playing referee over these ideas as far into the future as I can see.

The next topic of discussion would be the freedom of religion and conscience. I believe it fair to say that never in the history of man have so many religions and beliefs been accommodated in one nation. Furthermore, all these religions and the people who follow them live side by side in our communities in relative peace. For many years in Europe you were either a Roman Catholic or a member of a State approved religion. To be otherwise was considered blasphemy. Reformers and the Reformation Movement took centuries to break the established religion's hold on power. Old rivalries and bigotry die a slow death.

From the Pilgrims to our current day, America has been a destination sought for by those who wished to worship God after the dictates of their heart. The migration of people from their native lands for the purpose of freedom to worship shows us how wise our Founding Fathers were for putting this right into our Constitution. All these people came to America not to be Catholic-American, Methodist-American, Lutheran-American, Presbyterian-American, and so forth. Being an American means following your own beliefs and allowing your neighbor to do the same. Thomas Jefferson summed it up best. He told us, '...*if it neither breaks my leg, nor picks my pocket, then what does it matter to me?*'

After the War of 1812, a religious fervor gripped the nation. With so many religions welcomed in this nation and living side by side, the ministers of those churches began their own missionary programs. Their goal was to convert the non-believers and followers of other religions. They all had a common belief. Their church was the true church of Jesus Christ. In upper New York State there was even a boy of 15 that claimed God the Father and Jesus

Christ had appeared to him and told him none of the churches on earth were the true Church of Jesus Christ. What a firestorm this claim ignited.

Let's now discuss the 2nd Amendment. Which of all the Amendments in the Bill of Rights is the most important? Is it Speech, religion, expression, self incrimination, States rights, or to peacefully protest? I say it is the 2nd Amendment or the right to keep and bear arms. This Amendment is the muscle behind the other nine Amendments. It is the protector of all rights and liberty. How incredibly wise it was for our Founding Fathers to place this Amendment in our Constitution. For had they not done so would we be having this interview?

Following this train of thought, Sharron asked if I believed there should be any restrictions on firearms. My belief is any restriction on the sale and ownership of firearms is unconstitutional. The basis of my belief is this: at the time of our War of independence in 1775, all weapons were military grade. There were no differences between a military musket and a civilian musket. If the military or police have fully automatic weapons then law abiding civilians should also have access to them.

Sharron said she agreed with my conclusion, but she wanted to push me a little bit further on my beliefs by asking me if I thought there should be any restrictions on what a citizen should be allowed to purchase. My answer to this question is simple:

• Why is it reasonable and expected for American

citizens to pay for automatic weapons for our military and police?

• Why do many think it should be unlawful for *law abiding* citizens *to not* have these weapons?

• I have to pay for them to use but I do not have the same right as them?

• A government that does not trust its law abiding citizens with those same weapons, is not a government the citizen should trust with any weapons.

The true purpose of the 2nd Amendment is not so a hunter can shoot a deer. Its true purpose has always been so the citizen can throw off the shackles of a tyrannical government.

I asked, "Is this not the very thing we have just done?"

Some might ask if I believe the citizen should be allowed to own a jet fighter or an aircraft carrier. I say the citizen already owns all of those weapon systems. We paid for them. They are to be used to protect us, not to be used against us. The people we trust to wield such firepower should do so only under the strictest of our confidence and loyalty to the Constitution and the citizen, not the political class.

Sharron replied that my discourse was more than an interview; it was more a college course on the Constitution. She was right.

I guess I could have quickly passed over the Constitution and what I think and how I feel about it. I could have moved on to other historical events prior to our fall for the sake of time and this interview. I could have done this but I will not. There are many things in my life I love. I love my God, my Savior, my wife, my family, my friends, my country, and I love the Constitution of the United States of America. I want to ensure this divine writing is included in this interview.

I have had this thought for a very long time. If our founding documents had been included, promoted with respect and honor, and been given the depth of discourse they deserved, would we have had to go through the fall and fight our way back to this point? I repeat, the absence of our founding documents along with the denigration of our Founding Fathers from our education system was not an oversight or mistake. It was part of a master plan. One we have corrected and may it forever remain so.

It was time for a short break. Sharron turned off her recording devices. My wife had brought out some of her incredible chocolate chip cookies and some bottled waters for us to enjoy. I offered Sharron some of these refreshments and she partook happily. I could see by the ring on her finger she was married so I asked her about her family. She told me she had a good husband, three daughters, and one son. She showed me a picture of her family and told me her children were all very smart, had a lot of personality and were full of mischief.

How wonderful!

I would not give two cents for a child that didn't have a little sparkle of mischief in his eyes. When I see the sparkle, I know the wheels are turning in their head.

It was time to get back to our interview.

Sharron turned her recording devices back on and pulled out her notebook and asked me her next question. Was there anything else prior to the *1st* Civil War I wanted to discuss and how I thought it applied to what we had gone through after the fall? There were plenty of topics to discuss from our past that had consequences many years later. I decided to discuss slavery at this point in our interview. Slavery had been abolished for over 150 years yet the topic never ceased being discussed. Our nation's greatest sin prior to 1962 and 1973 had to be dealt with on a regular basis.

Less than five percent of the American population owned slaves. Leading up to the *1st* Civil War, only one political party owned slaves, supported slavery, and wanted slavery expanded into the newly purchased Western Territories. That party was the *Democratic Party.* The Whig Party was weak in its support for the Abolitionist Movement. It was now 1854 and a firm stand against slavery was needed. A new party was formed as the Abolitionist Party and was named the Republican Party.

It took from 1854 to 1860 before the Republican Party had sufficient numbers to make a serious run for the Presidency. In 1860 a Senator from the State of Illinois ran for the highest office in the land and won. He would be our

16th President. His name was Abraham Lincoln. I wish to discuss more about this incredible man, but at a later time. I am starting to feel a little tired but I want to discuss a couple more topics before I call it a day.

I wish to speak a little on the subject of what happens to people in general and more specifically to citizens of this nation when the Bill of Rights are not followed or enforced by government. Throughout history the persecution of people based on where they were born, the color of their skin or their religious beliefs has been in the hearts of men. Often times the practice of racism, bigotry, and intolerance are used for control of others and to gain power. The American Indian was exploited and persecuted in order to control them and obtain their lands. The Blacks were thought of as inferior due to their skin color and enslaved for 246 years. The Irish were looked down upon because many people believed them to be drunkards and trouble makers. The Chinese were considered as less than human and were put to work on the railroads and given the most dangerous jobs.

This is just a partial list of our violations against humanity. It is enough of a list that we as a nation should hang our heads in shame. Truth be told, we have corrected many of our not too distant past mistakes. We have also worked hard to not forget our mistakes and try not to repeat them. Nations of cowards never admit to their role in genocide, enslavement, and other human rights violations. They even look the other way when discrimination and persecution take place all around them.

In contrast to the nations of cowards, a truly great nation will make mistakes on a grand scale. The difference is when a great nation recognizes its mistake it will admit to it and take corrective action to never let it happen again. Some people who were affected by this injustice will accept an apology as payment in full. Others will expect continuous apologies and contrition for eternity and still never forgive.

My intent here is to point out the persecution and unlawful treatment of other people and groups based solely on their differences. If you will recall, I had spoken about the religious fervor taking place in America circa 1820 and a young man of 15 years old who had claimed to have seen and spoken to God the Father and His Son Jesus Christ. He claimed Jesus told him the true church of Jesus Christ was not on the earth at that time. But through this young man Jesus would re-establish His true church on the earth again. Can we even begin to imagine the hornets' nest of persecution this generated?

The persecution of this young man, his faith and the church he would organize started almost immediately and was relentless. From 1820 to about 1860 this small group of people who only wished to exercise their beliefs in peace were harassed, persecuted, robbed, beaten, and murdered. These things were done by mobs of men who called themselves Christians.

In fleeing persecution, this small group of people went to Kirtland, Ohio where they tried to make a peaceful life. The mobs followed with their violence and they soon left Ohio for Independence, Missouri. The persecution did not end at another State's border. In Missouri, Governor Lilburn Boggs issued an extermination order for all members of this group found in Missouri. The group fled for their lives to Nauvoo, Illinois. After the leader of this group was murdered while in jail, it was obvious their Constitutional Rights would not be enforced by any government. It was time to head west into the Rocky Mountains where it would be safe.

To this day, no other people in America have ever been sentenced to genocide based solely on having different religious beliefs. One must confess this group of people are unique and a curiosity to others not of their faith. But even after having had their rights violated and still treated with disdain, they have never shrunk from their duty to the Republic. In fact their belief in the Constitution is based on their belief the Lord had His hand in guiding the men who would write it. To this group, our founding documents are sacred texts.

It was growing late and we agreed to stop for the day. We would continue tomorrow and decided 10am would be a convenient time for both. She assured me we had all the time I needed to complete every interview as thoroughly as possible. She could see this interview taking several more days due to the depth of information and amount of background I was covering.

Sharron collected her recording devices and placed them in a bag. After gathering the rest of her items, she headed outside to her car. She would go home to those little angels she had shown me earlier in the photograph.

Tomorrow, we will talk about the 1st Civil War and the aftermath that followed.

Tonight would be a night spent quietly with my wife. We would have dinner, discuss some of the topics of the day, and enjoy another peaceful night. I look forward to my next interview. I realized I needed to do one more thing tonight.

THE SECOND INTERVIEW 1860-1900

I decided to sit on the porch the morning of the second interview. I had spent quite some time during the night writing notes for today's recording session. While waiting for Sharron to arrive, I reviewed my notes and the path my thoughts had traveled. I asked myself if anything of great historical value happened from 1860-1900 besides the Civil War. I could remember the Pony Express had begun in 1860, the *13th, 14th,* and *15th* Amendments were added to our Constitution, but what else? Maybe tomorrow's interview will be a short one, or maybe we will move on to the next interview timeline of 1900-1930.

A quick trip to my study and a brief scan of one of my U.S. History books proved very surprising about that time period being a quiet time in history. I was astounded. Major events had taken place in those decades and had completely slipped my memory. Worse still, I had placed some of those events in the wrong decades. This was not about teaching *an old dog new tricks,* it was reminding an old dog about old facts. I found my notepad and pen and began to write. The list in front of me was not really long, but it could have been.

The day was beautiful and the desire to spend all day here and enjoy this spring weather was overwhelming. The barking of the neighbor's dog drew my attention back to the present. A few moments later a car pulled up in front of my house and out stepped Sharron. She waived and said good morning. I returned her greeting as she opened the back door to her car and retrieved her recording devices. She had a great smile and she walked swiftly like an athlete would towards my porch. I opened the door for us and we went inside.

My wife met us at the front door. She had heard me talking to Sharron from the hallway and came to greet her. The typical pleasantries of "Good morning." and "How are you today?" passed between them. I then realized how tall Sharron was. She had to be close to six feet tall. My wife is about five feet, six inches tall and that is not short. But standing next to Sharron it was noticeable. We went into the study and Sharron set up her equipment as she had done previously. We settled into our seats and Sharron turned on the recording devices. It's showtime!

I looked down at my list and prayed in my heart I would find the proper words to describe the forty year time span I wanted to discuss. Then the pictures of the events I was to discuss filled my mind and the words began to flow. Inasmuch as you keep the commandments of God you shall prosper in the land. But if we do not keep the commandments of God we shall be cut off from His presence. We live in a land of promise. It is a choice land above all other lands on the earth. If we will be obedient, we will never be swept off this land and the Lord will protect us by His mighty power.

This land shall have no king ruling over it other than the King of Kings. This land shall not have slavery on it ever again. For if we were to embrace any form of slavery the judgments of God shall be poured out upon us and we shall pay for it in blood and destruction. This is where I wish to begin today's interview.

We hear it a little today, but leading up to our fall we heard it from everyone in the nation on how our nation was so divided. Whether they were on the left or the right, politicians and those who supported them decried our division. If ever an opposing view was given on any subject, he was considered divisive, and not a free thinker. Each side of the body politic blamed the other side when they would not support legislation that *always benefitted* the American people. If you don't support *OUR* ideas then *YOU* are divisive. Disagreeing on ideas is one thing. Literally dividing a country in half and going to war is *DIVISIVE* to the extreme.

The year is 1860. It has been six years since the Republican Party was organized and formed. The party platform has many things in it that we would recognize more than one hundred and sixty years later. The main belief and principle they will stand on in 1860 is the abolition of slavery and indentured servitude in the United States and its territories. The Democratic Party, which is *pro-slavery* wanted the Federal Government to protect their property, also known as *slaves*, from being freed. The Abolitionists wanted the same government to free all slaves and protect their human and Constitutional Rights. Some in Congress hoped to find a middle ground. When it comes to a moral position, there can be no middle ground.

The Southern States that wished to maintain the status quo had been making threats of secession if Washington D.C. moves to free the slaves. This is not a hollow threat. They have already begun preparations to form their own government and military if they decide to secede. Abraham Lincoln, a Republican, has been elected President at a most combustible time in our nation's history. Within weeks of his inauguration on March 4, 1861, the Southern States would declare their independence and form the Confederate States of America.

You are President of the United States and half of your nation has decided to go their separate way. What do you do now? If you agree to the status quo and the Southern States remain in the Union with slavery, then you will split the nation due to the Abolitionist Movement. You can insist the South remain in the Union but they must agree to phase out slavery over a specified amount of time. You will give them one decade to comply. They will insist on multiple decades to do so. You can agree to phase out slavery but forbid the expansion of slavery into the new States and territories. Or, you can go to war with the Confederate States and force them to remain a part of the Union and with victory on your side, you can abolish slavery once and for all.

These were the choices Abraham Lincoln had in front of him. Try as one might for a negotiated settlement, there was no solution both sides would agree to. The Southern States pushed for the expansion of slavery into the new States and territories even though the law forbade this. The expansion of slavery into States like Missouri and Arkansas was not pushed for by a plantation owner in Georgia. It was pushed for by the slave traders. It meant big business and even bigger profits for every new State that allowed slavery.

Sharron expressed how sad it made her to know that the lives of other people came down to the profits they created for others. I agreed and told her the older I get the more I understand that you should never get between some people and the money they want to possess. Without a strong moral compass to steer you, money will win every time. She then went back to taking notes and I continued speaking.

On April 12, 1861, the Civil War began with Confederate forces bombarding Union soldiers at Fort Sumter, South Carolina. What would ensue was four years of the bloodiest fighting America would ever know. This war would cost the lives of some 600,000 men and wound or maim several times that amount. The lives of millions of civilians would be affected in unfavorable ways. The cities had been destroyed, the farms were decimated, and livestock had been killed or taken as provisions for the victorious. Starvation in parts of the South was taking place. Was this not enough payment for the sin of slavery?

The North was victorious. The reconstruction of the South needed to begin as soon as possible. The healing of the nation would take some time to accomplish. The war had put family, friends, cities, and states at odds and with arms against each other. President Lincoln had saved the Union. But was the price worth all the suffering? Only time would reveal the answer to this question.

Throughout the history of the world when a victory is won over an opposing nation and their military, the victors are rewarded with the spoils of war. The victor sets the terms and conditions for the vanquished. Terms could range from compassion, or being forced to pay tribute without end, to all forms of human abuses and decimation, or full out genocide placed on the defeated people. All these punishments were desired by different groups of Americans as further payment on the South. President Lincoln chose compassion, love, and forgiveness. He knew what so many others didn't. They were blinded by their hate. The South would be a part of the Union again and the people in those States are still American citizens. President Lincoln would not live to see the completion of his work.

It is now 1866 and the *13th* Amendment is the law of the land. Four million slaves have been freed. In order to help them become self sufficient and prosper, President Lincoln awarded each of these *Freedmen* 40 acres of land to farm. They were also given an army surplus mule to work their land. Much of that land came from their former Masters who were the plantation owners. Even though there is no way to pay back 200 plus years of human dignity being lost, this stipend would have to do, for now.

I need to make a point here before we move on. Since our founding in 1789 we have had elections for President every four years. The person who received the majority of Electoral College votes was made President and the runner-up was made his Vice President. Since your opponent was from the opposition party, I have always been amazed there were no assassinations by the Vice President's party so he

could become President. This system was later changed
to a President picking his running mate and ending the
potential never ending cycle of assassinations.

Upon President Lincoln's death his former adversary,
Andrew Johnson, a staunch Democrat Party loyalist,
became President. Johnson then reversed Lincoln's policies
as quickly as he could. The 40 acres given to the *Freedmen*
was taken from them and given back to the plantation
owners by Johnson. Their ability to support themselves
was taken away and placed back in the hands of those who
had enslaved them. The slaves were free but what were
they now? Were they citizens of the United States or just a
large group of *Freedmen* living in America with no rights
or protections? The answers to these questions depended
largely on where you lived in America and which political
party controlled your State and local government.

It was time to further expand the liberties and rights
framed in our Constitution. Another Amendment was
needed to settle this question concerning the status of
citizenship of former slaves, once and for all. The States
that did not recognize slaves as citizens would be given
another wake up call. In 1866 Congress passed the *14th*
Amendment giving full citizenship to the former slaves
in America. Almost every Republican voted in favor. In
contrast few Democrats voted for the *14th* Amendment. It
would take two more years for it to be ratified by the States
and become part of our Constitution.

Even though former slaves had been granted full
citizenship by the *14th* Amendment, their rights were

being denied in many Southern States. Black Codes, or Jim Crow Laws, such as poll taxes and requiring Blacks to read and write in order to vote were being implemented by Democratic Party controlled State and local governments. This was done to further deny former slaves their rights and force them to remain dependent on the plantation owners. These grievous actions needed a national remedy. The *15th* Amendment would be considered shortly after the *14th* Amendment had been voted on. Yet before we address the *15th* Amendment we need to discuss the *14th* Amendment further.

For more than one hundred and fifty years the *14th* Amendment has been used *illegally* and *incorrectly*. This was never more evident than in 1968 when it was used as the basis to grant citizenship to anyone born in America whether their parents were in this country legally, or not. This very topic was heavily debated when the *14th* Amendment was introduced in Congress in 1866. There was concern this amendment would be used to abuse immigration laws. A great deal of debate concerning the language, content, definitions and implementation took place. The blanket granting of citizenship to any group of people let alone an individual was of great concern to many Congressmen.

The granting of citizenship to any child born in the United States regardless of its parents being here legally was not canonized in law by Congress and the President. It was not placed in our Constitution by way of Amendment. It was not even declared a right to illegal alien children by the Supreme Court of the United States. It was implemented around 1968 by the *federal bureaucracy* and *unelected bureaucrats*. This should have been corrected immediately by Congress and the President but it was not. This one act of *unauthorized interpretation of the law by bureaucrats* should have had one question attached to it by Congress: Does this interpretation benefit the American citizen?

Statesmen would have answered, no. They would have then corrected this *illegal action*. This is one of the topics added to the list of things leading to our fall. I will discuss this topic in greater detail during the interview that correlates to those time periods.

Looking back on his original positions of saving the Union, President Lincoln must have reflected on how his position had changed during the war and to this point in time. To paraphrase his original words here, he had said, 'If I could save the Union by maintaining slavery I would do it. If I could free some slaves and not others and maintain the Union, I would do it. If I could free all the slaves and maintain the Union I would do that.' The war was over, the Union was maintained, and the only moral option was implemented. The slaves were free.

I am sorry Sharron. I know I am jumping around here concerning the so called *'Civil War Amendments.'* But as I remember certain important aspects of the *13th*, *14th*, and *15th* Amendments I want to be sure they are included in this record. I will try to do better as we continue. Now, where was I? Oh yes, now I remember.

President Lincoln had written the Emancipation Proclamation during the war but I am sure he knew a Presidential order would not have any long term enforcement. A law passed by Congress could be overturned with a new Congress and President. Something was needed to ensure that slavery in America would never happen again. The *13th* Amendment to the Constitution was ratified and made supreme law of the land on December 31, 1865. Slavery and indentured servitude would never be legal in America again.

President Lincoln would not live to see this Amendment added to the Constitution. Less than a week after the Civil War officially concluded an assassin's bullet ended his life. Radical Southern dissidents had their revenge and they paid for it with their lives. This would not bring back the life of President Lincoln. He would not be allowed to guide the nation through reunification and reconstruction. A tremendous opportunity had been lost. Vice President Andrew Johnson, a Democrat, was then sworn in as President. He would not follow in the footsteps or maintain the policies of his predecessor.

I believe it is very important to discuss the *13th* Amendment in greater detail here. With the end of the Civil War nearing and the Union Army being victorious, one might think the *13th* Amendment would be a logical step on the part of Congress to pass. But when has there been a Congress ruled by logic? The debate on this Amendment was fierce. The Abolitionist Republicans fought with everything they had to push it across the finish line. On the other side of the debate was the Democratic

Party. When the vote to abolish slavery was taken, every Republican had voted for it. *By contrast, every Democrat, except four, had voted against the abolishment of slavery.*

You might think this sounds logical because of how the Southern States felt about this issue. Here is the truth we were never taught in school. At the time of this vote, the Confederate States had not been reintegrated into the Union. *Those Democrats who voted in opposition to this Amendment were Northern Democrats.* Had the South been allowed to vote on the *13th* Amendment there may have been a different outcome. In the coming years there would be more amendments added to the Constitution dealing with the slaves and their rights.

We will jump ahead a couple years now. Even though the slaves were free and it was perfectly legal for all males to vote in an election, Black males were forbidden to do so in some parts of the country. The Civil War was over and the pro-slavery States had lost. The *13th* Amendment freed all slaves in America. The *14th* Amendment granted full citizenship on the freed slaves. Yet the Southern Democrats still looked at Black Americans as inferior and unable to choose a person they wished to represent them in national, State, and local governments. It is so very important for us to know the true history of this time period and how it would affect us later in the 20th and 21st centuries.

By the time the *15th* Amendment was ratified which gave Blacks the right to vote, the former slaves had been enduring a living hell by the Democratic Party. The denial of Constitutional Rights was only the tip of the iceberg. After the war in 1865 and the passage of the *13th* Amendment, Southern Democratic officials disarmed Blacks and violated their 2nd Amendment Right to protect themselves. Then the Democrats unleashed their terrorist organization called the Ku Klux Klan on Blacks to keep them in their place. Black Codes or Jim Crow Laws were implemented to disenfranchise Black voters. Those Black males that did vote did so in fear and their votes were usually 'lost.' The year may have been 1870, but there was little if any protection from a Federal Government that only a few years previous had stood for freedom, liberty, and the equality of slaves.

Sharron commented on how many topics of interest could be discussed concerning the five years after the Civil War and we could spend hours on this time period alone. She was right of course. What an amazing time in our nation's history. Everything that transpired in those years would have long term ramifications for over a hundred years. Slavery may be over but State endorsed racism and segregation would last long into the future. We were now ready to move on to other events that took place from 1870-1900. I looked down at my notes and began to speak again.

With the Civil War coming to a close, Congress was once again looking to acquire more land to call ours. From 1800 to 1848, we had added over a million square miles of land to our nation. Two years after the Civil War we added an additional 600,000 square miles to our total. The 1867 purchase of the Alaskan Territory from Russia was thought of as a waste of money by some in Congress. It would be several decades before the wisdom of this purchase would be made self evident.

In 1870 there were 38 million people living in America. We had almost four million square miles of land we called our own. If you do the math, it breaks down to about a 10th of a square mile of land for every person in the country. Breaking this down further it is about 2,788,000 square feet or about 64 acres for every man, woman and child. We had ample room for many times the number of people already living in America. We needed more people, and they were on their way here.

As the number of immigrants grew, the push west into unsettled lands was at a hectic pace, except for one thing, the hectic pace was slow. Covered wagons and walking west to settle lands and make claims on land took months. In 1870 the Union Pacific Railroad pushed west from the Eastern States and the Central Pacific Railroad pushed east from the Western States and joined near Ogden, Utah. You could now travel from the Atlantic Ocean to the Pacific Ocean in comfort. Travel time from New York to San Francisco on a horse was about three months. It was even longer by about a month in a covered wagon. The trains of the day could cover the same distance in about a month depending on mountain weather. It was now three times faster to travel from anywhere in the East to anywhere in the West.

In the 1870's we saw many new creations and inventions that would benefit not only Americans, but the entire world. Unfortunately, we saw many of the old practices of inhumanity also take place. For years the American Indians had resisted and fought the Federal Government's request for them to live on reservations. Now the Federal

Government ordered all remaining tribes to report to and live on these reservations. This was tantamount to a declaration of war on the Indians. These wars would pit the U.S. Army against our Native Americans, the most famous of these battles being at Little Big Horn. There was no other outcome from these wars other than full compliance by the Indians to the federal mandate. Disgraceful is the only word I can use for the actions during this time.

Quickly, let's highlight some other events that took place during this decade. One of my personal favorites was the invention and formation of a professional sport called baseball. The National Rifle Association was formed to promote and protect Gun Rights. The manufacturing and transmission of electrical energy was harnessed. The cylinder phonograph player was a modern marvel in this decade. Even though there were patents on Intellectual Property Rights due to the Patent Act of 1790, 1871 would see the formation of the Patent and Trademarks Resource Center Program. The inventions and creations of this nation would continue to be unleashed into the world.

It is now 1880 and there are 50 million people living in America. We are growing by 1.2 million people a year and those numbers will gain momentum soon. There is a different attitude among the Americans than what you would find in Europe. The centuries of imperial rule has driven the spirit of man into the depths of despair. There is no shine in the eyes and faces of many Europeans. This cannot be said about Americans. There is a 'we can do anything' attitude and feeling that permeates the entire nation. Some of this swagger comes from a time when a bunch of rebels defeated the greatest and most powerful empire on earth and won their freedom. This attitude is contagious and the immigrants are infected with it almost immediately upon their arrival.

It is during this decade that France will attempt to connect the Pacific Ocean with the Gulf of Mexico. They will not succeed. We will not see the need for this venture for another 20 years. When we do decide to accomplish this engineering marvel, we will see it to fruition. This topic will be discussed a little later.

In 1886 the Statue of Liberty was opened to the public with great fanfare. It had taken the French Government 12 years to design, build, disassemble, ship to New York, and re-assemble. This was to be a gift to our nation with very praiseworthy ideals attached to it. It told the rest of the world, especially Europe, to look to America for guidance on how the chains of tyranny can be thrown off and a people can prosper. We were only a hundred years old and the world already wanted to follow us.

In the 1880's the West was still wild. With all the advances in industry and commerce one might think we had civilized the entire nation. This was not the case. There would be many historical outlaws during this decade. The Jesse James Gang, Billy the Kid, and the shootout at the OK Corral were but a few gun slinging legends that would color the canvas of the Wild, Wild, West.

Other interesting events happening during the 1880's include the creation of Coca Cola, the telegraph and telephone, and the first motion picture, The Oklahoma land rush also occurred at this time. There were many other inventions and events taking place during the 1880's; suffice it to say we were growing into every part of the land we could inhabit and inventions were helping us all along the way.

With the decade of the 1890's upon us we started it off with 62 million Americans living within our borders. It was during this time Congress decided to further protect Intellectual Property Rights. They authorized the formation of the Copyright Office within the Library of Congress. When Congress added this protection to our creations, we would continue to be the most creative and inventive people in man's history.

At this time I think we need to discuss in some detail the importance of this system we put in place to protect individual's ideas and creations. It is because of our Founding Fathers and many other leaders in our nation's history who knew they should look back to the past so we could move forward into a prosperous future. Is it any wonder that in the history of the world it was ruled by monarchs and we see little inventions and creations taking place? Why is this?

Sharron spoke up and said it was because of incentive. She was correct. What incentive does an individual have to invent a better mouse trap or create a work of art when your life and everything you do is considered property of the crown? The right answer is little to no incentive. We had the Bill of Rights to ensure our freedom, but what would we do with that freedom? Once again, the right answer is anything our hearts would desire and our minds could conceive.

"What was the true genius of the Patent Act of 1790 and the formation of the Copyright Office?" I asked. Sharron stated, "They were Federal Government agencies established to protect the individual and not empower the State."

"Exactly right," I said.

She then added, "The true genius of such a system guarantees by law you will benefit from your ideas. If someone else were to infringe on your patent, they would have to pay you for damages due to their infringement." She was right again. "One more question for you. If there was no Patent Office within the Federal Government until 1975, how were patents protected?"

She answered immediately, "The States agreed to cooperate on patent protection." She really did know her history.

I said, "I'll try again later to stump you, Sharron."

With a smile she said, "Try all you want."

The protections of ideas were now in place. Along with these protections came an inventions boom. Everyone wanted to invent something everyone else would need or want. If the pursuit of happiness meant becoming wealthy from your idea and enjoying the fruits of your labor was your definition of fulfillment, then by all means, get inventing. Americans were just hitting their creative stride.

To finish off the decade and the century we saw the creation of basketball, the formation of the first professional football league, and the incorporation of General Electric.

By the way, we also had a minor war with Spain.

The Spanish American War lasted for a mere four months and was completely one sided. The military might of Spain was no match for that of the United States. Cuba had been fighting Spain for their independence for several years. We were supportive of the Cuban rebels. Spain declared war on us and we in turn declared war on them. Four months later Spain would abandon their colonies and return home. Cuba was free and we added Puerto Rico, Guam, and the Philippine Islands to the list of our territories.

Sharron, can you turn off your devices for a moment please? Sharron did as asked and then I told her it was 12:30 and I was ready to eat. I asked her if she would also like some lunch.

She said, "I would love some."

My wife had made us some egg salad sandwiches courtesy of our chickens. I guess those hens are good for something from time to time. The three of us spent lunch enjoying our sandwiches and getting to know each other better. A great lunch and some good conversation was a welcome break. After lunch we stepped outside to enjoy the spring air. Then it was time to get back to work. Break time was over.

THE THIRD INTERVIEW 1900-1930

With stomachs full from a very tasty lunch and our minds clear from some fresh air, we returned to my study and took our seats. Sharron turned on the recording devices, retrieved her notebook and pen and I began to speak. Looking at the dates I had written down, 1900-1930 caused me to pause and think for a second. This time period we are about to discuss is where and when it all began. She looked at me with some puzzlement. Obviously I needed to clarify my statement a little more. I believe if there is a period in time where we could point to and say this is where our fall began; then 1900-1930 is that time period.

Our accomplishments over the past 125 years had truly been remarkable. No other civilization had progressed so far and as fast as this nation had. We had been blessed by God beyond our ability to show Him proper gratitude. With the dawn of a new century upon us we were looking to the future with even greater expectations. We had expanded our borders from sea to sea and if we had desires to expand any further it would require us assimilating Mexico and/or Canada. This was not our desire. The borders of North America were set and in place for now.

It was now the 20th Century. What was on our minds and lists of things to pursue? We turned our focus and attention to science, inventions, technology, medicine, education, the arts, economics, and the advancement of a civil society. It was not uncommon for the philosophies of man to be discussed and given to heated dissent. Some of these ideas were being considered and given acceptance in some parts of Europe and Asia. One of the more popular writers of these philosophies was Karl Marx. Our nation has great oceans to protect us from invading armies but an idea cannot be stopped by any barrier.

By 1900, 76 million people called America home. We were growing at over one million people per year. When Congress does something right you need to give them credit for it. It does not happen very often. In 1900 Congress placed the United States of America on the gold standard. Our paper notes placed in circulation would be tied directly to the reserves of gold and silver in our treasury. By way of example this meant if you had a $20 note or bill in your hand, there was a $20 dollar gold coin in the treasury backing the value of your note. Sharron then asked how much a $20 gold coin weighed. I told her it weighed one ounce. She seemed surprised at this answer knowing what an ounce of gold was valued at just a few years ago. This same valuation of money held true to other denominations of currency. A one dollar note was worth one ounce of silver and so on. This one act of Congress made our currency one of the strongest and most valued in the world. Furthermore, this law constricted the ability of the government to deficit spend the people's money on frivolous projects.

In 1901 President William McKinley was removed from office, not by the ballot but by an assassin's bullet. It had been 35 years since Abraham Lincoln's assassination and it makes me wonder in 35 years why we had not done more to protect our President. This should have been the number one priority of law enforcement agencies within the Federal Government. Upon President McKinley's death, Vice President Theodore 'Teddy' Roosevelt, a Republican assumed the Presidency. It is with him we see the move towards an all powerful Federal Government.

Just as a point here, it is interesting to note that in thirty years President T. Roosevelt's Nephew, Franklin D. Roosevelt, a Democrat, will also become President of the United States of America. He will advance the Progressive Movement and expand the role of government further than his uncle could have ever imagined.

President T. Roosevelt championed legislation to fight large corporations from conspiring to fix prices and profits with anti-trust laws. He would also move to end monopolies in the United States. During his first term in office the first movie theater opened in Los Angeles. Hollywood would soon become the movie capitol of the world. Willis Carrier invented the air conditioner in this same year. How did we ever live without it? The ritual of fans and open windows gave way to cool comfort in the summer. Neighborhoods also changed with this invention. No longer would we sit outside on our porches and visit with our neighbors while our kids played. We would sequester ourselves in cool rooms and houses and not care much about the outside world.

Several milestones occurred during 1903. For starters, the first World Series in baseball was played. Of much more significance: it may have only been just over 800 feet, but Wilbur and Orville Wright proved their flying machine worked and man could join the winged animals and fly. It would take several more decades to perfect and fully commercialize air travel but this first flight changed the world. Horses, sailing ships, trains, and cars would be obsolete modes of transportation when distance coupled with speed was of the highest importance.

Fabian Socialism may have originated in England circa 1880, but the precepts and ideology were not isolated there. Though the *Fabians* decried *Marxism* they did advocate for a gradual embracing of *Socialism*. All that was needed in this country was a leader, some supporters, and some willing pawns to be used by the leader to create a new party and push for the fundamental transformation of America. President T. Roosevelt would be that leader and his party would be called the *Progressive Party*. The term Socialist was taboo in America but *Progressive* didn't feel all that scary. *Progressivism* was and still is in *opposition* to our Constitution.

In1904, we told the world America can and will accomplish the impossible. Commerce between nations was king and shipping goods from Asia and Europe around the southern tips of Africa of South America added time and expense to every product imported and exported. We also needed a quicker way to move our naval ships from ocean to ocean. The only solution was to build the Panama Canal. Where France had failed we said we would succeed.

America called upon our best minds to design, engineer, and construct this mega structure.

At this time, I have a question to propose. What do men with power desire most? More power is the answer. The election of 1908 showed this statement to be true. President T. Roosevelt had completed the term of William McKinley who had been assassinated in his first year as President. Then President Roosevelt won his election in 1904. He had served for almost a full eight years. This was the tradition set by George Washington. President T. Roosevelt decided to break tradition and run for third term and if he won he would be the first President in our nation's history to serve for nearly 12 years.

Theodore's bid to break tradition along with his changing viewpoints on national and international politics was rejected by the Republican Party and its voters. When William Howard Taft, also a Republican decided to run for President, he had his Party's support to challenge his mentor and a sitting President of their Party. Taft would defeat President Roosevelt in the primary and go on to win the General Election. Theodore was defeated but he would return in 1912 to stir the pot in the General Election and hand the Presidency to Woodrow Wilson.

Years ago I was a Scoutmaster for 10 years in the Boy Scouts of America. Prior to that I had been a Cub Scoutmaster, merit badge counselor, and spent 10 years as a Cub and Boy Scout. I even earned the Eagle Scout Award as a Boy Scout. Why do I bring this up? Well, in 1910 the Boy Scouts of America was founded. This is a special year to me and possibly millions of other Boy Scouts. My sons are all Eagle Scouts and my daughter was a merit badge counselor and scout camp program director. I believe in the Scouting program that is up until 2010 when everything in the B.S.A. changed. It was grotesque what the National Council did to the B.S.A. over political correctness. The 100 years of tradition and turning boys into men was abandoned for social acceptance. I could go on for a while venting my displeasure on the National Council but I believe I have said enough on this topic for now.

It is surprising that in our first 120 years as a nation, Congress never set the maximum limit of seats or Representatives permitted in the House of Representatives. The Senate had definite numbers allowed in their chamber. Two Senators from each State were allowed in the Senate. No more, No less. In 1911 Congress affixed their maximum seats at 435. As our population grew, there would be adjustments as to how many people each seat represented but there would not be any seats added or subtracted. The Senate was not free from changes in this decade. The status quo would soon be turned upside down.

As a side note, this was the year when the Eugenics Movement made one of its boldest moves into the light of national discussion and debate. The Governor of New Jersey and future President of the United States Woodrow Wilson, a Democrat signed a bill into law ordering the forced sterilization of the 'feeble minded.' I have only one word to use for the entire Eugenics Movement: *EVIL*. The world would vilify the NAZIS for what they did in World War II, but they learned their ideology from Margaret

Stanger, Woodrow Wilson, and the rest of the *Progressive Movement* ruling class of this era.

There are many presidential election years to look back on with regret and disdain. The 1912 election year is definitely one of them. The Republican Party nominated President William H. Taft as their candidate for re-election. The Democratic Party nominated Woodrow Wilson to challenge President Taft. A third Party would challenge both the Republicans and Democrats for the Presidency that year. It had been four years since his defeat in the Republican Primary and those years were not spent in quiet, peaceful, or anonymous civilian endeavors. Former President T. Roosevelt, now a *Progressive Party Candidate*, was back with a vengeance. He founded and chaired the *Progressive Party*. It was not a surprise when he was nominated as their candidate for President.

Let us discuss the *Progressive Party* for a moment here. The nickname of this Party was the *'Bull Moose Party.'* How did it get such an obscure name one might ask? When Theodore was interviewed by the press, a reporter asked him if he was healthy enough to be President again. Roosevelt answered by telling the reporter he was as strong as a Bull Moose and the name stuck. If we were to look at the *Progressive Party Platform* with eyes from the year 2000, it would seem quite ordinary and benign. But in 1912 the *Progressive Platform and ideology* scared the hell out of many Americans. Americans love change from time to time and after 12 years of Republican rule, change was in the air again. Compared to Theodore Roosevelt, Woodrow Wilson seemed like the type of safe change the nation wanted.

Had he been honest about his beliefs, Woodrow Wilson would have never been elected either. The truth is he was as much a Progressive as Roosevelt but was smart enough to keep his beliefs to himself during the election. The Woodrow Wilson era would lay the foundation for the next 100 years of *Progressive ideologies* and their agenda being implemented in America. It was this destructive ideology and implementation of their agenda which led to our downfall.

I asked Sharron, "If there was one year you could point to and say that was the year America came to a crossroad and decided to take the wrong path, which year would that be?"

She thought about the question for a minute and said, "The first was 1913 and the other was 1933. The 1933 first term of Franklin Roosevelt began an era of unbridled federal power and control over America. I think 1913 was more destructive due to it being the year Woodrow Wilson was inaugurated and the *16th* and *17th* Amendments were added to our Constitution."

I had to agree with her assessment. She continued to amaze me on her grasp of American history.

Let us look at 1913 in greater detail. Woodrow Wilson has been inaugurated as President. Over the next eight years, he will imbed the ideology of *Progressivism* into the Federal Government. He is a racist and a supporter of the Ku Klux Klan. He will segregate the Federal Government into white and colored departments. He will also do this within the military. He is everything a President should never be but as a Democrat his beliefs and behavior are accepted and championed.

The *16th* Amendment is one of the most destructive Amendments added to our Constitution. By voice of the people the Federal Government could now lay tax burdens on those same people. The States and the people voted to enslave themselves to their own government. Congress could now find any source of tax revenue it deemed necessary for their use. The only roadblock was the U.S. Senate which was controlled by the States. Only they could stop any abuse the House of Representatives could try to impose. *Progressives* knew they would need to change this part of the Constitution in order to further their goals.

It had been almost 50 years since the *13th* Amendment abolished slavery for 4 million people. As of 1910 there were 76 million Americans. They, along with their States, now voted to become a 'percentage' of a slave based on their tax bracket. Truth be told, any percentage of a slave, is full slavery to the government.

The *17th* Amendment, which elected Senators by direct, or popular vote eliminated the ability of the State Legislatures to thwart the never ending hunger for benefits from the *people's chamber,* also more commonly known as the 'House of Representatives.' The States could no longer exercise their ability to implement the checks and balances on federal power our Founding Father's placed in our Constitution. Although previously appointed by their State's Legislatures, the people would now elect their Senators by popular vote, as they do for the House. The States' Legislatures have been completely removed from the national legislative process.

Though it would take years or even decades for the ills of this Amendment to take hold, it would and with destructive results. States could now be financially crippled by un-funded mandates and liabilities placed on them by their elected officials.

I think it is imperative to illustrate how difficult the process is to add an amendment to our national constitution, let alone two amendments within one year. The process requires 2/3 of Congress to vote for the Amendment and ¾ of the States in order to ratify it. One might ask themselves, 'Why did the Founding Fathers make this process so difficult? Why didn't they use a simple majority in Congress and the States for the amendment process? Why indeed?'

Has any true Democracy ever succeeded?

The answer is no.

When people can vote for 'entitlements' with a simple majority, there will be no end to the burdens placed on the backs of their fellow citizens who are also expected to pay for those 'entitlements.' This is one of the reasons why Theodore Roosevelt was not successful for what some would consider his third term as President. His *Progressive Party* was not given wide support from the people in 1912. Their ideology was more of a *Fabian Socialist* platform with one additional belief. They believed the constitutional amendment process of super majorities should be eliminated and replaced with a simple majority rule.

I am certain that had *'We the People'* not seen through the Progressive Party platform and ideology in 1912, the collapse of this nation would have occurred many years earlier.

It was not all gloom and future doom in 1913. Americans were changing the world. Henry Ford invented the first assembly line for his cars. Up to this point, all products were handmade and required a great deal of time, effort, expertise, and expense to produce. The Ford Motor Company would revolutionize rapid manufacturing for the entire world. Soon, all products throughout the world would adopt this new method to increase efficiency and profitability. Capitalism was alive and well in America and was being spread to other nations.

This year would not end on such a high note. Since our nation's founding there has been a great deal of discussion and discord on the necessity of a central bank. The discussion, debate, and indecision of the past ended in 1913. Congress authorized the Federal Reserve System and we now had a *central bank* for our currency. This new 'central bank' was charged with the obligation to protect the value of the U.S. dollar. To give this non-government agency legitimacy, the President would nominate the head of the Federal Reserve Board and the Senate would advise and consent to the nomination. Congress gave its Article I Constitutional authority and obligation to 'value the currency' of the United States to a group of bankers. There would only be a moderate amount of congressional oversight on this central bank.

When a ship is moored to the dock it can move a little with the currents and tides. Now visualize the ship as our nation and the dock as our Constitution. The ropes that hold the ship to the dock are strong and firmly attached at both ends from 1791 to 1913. With the implementation of the *Progressive Agenda* and the ratification of the *16th* and *17th* Amendments along with the formation of the Federal Reserve System, our nation was cutting each of the ropes that held her safely in place. There were not many ropes holding the ship to the dock and the ones left were being put under greater and greater strain every year.

Thomas Jefferson had warned us, as did many of our Founding Fathers, to not get involved in European entanglements and squabbles. One of these occurred in 1914 when World War I broke out. We declared this to be a European problem and would stay out of this squabble for another three years. When we did get involved, the power structure of the world would change.

The following year, 1915, Congress authorized the formation of the U.S. Coast Guard. In order to free up the U.S. Navy to fulfill their duties, the Coast Guard was tasked with the job of securing our coastlines and water ways. Their job would include the interdiction of 'rumrunners' during Prohibition. They would also aid in search and rescue operations at sea.

Championed by the Democratic Party for her vision and promotion of reproductive rights and a true believer in the *Eugenics Movement*, Margaret Sanger opened Planned Parenthood in 1916. She was a racist and an anti-Semite who believed the Black population should be eliminated through abortion. This evil ideology is clearly made evident in placing 8 out of 10 clinics specifically in minority communities. I believe 1916 was one of the darkest years in the soul of our nation.

Presidential elections occur every four years, but it always seems they happen more often than that. This was the case in 1916. Woodrow Wilson won a second term with the slogan, 'He kept us out of war.' The following year we would enter World War I or the 'War to End All Wars.' During this year, we purchased the Virgin Islands from Denmark. Congress then created the U.S. Forest Service to manage and protect our national parks and monuments.

Before we move on to 1917, I want to speak a little more about Woodrow Wilson and his Presidency. Who was Woodrow Wilson? To this day, he has been the only President to have a PhD. If my memory serves me correctly, I believe his doctorate was in history and/or political science. With his PhD came an heir of superiority found among many with high levels of education. He believed the most intelligent people should lead or rule over the common folk. And who would these intelligent people be? Why those who held degrees on pieces of paper from a school of high regard, *of course.*

Being from the South influenced him greatly concerning his views on Black Americans and those of color. As President he showed the movie, 'The Birth of a Nation' in the White House. This was a white supremacists movie declaring white superiority in America. The Ku Klux Klan features prominently in this film. I think it only fair to claim he was a racist to his core.

Prior to becoming President, one of his core beliefs was that the American system of delegated and enumerated powers was *not in conformity* with modern times. He believed the Legislative Branch held too much power and the Executive Branch, especially post Civil War, held too little power. He wanted to change our system of government to a British Parliamentary form of governance with a Prime Minister holding great influence and power. He would change his views slightly after watching what Teddy Roosevelt had accomplished by being a forceful Commander in Chief.

Less than four months after his second inauguration, the United States entered World War I. We sent over two million men to bolster the ranks of the British, French, and other allied nations. Germany, Turkey, and Hungary did not have the resources to combat the combined Allied Powers and would soon surrender. This is when President Wilson would put forth his dream of the League of Nations. He believed war could be avoided if nations would sit and talk over their grievances instead of marching into war over them. Many nations did agree to join the League of Nations. Our Senate did not agree to ratify this treaty on the grounds of possible loss of national sovereignty. In November of 1918 the armistice was agreed to by the warring parties and the guns fell silent. It had only taken one and a half years for America to push the war to a conclusion.

The year is 1919 and the location is Versailles, France. The leaders of the world have gathered to formally conclude World War I. Every major and minor power is there to try and acquire something from this group. Vengeance was on the agenda from the victors. Their belief was they had the ability to crush the pride of the German people and subdue them under burdensome war reparations. Where the Roman Empire had failed over a millennium ago, the Allied Powers would succeed today. After the treaty was signed and the victors had their blood, they had no idea they had just sown the seeds of another world war in only 20 years.

Had the Allied Powers received the surrender of Germany with humility and empathy for the German people, perhaps 80 million lives could have been spared in the next Great War. After our own Civil War we could have sought vengeance on the South but love, sympathy, compassion, with the desire to reunite the Republic under one flag, won the debate. Perhaps Europe should have followed our example in Versailles.

The European powers rolled out a map of the world and began to draw lines on it and declared the land within those lines to be nations. Many of the Middle East nations had never been recognized as such prior to this time. Kings of territories with undefined lines fought for extended lands and resources. Suddenly these kingdoms were nation states that had definite borders. Worse still these same European powers divided up the world into spheres of influence and control. National sovereignty was not acknowledged unless you were one of the power brokers. Such hubris on the parts of the European powers would have long term consequences.

Let us now return to America. In the conclusion of 1919 we added yet another Amendment to our Constitution. Our Founding Fathers had warned us not to use the amendment process in our Constitution for light or trivial things. But we did it anyway. World War I was over. Two million men were coming home to a nation in recession and heading towards a depression. Yet the biggest concern at this time was to end the consumption of alcoholic beverages. I find it difficult to understand why we went through the amendment process to do this. The 18th Amendment would prove the theory of unintended consequences to be true.

The decade came to a close with the ratification of the 19th Amendment. This Amendment secured the right for women to vote in this nation. Just a side note here concerning this Amendment. Most of the Democrats in Congress voted again to deny another group of Americans their right to participate in their elections and government. It may not be their intention, but it seems the Democratic Party is bound and determined to be on the wrong side of history when it comes to freedom, liberty, and natural rights.

So we arrive in 1920 and there are 100 million Americans doing their best to survive the economic devastation of the depression. With another Presidential election upon us, a change in national politics is in the air. Woodrow Wilson had failed to place the United States under a one world governing body ruled by elitists. America will remain sovereign and free because the Senate refused to place America in the League of Nations. Warren G. Harding, a Republican is elected President and Calvin Coolidge, also a Republican will serve as his Vice President. Harding will only live for two and a half years of his first and only term.

Next, I would like to discuss more about Calvin Coolidge and his Presidency. He was one of my favorite Presidents of the *20ᵗʰ* Century. Other men who I respect and were Patriots would include Ronald Reagan a Republican, Harry S. Truman a Democrat, and John F. Kennedy also a Democrat. We will discuss each of them in later interviews but for now let's focus on Calvin Coolidge.

If I were to ask a group of people to tell me about the Great Depression, I would get a fairly wide range of answers concerning the depression of the 1930's. This is not the depression I would be referring to though. The depression of 1920-1921 in many ways was deeper and spread wider over the U.S. economy than the 1930's depression. So why have so few people heard about this depression? One word sums it up, duration.

It is 1920 and the worst economic depression in American history has struck. The voters once again have turned to Washington D.C. to fix their woes. They have elected you as President and want you to wave your magical Presidential wand over the nation and restore everything. What do you do?

Governments only have a limited amount of tricks up their sleeves to repair such problems. They can get out of the way and let the free commerce market, also known as Capitalism, clean up the mess or they can institute programs, raise taxes, spend debt ridden stimulus money, or take total control of the nation's economy. I ask again, as President, "What are you going to do?"

Harding and Coolidge opted to let Capitalism fix the problem. They did this by cutting taxes in half and by shrinking the Federal Government by half. In other words, they got the government out of the way and let the economy restore itself. Free commerce, free markets, or Capitalism is not pretty, but it is incredibly efficient. Within two years the depression was over and we began what is called the Roaring 20's.

Let's highlight some events of the 1920's and move on to the end of the decade. In 1922 the Lincoln Memorial was dedicated. In 1924 Calvin Coolidge is elected President for the first time. That same year the first Winter Olympics is held. In 1927 Charles Lindbergh flies non-stop from America to Paris. Herbert Hoover, a Republican wins the Presidential election in 1928. He would be sworn in March 4, 1929 and seven months later the stock exchange would crash precipitating the Great American Depression.

I almost forgot one more event from 1927. Earlier we had discussed a little bit concerning the Eugenics Movement. As a reminder, Woodrow Wilson was a eugenicist and while Governor of New Jersey signed a bill into law forcing the 'feeble minded' to be sterilized. Well, it took time for this to wind its way through the courts but it eventually landed in the Supreme Court of the United States. The court gave its stamp of approval to the eugenics ideology by upholding the compulsory sterilization of the 'feeble minded' as Constitutional. The initial step towards ridding society of its unwanted or the unproductive had begun with this ruling.

Before we conclude this portion of the interview and move on to the 1930-1950 interviews, I would like to go into further details concerning three topics. The first will be the *18ᵗʰ* Amendment, followed by Calvin Coolidge, and finally the stock market crash of 1929.

A short time ago we discussed the *18ᵗʰ* Amendment. Here we will discuss this Amendment as being the *'poster boy for unintended consequences.'* Alcoholic beverages have been consumed by man for thousands of years. When a nation criminalizes such behavior, there will be consequences. Every time a product or service is made illegal, black markets will appear over night to supply the demand. Criminal organizations will control the supply of goods and services and make a fortune doing so. This windfall of income will create organized crime, (the union of criminals, politicians, and law enforcement) to benefit and profit from each other. Finally, violent crime will escalate as criminal empires fight for more control over goods and services. Is this not exactly what happened during Prohibition? Future generations should take note of this example.

Calvin Coolidge was one of the last pro-Constitutional Presidents. He was an ardent proponent of small government, low taxes, individual liberty, personal responsibility, rugged individualism, and free market Capitalism. He knew the simple truth of the smaller the government, the greater your freedom. The opposite is also true. He knew the individual and Capitalism could solve almost any problem found within this great nation. There would be other Republican Presidents after Calvin Coolidge. Many would not be as firm in their beliefs as he was or in the Party Platform which included these ideals.

Calvin Coolidge was one of the finest examples of a true American Patriot.

All economies have highs and lows. When they are at their highs, everyone takes credit for it including politicians. When economies hit their lows, it is always someone else's fault. Truth be told these highs and lows are all cyclical and will happen every 7-10 years. The stock market crash of 1929 was predictable and has happened many times in our economic history. Our economy had come roaring back from the 1920-1921 depression and everyone was benefitting from it. Herbert Hoover had followed Calvin Coolidge into the White House. But the decade that came in with a roar, would end in a whimper.

What happened from 1921-1929? With the Hardy-Coolidge tax cuts in place, Americans had more money in their wallets and purses to spend, save, or invest. All Americans could see the stock market soaring as people bought products and companies made profits. Nobody wants to be left out of a good time. Many people took their extra money and jumped into the stock market. This made the price of stocks soar. Then more people wanted to benefit which made the stock market soar even higher and so on it went. The problem was there were not enough profits in the companies to support their inflated stock prices. The balloon had stretched as far as it could and then it popped. So what caused the stock market to crash in 1929? In my opinion, unfettered greed on the parts of individuals and companies was the true cause.

There is a monster that lives among all mankind. When this monster escapes from its cage it will devour everything and leave little or nothing behind. This monster is called greed. Regardless if you are in the stock market, real estate market, commodities market, or any other business this monster will wreak havoc and mayhem from time to time. History repeats itself and the lessons of economic euphoria and depression must be learned by each generation. When the school of hard knocks is called into session, man must face his consequences. Will he run to government for help and protection or will he face the pain and growth head on? Confronting one's consequences and conquering them is always a better choice. President Hoover had these same choices during his Presidency. He would do everything wrong concerning the economic crisis of 1930. More on this subject matter tomorrow.

It was getting late in the evening and I was getting tired. I asked Sharron if we could meet at 10a.m. again tomorrow. She asked if it would be alright to meet earlier tomorrow because her daughters had a school function at 6p.m. and she wanted to be there if possible. I told her by all means we could begin early. I also told her how important it was for her to attend every activity involving her children. I had missed so many of my kids' functions due to work and other commitments. Not a day goes by that I do not feel remorse for having missed so much. She collected her things and went to her car and drove away. As I closed the door, I knew I had some research to do for tomorrow. The Great Depression and World War II were up next.

THE FOURTH INTERVIEW 1930-1950

It was 7am and I had been awake for over an hour. It was not long ago that I would rarely go to bed before midnight and get up at 4 or 5a.m. I never slept. I always had something to read, research, ponder, or discover. I did not want to leave this world knowing I had spent 25-33% of it with my eyes closed and unconscious. After my 3rd interview yesterday, my wife and I had dinner, listened to some music, and I went to my study to take notes on today's subject matter. This 4th interview weighed heavy on my mind and soul. I wanted, no, I 'had' to be as accurate as humanly possible with my facts and beliefs about the next time period that we would discuss.

One of my dearest friends would have told me I had 'luggage' on my face. She was probably right. I was a little tired this morning. Why I was tired, I wasn't sure. Perhaps it was the interviews the day before or if the clouds and rain had anything to do with it? Regardless, I had work to do around the house and an interview in two hours. I had to get cleaned up, have breakfast, feed the critters, and perform a few house maintenance chores within the allotted time.

I had completed my list of chores when the neighbor's dog started barking. A quick glance down at my watch told me it was 8:50a.m. A moment passed and Sharron's car pulled up in front of the house. Setting up for the interview was becoming routine. In just a few minutes we were ready to begin. I had decided the night before to be a little more interactive with Sharron. I would test my interviewer's knowledge on the 1930's and the 1940's.

Sharron, it is 1930 and Herbert Hoover is President. The stock market has collapsed and the economy is in a deep recession heading towards a depression. Tell me what you know about this year, if you would please.

She paused for a moment to collect her thoughts and began to speak.

"As I recall, in 1930 the recession was in full swing and we were headed towards a depression. The people were in a panic and scared concerning their future. Hoover was President and had some tough choices to make. He could follow Coolidge, his predecessor by cutting taxes and government spending in half, then let the free market correct itself. Or, he could use the government to try and right our economic ship."

The smile on my face was quite apparent to her as she nodded a knowing grin, and I broke in, "He chose unwisely." We both broke into laughter.

I told her how impressed I was with her knowledge of American History. She thanked me for the compliment and I began to speak.

It had always puzzled me how President Hoover reacted to this economic downturn. He had been Secretary of Commerce under the Harding and Coolidge Administrations. He had witnessed and been part of the miraculous recovery from a depression by getting government out of the way of people. Now, during his administration he would come to the opposite conclusion that *only government could fix this crisis.*

I can only come to two conclusions. He did not have faith in the American people and/or he had even less intestinal fortitude *{or guts}*, to do the right thing.

Presidents Harding and Coolidge had one thing in common. They both had full faith that the American people and Capitalism would correct any economic downturn no matter the severity. Hoover allowed fear to conquer him. Faith is the antidote to fear and the opposite is also true. 1930 was an election year for Congress and to save their *'cushy, do-nothing jobs'* the people must see them trying to solve this crisis. President Hoover's re-election campaign would start in two years and if he had not solved the problem by then he would be a one term President. The solving of this crisis never seemed to be about what was right for the American people. It was about politicians protecting their power and income.

As if the situation in America wasn't bad enough, there was also a run on the banks. People panicked at the thought of losing everything and withdrew all of their money from banking institutions. It was as if a snowball was rolling down a mountain picking up snow and growing larger and larger one bank at a time. By the time the avalanche had slowed, many banks had closed, never to reopen.

There is nothing like a crisis *'whether it is real or fabricated'* to loosen the purse strings of Congress. Constituents called for Congress to fix this mess. Now remember, the *17th* Amendment empowers people to *directly* elect their Senators. This started working just as those who crafted this Amendment desired. Congress was on a spending binge and the Senate would give the people whatever they wanted. Everyone should have been scared at first and then taken a deep breath and slowly walked the correct and proper solutions through the Federal Government. All of this was just a prelude to what the future would bring. Every crisis would supposedly be solved by what was actually the *wasteful spending of taxpayer dollars.*

The Federal Government would now go into deficit spending and add more red ink to our national debt. The Hoover Administration would give direct loans to banks, State Governments, and create a host of federal relief programs to try and end the economic downturn. This plan would not work as one might expect. Even government work programs such as the building of Hoover Dam would not bring the nation out of a recession/depression.

We should not forget about the effects of bad legislation. The 1930 Smoot-Hawley Tariff Act was passed during this time to not only stop other nations from taking advantage of America, but to also raise revenue for the government to spend on relief programs. All this 'Act' did was to make a bad situation even worse. Nations all around the world retaliated with their own tariffs on American goods and very quickly world trade almost came to a standstill. What little economic activity had survived to this point from exports ended and the work force employed to manufacture those exported goods was added to the rolls of the unemployed.

Unfortunately, 1931 would see more of the same failed government policies and programs. This created more deficit spending and a great deal of red ink on the federal ledger. A few other highlights from this year would include Nevada legalizing gambling, the start of construction on Hoover Dam to harness the power of the Colorado River, and Congress officially making the 'Star Spangled Banner' our National Anthem.

The 1931 Davis-Bacon Act passed by Congress and signed into law by President Hoover was another instance of the Federal Government getting involved because of special interest lobbying in the free market. They had no business or authority to do so. The 'Act' was to ensure all laborers and mechanics on government projects were paid the prevailing wage of the local community. This would not allow businesses from other jurisdictions to undercut the local businesses or labor market. In contrast, all non-government projects are put out to bid and the company with the best bid won the contract. Government, by inserting themselves into this process, distorts the market and costs the tax payer more money to do the project. This is not government's role or responsibility.

There may very well have been a more sinister reason for this 'Act.' Racism. Black owned businesses and laborers were winning a high percentage of the government contracts prior to this 'Act.' There was nothing wrong with their bids or final product except they were winning and white owned businesses were losing. I believe the Davis-Bacon Act was intended to exclude Black owned businesses from participating in the government contract *tender process*.

1932 began right where 1931 ended. America was in a full blown depression. The Federal Government had accomplished nothing to alleviate the deteriorating situation other than adding a lot of red ink to the national debt. This is not an accomplishment that brings the American people confidence. Nor can it aid in the successful re-election of a President. With unemployment growing, businesses closing, banks failing, and desperation escalating throughout the nation, the time was ripe for a Progressive Democrat to capture the White House. He would use lofty promises and media propelled propaganda to accomplish this goal. Americans were desperate and were willing to try anything and anyone that promised to fix their problems, even if it meant the fundamental transformation of their country.

President Hoover's failures were Franklin D. Roosevelt's catalyst to the Presidency. The American people are very forgiving when a person makes mistakes. However, they will almost never reward failure with a second term as President. F.D.R. would win the Presidency of the United States in an Electoral College landslide. What President Wilson had started with the agenda of the Progressive

Movement, F.D.R. would accelerate. Where President Hoover left off with his big government solutions to everyday problems, F.D.R. would expand his programs into a federal leviathan. The Republic would see changes in the lives of everyday citizens the Founding Fathers would have never, ever allowed.

Sharron, before I continue, I must inform you there are a few Presidents for whom I feel a great deal of contempt. Woodrow Wilson is one of them and the next in line for my disdain is Franklin D. Roosevelt. We will discuss other Presidents later as our interviews continue, but I wanted you to know if I start sounding a little annoyed with F.D.R. and his ideology, I have good reason. I will endeavor to explain why I am so adamant, in a clear, concise and unemotional manner.

She told me, "I understand your feelings because I have similar feelings for many of our former officials."

"Good, now I can continue without worrying about offending you," I said.

President Roosevelt wanted to expand the government with over a dozen new programs and relief agencies to show America he was doing something to fix the economy. He had a problem. Congress was not willing to go along with the amount of deficit spending he wanted. A couple of factors made it difficult for Congress to go along with F.D.R.'s deficit spending. First there was a decline in federal tax receipts because fewer people were working and paying taxes. The other was America had been placed on the gold standard 30 years earlier to inhibit such wild spending. For the past several years, Americans had been buying gold and silver as a hedge against inflation. Gold and silver has always been a secure commodity in bad times. The gold and silver the Federal Government held in its depositories was not sufficient to cover any more deficit spending.

President Roosevelt was at a crossroad. In order for him to grow the Federal Leviathan he envisioned, he needed money, a great deal of money. His problem was the revenue sources were all depleted. Then there was also that pesky gold standard obstruction. If there was just some way to get the gold out of the private sector and into the depositories of the Treasury, his expansion could continue. But how would he do this? He could have Congress legislate a law for people to "sell" their gold to the government, but that would take a great deal of time with an uncertain outcome. He could confiscate the gold and silver claiming a national emergency but this was a high risk move that could bring down his Presidency. Or, he could issue an Executive Order declaring the ownership of over $100 worth of gold to be illegal and the people would be forced to sell their gold to the Federal Government. What would he do?

Sharron, have you read the original Constitution? She replied she had read it several times and thought it to be an inspired document even with the scars of improperly crafted Amendments. I had to agree with her assessment. Then I continued. I have read the Constitution of the United States of America many times in my life and have never read in any article, section, or verse a line where the President is granted the authority to declare any item legally purchased to suddenly be illegal and to mandate it be surrendered to the government.

Only one word comes to my mind when I read about actions such as this. Tyranny.

What did Congress and the people do about this unconstitutional action? They did nothing, nothing at all. Congress should have acted immediately on this and overturned the President's illegal action, but they sat by quietly. I wonder if they were all in on the scheme to deprive Americans of their property? If they weren't in on the scheme then they were duplicitous in their non-action.

What about the American people? Did they not see this overreach of Executive authority? Did they not think for one moment to revolt against such tyranny? Perhaps many of them thought since the government was only coming for those who had gold and they had no gold, this order did not impact their lives. They should have looked through the lenses of liberty and thought about stopping this action before the government came for someone or something else.

So now the people did what the government told them to do instead of demanding the government do what the people told them to do. They sold the government their gold at a fixed price of $20.67 an ounce. This is why I believe Congress was in on this scheme. Within a year of collecting all the private gold in the country, Congress re-valued an ounce of gold at $35.00 an ounce. The government suddenly made a profit of almost 70% on their investment and had a great deal of money to spend and fund the President's programs. If a private business had done anything remotely like this, the owners would have gone to prison and the assets would have been confiscated by the government as an additional penalty for the crime. Yet when governments do this, there never seems to be any crime committed. Amazing isn't it?

Sharron felt she had to speak up. She could see why I had such contempt for F.D.R. and could hear it in my voice. She asked if there was anything F.D.R. did as President that I felt was right. I told her there was, but that topic would be covered later in his Presidency. For now, I would concentrate on the early years, and when I say early, I mean early. His Presidency was only a year old when he took this action. There would be more actions as the years passed.

Sharron then added, it seems like F.D.R. was trying to fulfill the Progressive mission of his uncle Theodore Roosevelt and complete some of Woodrow Wilson's goals. She was absolutely correct. Theodore Roosevelt was not only an uncle to F.D.R., but also a hero figure. We could spend more time on this topic but we are only in 1933 and have 17 more years to discuss for this interview.

President Roosevelt now had a lot of money, most of the gold, a complicit Congress, and the ability to expand government. He would do just that. He introduced his 'New Deal' programs to America and they sounded good enough to endorse by most people. He would create dozens of new agencies and give the bureaucracy unforeseen and un-acceptable powers by our Founding Fathers to control and regulate the economy and people's lives. The only people to truly benefit from these programs were those who worked in and for the government.

I have spoken a couple of times about F.D.R.'s 'New Deal' programs and agencies. Perhaps this is a good a place to list a few of them for this interview. There are the Agriculture Adjustment Act, the Civil Works Act, Civilian Construction Corps, Federal Emergency Relief Act, Federal Deposit Insurance Corporation, Nation Industrial Relief Act, National Youth Administration, Public Works Administration, Tennessee Valley Authority, and the Works Programs Administration. Each of these programs required vast amounts of taxpayer dollars to operate on an administrative basis even before any so-called aid could be given to the citizens. But this was the point of most of these programs. Aid to the citizens was secondary to the goal of government involvement and control of the individual and their lives.

1933 was the 20 year anniversary of America adding two of the most destructive Amendments to our Constitution. The 16th Amendment which gave Congress the right to levy taxes on income and any other source they deemed necessary. It has proven to be a disaster for the American citizen but would never be repealed. The *Progressive Ideology* of wealth redistribution is the ultimate form of control the left would not relinquish until the fall. The 17th Amendment which elects Senators by direct vote of the people has proven to be something that our Founding Fathers never intended: lawmakers only answerable to the people and only concerned about their re-election. There would be no cake and ice cream to celebrate these wrecking balls on society. Also, the *18th* Amendment was 14 years old which outlawed the consumption of liquor in America. The only thing this Amendment has done is create organized crime and corrupt our justice system. Happy 1933!

Finally, Americans had had enough! One might think they'd had enough of the depression which was deepening or their States being removed from the federal law making process due to the 17th Amendment or was it having their pockets picked and enslaved to the Federal Government by the 16th Amendment or perhaps it was the growth and intrusion into their everyday lives by a Federal Government leviathan. It could have, and should have been every one of these issues but it wasn't. What Americans had finally had enough of was not being allowed to have an adult beverage due to the 18th Amendment. So the 21st Amendment was ratified and Americans could now enjoy a good drink or two or more and forget their woes for a period of time.

The Great American Depression was still going strong in 1934. The only positive action taken by Congress this year was the formation of the Securities Exchange Commission or S.E.C. The Constitution gives Congress the authority to regulate commerce under the Interstate Commerce Clause. Our Founding Fathers placed this clause in the Constitution not to control every aspect of commerce, but in 1791 definition and usage, to make or keep regular, meaning to fight fraud and monopolies from occurring. The S.E.C. was tasked to do just this thing. All forms of fraud, insider trading, deception, anti-trust, monopolies, and price fixing must be stopped and prosecuted in order to maintain integrity within the markets.

In other parts of the world there are movements towards dictatorships and bloodshed. In Germany, the National Socialist Workers Party or NAZIS are in power and spreading their control into every aspect of German life. In Italy, the Fascists led by Benito Mussolini are doing the same things as Adolf Hitler in Germany. Japan is expanding its power and reaches into China, Korea, and other parts of the Pacific Ocean. The drums of war are beating all around us but we are not interested in them because we have problems here at home to solve.

When 1935 rolls around, the further expansion of the Federal Government into our lives continues. President Roosevelt and the Congress have all but spent the surplus windfall of money from their confiscation of the people's gold. They needed a new source of revenue to sustain and grow their control of the nation. Another tax would be political suicide in this environment, but a tax with a benefit attached to it should be acceptable to the people. Better still, a tax with a cash benefit would even be easier to sell to the people. The people may even want or demand such a tax and cash benefit program. The best of all scenarios would be a tax and cash benefit program the citizens demanded and it would make the people dependent on government for their retirement years.

The Social Security Act fulfilled every aspect of the best scenario. You and your employers would pay into this loosely defined 'trust fund' all of your working life. When you were allowed to retire at age 62, you would receive a guaranteed check every month until you died. This was sold as a supplemental income benefit meaning you should plan for your own retirement and this check would help you during your retirement years. The move towards people being totally dependent on the government for all their needs and some of their wants was moving forward.

For years I have called the Social Security Act the largest 'Ponzi Scheme' the American People have ever been subjected to. A 'Ponzi Scheme' is when the investors at the front of the line receive the highest return for the lowest monetary investment and the investors at the end of the line, who have paid in the most, receive little if anything when the scheme collapses. That is a 'Ponzi Scheme' and if you did this very same thing in the private sector you would go to prison for life. No such penalty exists for the government or politicians who concoct these schemes.

Sharron had a question for me at this point. She asked if I thought the people who designed this scheme knew it would eventually collapse under its own weight. This was not only an excellent question but it was one I had asked myself several times over the years. My conclusions were that the designers of this tax and benefit scheme were well aware that if conditions remained the same as at the time the program was implemented, then the program could endure. Change one parameter in the equation and there would be stress placed upon the program. Change two or more parameters and collapse is inevitable.

Let me explain.

When the first Social Security Checks went out there were about 30 people paying into the system for every person receiving a benefit check. This was a healthy ratio. Then more people started retiring and this placed some strain on the system but it was still healthy. Then the benefits were increased. So now you have people totally dependent on the government for their retirement receiving more cash benefits with fewer and fewer people paying into the system. Disaster is on the horizon. I am positive this was a known scenario when this program was implemented. But the truth about the program might be even darker and more evil than this.

When the Social Security Act was signed into law, the age one could retire and start receiving benefits was placed at 62. In 1935 the life expectancy of Americans was 61. Could this program have just been an elaborate scheme to get people to pay taxes with no intention of payment? Furthermore, if it was a true trust fund then why were the taxes paid into the government for this program never placed in a trust fund that was untouchable by politicians? Instead, it was counted as general revenue. Deception lies, thievery, and corruption were all hallmarks of the Roosevelt Administration and he had only been President for three years.

In 1936 the world's greatest athletes gathered in Berlin, Germany for the Summer Olympics. They had trained most if not all of their lives to be faster, stronger, and better than anyone else. Those who had trained the hardest and had the most talent were rewarded with a gold medal. In sports, you are rewarded for your accomplishments. Winning is everything. Failure is its own punishment. This is how it should be in life and especially politics.

1936 was a Presidential election year. President Roosevelt by all measures had been a four year failure at his job. He should have been another one term President just like his predecessor Herbert Hoover. The country was still in a depression, he had confiscated all the private gold in the nation, he grew the bureaucracy and the burdens placed on the American people, and he crafted a 'Ponzi Scheme' to steal even more money from the taxpayer called Social Security. Even with all this proof of him being a failed President, the people decided to reward him with another four years in the Oval Office. This confirmed Progressivism had taken root in America and we were heading down the wrong path as a people and a nation.

Sharron, have you ever seen the old black and white film of the Hindenburg exploding over New Jersey? She had. Do you know what year that incident happened? She told me no. I had finally stumped her. I know this was an obscure question but I was seeing how much she had paid attention in history classes. It is hard to believe it happened in 1937. That was almost a hundred years ago. That was the same year the Golden Gate Bridge opened to the public. There was one more event that took place in 1937 and we should examine it closely.

One of the most important duties of the President, next to being Commander in Chief of the armed forces, is to appoint judges to the federal courts. A President can secure his legacy by appointing judges who share his beliefs and ideology. His appointments do not automatically take their place on the bench. After he has made his choice, his nomination is sent to the Senate for review. There they will determine if his choices are in the public good and give their advice and consent to his nominations. There is much at stake in these confirmation hearings for an appointment to a federal court is for life. This is done to insulate the courts from elections and public opinion polls. This is not a perfect system but it is the one we had.

Every President has to contend with a federal court and a Supreme Court that is not always in agreement with their ideology and agenda. This is good. There should always be opposition in all things especially politics. All Courts, up to and including the Supreme Court, would ideally be ones that base all their decisions on the original intent of the Constitution and not on personal beliefs. To have such a court system would be almost impossible. Staying as close to the Constitution is the best way to maintain freedom and liberty. The Supreme Court of the United States or S.C.O.T.U.S. had not been as friendly to F.D.R. as he wished. So he formulated a plan to aid him and his agenda.

The President's plan was to increase the S.C.O.T.U.S. by six Justices, making it 15 Justices instead of the nine we had always had. Now Congress is the *only* branch of government with the authority to create courts, close un-needed courts, configure or re-configure courts, or completely change the federal court system. Congress saw exactly what the President was attempting. He was trying to pack the S.C.O.T.U.S. with like-minded Justices who would be more favorable to his *Progressive Agenda*. Had he been allowed to expand the court he would have automatically had six of the eight votes necessary to ram his agenda through. F.D.R. would have only needed two of the remaining nine Justices to go along with the other six. This was a wake-up call for every person in the nation on what type of President he was. I believe he was seeking a Monarch-style Imperial Presidency or South American styled *strong man dictatorship.* Regardless, this was an evil attempt to distort the court.

Before we move on to 1939, we should review the conditions of 1938. Speaking of 1938, one of my favorite movies is the 1953 version of H. G. Wells' 'War of the Worlds.' I know the special effects were quite primitive compared to the technology used in today's films but it still remains one of my all time favorite movies. The ground breaking Orson Wells Radio Show, which inspired the movie was broadcast in 1938 and performed by Orson Welles. The radio play was done so well that many Americans actually believed the Martians had invaded. What panic this play caused. This is a tribute to the power of imagination and radio.

The Great American Depression is now in its 8th year. Unemployment is hovering around 25%. F.D.R. has created a massive federal leviathan to 'fix' the economy. In order to feed this monster he has raised taxes on the rich as well as those who are still employed. He created the Social Security Administration to collect even more tax money from Americans promising to aid them financially when they retire. He was using that money to fund the bloated bureaucracy. He and his fellow Democrats then placed another burden on the backs of all employers in the nation by mandating a national minimum wage. The Constitution does not grant the authority to implement such a law but this did not stop his Presidency from doing so. In order for employers to comply with this law, they were forced to lay off more workers and seek alternatives to the increased labor costs.

On the world stage, by 1938 Germany has already annexed Austria and the Sudetenland. Japan has invaded China, Korea, and other parts of Asia. Italy has moved to reclaim its former Roman Empire. World War II would not officially begin until the autumn of 1939 when Germany invaded Poland. France, Great Britain, and other European nations would declare war on Germany for its aggressions. The Axis Powers of Germany, Japan, and Italy would in turn declare war on all nations aligned with France and Great Britain.

1940 was a Presidential election year. The people of America have been suffering from the depression for the entire Roosevelt Presidency. F.D.R.'s policies and his 'New Deal' programs have proven to be a failure. He had been given the chance to correct the course and right the ship of America and failed. In fact, every program and part of his agenda has done nothing but prolong the depression and increase the nation's suffering. America was ready for another change in leadership.

Roosevelt had served his two terms and another Democrat would be needed to continue his legacy. This should have been an easy victory for any Republican to win. Political failure is a shoe-in for your opposition. The one thing nobody could anticipate was F.D.R.'s thirst for power. He decided to break tradition and run for a third term as President. I guess if you are a Roosevelt you believe the nation will come to a halt if you are not in charge. Arrogance and hubris must be in the Roosevelt genes. His gamble paid off and FDR won in a landslide. America had changed. We were unmooring our nation from the Constitution at a rapid pace.

Europe and Asia were in deep trouble in 1941. The Axis Powers were expanding their empires throughout the world. China had fallen to Japan, France had fallen to Germany, and Great Britain had been chased off the European mainland by the Nazis. Britain was now standing against the Germans alone. They were in desperate need of food, fuel, medical supplies, and military equipment. The only nation who had an abundance of all these items was America.

World War II has been going on for two years and America has been on the sidelines. We were perfectly happy to let Europe and Asia fix their problems and fight their own wars. England, China, and Russia needed help. Congress finally crafted the Lend-Lease Act which allowed us to help but we would have to walk the razor's edge and not be pulled into the conflict. This action by the U.S. was not unnoticed by the Axis Powers.

December 7, 1941 truly was a day that has lived in infamy. Japan had sent four aircraft carriers filled with fighters, torpedo bombers, and dive bombers to attack and destroy the American Pacific Fleet in Pearl Harbor, Hawaii. The formal declaration of war from Japan against America did not arrive until the attack had been completed. The following day the United States declared war on Japan.

Germany followed by declaring war on America and we then declared war on Germany and Italy. The sleeping giant of America was awake now and was very angry.

What followed next is one of the most disgusting events in American history.

In 1942 President Roosevelt issued Executive Order 9066 stripping an entire group of people of their Constitutional Rights. What had they done to warrant such a draconian action? They were Americans of Japanese descent. These people were rounded up and placed in internment camps for most of the war. They were never given back their homes, businesses, or livelihoods. In fact, they were never compensated for the illegal actions of a rogue President.

You know Sharron, it never ceases to amaze me on how the Democrats are always on the wrong side of natural laws, basic human rights, and our Constitutional Rights. She said she agreed with me but she also had a question on how I would define each of these terms. She asked me to explain what natural laws are.

Natural laws are given to all mankind by God. He would never infringe on those rights because they are based on free will, choice, and self determination. Life, liberty, personal property and the pursuit of happiness are a few of these rights. Basic human rights are rights recognized by all civilized people. They are an extended version of natural law and rights. Constitutional Rights are written into a nation's founding documents. They are not the same from nation to nation but our Constitution lists them very specifically and it is the government's duty to protect those rights. Every person in every nation should have the same rights as we do in America because these are God given rights. The difference is man has inserted himself between man's God given rights and the desire for control over their citizens.

I hope this helped. She said it was a great definition of rights and thanked me.

In 1942 the first battles between American soldiers and the Germans in North Africa and the Japanese in the Pacific took place. We took heavy casualties going up against battle hardened German and Japanese soldiers. It may not have been a great showing of American military fighting power, but we would catch up quickly with these enemies who had been fighting for the past couple of years. To become a battle hardened soldier you must survive your first battles and learn how to fight and survive. Our time was coming very soon.

It is said that man's technological advances come quicker during times of war. This is probably very true. Each side in a conflict must find a faster and more efficient way of killing their enemies in order to conquer and survive. This sounds horrible but it is the true nature of military conquests. To this end, America was in a race we had to win. We had the most powerful military industrial complex man had ever known, but each side was trying to obtain the first nuclear weapon to use in order to claim victory. Such a weapon would render useless the other side no matter which side that was. We had to be the first to harness the atom or we could lose this war. It was during this year that we split the atom, and we were on our way to having the first weapon of mass destruction.

It is strange how the world can be at war but here in America life goes on pretty much as normal. In 1943 one of our most important Founding Fathers had a memorial dedicated to him. The Thomas Jefferson Memorial is one of the most beautiful tributes to this great man and patriot. America would spend the rest of this year island hopping in the Pacific fighting the Japanese on our way to their home islands. We would also begin our march through North Africa, cross the Mediterranean Sea and land in Italy to fight the Germans. Our soldiers were now battle hardened and ready for the final push across the Pacific and into German held Europe.

The date is June 6, 1944. It is D-Day. The full scale invasion of the European theater of war is taking place. We have already liberated Italy from the Germans and our landings in France will place tens of thousands of soldiers on the continent ready to fight the Germans. As the Russians pushed towards Berlin from the East and we fought our way to the same goal from the West and South, the outcome of this war should have been obvious. Germany would lose to the Allies. It was just a matter of time and how many people would have to die before they surrendered.

This war has the full support and cooperation of America's military manufacturing industry. We are building ships, planes, and all other armaments at a breath taking pace. No other nation has the ability or capacity to fight a war on two fronts and have more supplies, equipment and men than we need in order to win a conventional war. We also have an ace up our sleeve.

Congress took steps this year to ensure what had happened at the end of World War I would not be repeated. When that war ended, we had soldiers come home to a nation in a recession and there were few jobs and fewer prospects for making a better life after having served their nation in war. When this war ended, there would be two million men coming home to reclaim their civilian lives. Congress passed the G.I. Bill of Rights during this year guaranteeing education, healthcare, housing, and other benefits for all veterans. I believe this was a good and proper thing to do for the best of Americans.

Lest we forget with this World War going on, we were in a Presidential election year during 1944. Even though his health was failing rapidly, F.D.R. ran for President again and won. Roosevelt's four term Presidency would be the last one in our nation.

One of the most alarming times in American history happened in 1944. It was not another war or economic catastrophe; it was a proposal by F.D.R. called the *2nd Bill of Rights*. The original Bill of Rights guaranteed individual rights and included some group rights such as the right to assemble and air grievances. The States were also guaranteed specific rights but the individual was where all rights started and ended. Governments were charged with doing all they could to protect the individual and their rights.

Among Progressive and Socialists, our Constitution was often referred to as an antiquated Charter of Negative

Rights. This disparagement would also include the original Bill of Rights. They had real contempt for our founding documents. For the most part, government is supposed to be dormant, inert, or neutral in our lives. Not pro-active or engaged in every aspect of our lives. F.D.R. and his like-minded Progressives did not want limits placed on the *Federal Government.* To them, the *Progressive Ideology* was god and government was the means by which they worshipped god.

F.D.R.'s *2nd Bill of Rights* took an opposite view from our original Bill of Rights. Progressives and Socialists considered it a charter of positive rights. There were specific rights listed that the Federal Government and all other governments were obligated to provide to the individual. You were guaranteed a job, good wages, and a right to succeed in business, a home, medical care, protection from economic fears, and an education.

This was just another attempt by Democrats to control every aspect of the individual's life. It came right out of the writings of Karl Marx. It was rejected by Congress in 1944.

My question is this, how does the government guarantee and provide everything in F.D.R.'s '2nd Bill of Rights' and who foots the bill?

On April 12, 1945 President Roosevelt passed away and Harry S. Truman, a Democrat was sworn in as President. A month later Germany surrendered unconditionally to the Allied Powers. The war in Europe was over. The plans for a final push to end the war in the Pacific and invade

Japan are being made by the military. Once President Truman was sworn in, he was given full access to America's atomic weapons project known as the Manhattan Project. He would soon have to make one of the most difficult decisions a Commander in Chief has ever had to make.

Earlier in this interview you had asked me if there was anything F.D.R. did as President that I approved of. I told you there was and I would tell you about it later. It is now later. He was a good wartime President. After war was declared by Congress, he turned the war effort over to those who had trained their entire life for such an endeavor. He would oversee the effort as a Commander in Chief should but he allowed the military to fight the military's war.

While the President was learning more about our atomic bomb, the plans to invade Japan began to coalesce. The death and casualty estimates horrified everyone. It was estimated one million American soldiers would lose their lives or be wounded in order to conquer Japan. This was unacceptable. There was another option on the table but it was just as horrifying. The difference was between choosing the lives of Americans or Japanese dying. It was time for President Truman to pull out the ace from up his sleeve. What he would do next would save a million American soldiers and countless millions of Japanese.

If I remember correctly, there were six cities on the list of potential targets for use of our new weapon. These cities were removed from the daily conventional bombings taking place. No one knew what the bomb was capable of and a clean target was necessary for bomb damage assessment.

The use of an atomic bomb was as much an experiment as it was a tool to end the war.

It was not taught in schools after the war that we had prepared a leaflet warning the inhabitants of each city on the list that they were targeted for destruction. We even went as far as informing the Japanese civilians in those cities we had a new weapon that could destroy their city in one day. We then dropped millions of these leaflets on each of the cities. Although we wanted the people to flee from our targets, the leaflets were ignored.

We had done more to save innocent lives than any other nation in the history of the world. War is supposed to be inhumane to your enemy. Fighting other soldiers like wild animals is one thing. Vaporizing unsuspecting civilians is another. We chose mercy. We had warned the civilian population and their government of the impending doom and destruction. All we required from them was their unconditional surrender and we would forego the bombings. Japan stood defiant.

We were now obligated to follow through on our threat. On August 6, 1945 the first atomic bomb was dropped on Hiroshima, Japan. In a flash of light and an inferno the temperature of the sun's surface, 70,000 people died and the city was destroyed. We sent word to Japan demanding their surrender or else we would repeat this bombing on another one of their cities. They stood defiant. On August 9, 1945 we dropped another atomic bomb on the city of Nagasaki, Japan. Some 50,000 people perished in this attack and once again the city was left in rubble. We once again demanded the unconditional surrender of Japan or else we would continue our bombing of their cities. This time they responded and agreed to our terms. The war in the Pacific was over and within a month World War II would be officially concluded.

With World War II now concluded, America stood at its pinnacle of power both economically and militarily. No other nation in the history of the world had fought a war on two fronts covering the entire world. If we had been any other nation in history, we would have used this power for further conquests and expansion. How would we use our power and prestige?

The United Nations would hold their first meeting in 1946. Where the League of Nations had failed in their stated goals, the United Nations would try to succeed. This time America would join this international governing body and help it to fulfill its goals. It would be put to the test very soon to see if they could avert another war or if this was just another bureaucracy giving speeches and passing resolutions that sovereign nations would ignore.

In 1945 we had used the first atomic weapons on another nation. The destructive capabilities of these weapons would be experimented with for years. The thought had occurred to someone that maybe splitting the atom could be used for a creative and productive purpose. To this end the U.S. Atomic Energy Commission was formed in 1946 to discover and regulate the use of atomic energy for peaceful purposes. The first nuclear reactor was not far off in the future.

World War II ended in 1945 but two years later in 1947 much of Europe was still in shambles. The war had left economies, housing, food production, infrastructure, and basic government functions underfunded and overwhelmed. Europe was looking for answers to their problems and help so they could return to normal. In dire situations like this, a nation can turn to anyone who says they will fix the problem and make their lives better. This is what happened in Germany after World War I which led to the rise of the Nazi party 20 years earlier. Now an entire continent was looking for help.

The Communists, backed by Stalin and Russia, were rising in popularity. If conditions were left as is and nations were not aided, most of Western Europe may become Communist and worse still they might become Soviet satellite nations. This is when America implemented the Marshall Plan and spent billions of dollars rebuilding Europe and securing their democracies. This action stopped the Soviet expansion in its tracks.

We could rightfully claim we defeated Communism without firing a single shot. It cost us billions of dollars we would never be paid back, but in the end I believe it was the right thing to do and the right time.

It is unfortunate that many people were never taught how Berlin was a divided city after World War II. The Soviet Union, Americans, British, and French all had their sections of the city they were in control of and could influence. This was not a good situation because Berlin sat in Soviet controlled East Germany. In 1947 the Soviets stopped land access to Berlin through East Germany. Stalin wanted complete control over the city by starving out the allies and the German people into submission. Stalin was playing high stakes chess.

With the land access severed, there was only one way to supply the Allied sections of Berlin with food, clothing, fuel, and all other necessities that were needed. They would be delivered by air. Every air worthy cargo plane was put into service. Every nation who wanted to participate was welcomed. This operation was one of America's and our allies' finest hours. The Berlin airlift would go on for two years and it would deliver 2.3 million tons of supplies to the city. The Soviets could have shot down the planes for violating their airspace but this would have started another world war. Stalin had hoped the allies would tire of the airlift but we did not. He eventually granted land access again and the supplies flowed as in the past.

When Woodrow Wilson segregated the military and the Federal Government during his Presidency, it would have been proper for all Presidents following him to overturn his racist actions. It would take 30 years for President Truman to right this wrong. In 1948 he re-integrated the military and Federal Government. I do not have good feelings for the Democratic Party but Harry S. Truman is one Democrat I can admire for doing the right thing when hard choices had to be made.

The Potsdam Accords forbid the Soviet Union from invading neighboring nations and turning them Communist. There was nothing in the accord that stopped them from turning a nation Communist from within. This is exactly what they did to several nations after the war. The process would usually take about three years and the nation would go from a Capitalist nation with some social welfare programs to a full blown Communist ally of the Soviet Union. These nations would eventually join the Soviet controlled Warsaw Pact.

America and Europe needed a counterbalance to this possible Soviet bloc invasion force being built by Stalin. In 1949 the North Atlantic Treaty Organization or N.A.T.O. was formed. America, Canada, Britain, France and other European nations signed on to this treaty. Any attack on any member nation would be considered an attack on the entire organization and member nations would all respond in force. Treaty nations would train their militaries together and share advanced technologies in preparation for a conflict with the Soviets.

After World War II, the Soviet Union was granted administration rights over North Korea above the 38th Parallel. America took administrative control over South Korea below the 38th Parallel. In 1949, America turned full control of South Korea over to the South Koreans. Nature hates a vacuum. Something will rush in to fill a vacuum. That is exactly what the Soviet controlled North Koreans did. They rushed into the south and occupied South Korea claiming it as their own. This would be the first major test for the United Nations. Would they solve this issue peacefully or would this action by the North Koreans require blood to resolve? This is where we will begin in our next interview.

I informed Sharron that the next interview covering the 1950-1980 time period would be a very bumpy ride. I asked, "Sharron, are you hungry and would you like some lunch?"

"I would love some lunch thank you," she said.
I countered, "Let's go see what my wife is cooking up for us today."

I thought I could smell garlic in the air. Today we would enjoy personal pizzas with pepperoni and garlic on them. I would enjoy an ice cold Pepsi. When I offered Sharron one she accepted it with joy.

She said, "I am a real Pepsi fan. Growing up we never had Coke in our house. Dad liked Pepsi. Not Coke, He called it N.O.G. It meant Nectar of the Gods."

We then got to the serious business of enjoying pizza and Pepsi.

With lunch now concluded, we went outside on the porch to enjoy the smell of rain in the air. There is something about rain that makes me feel refreshed and tired at the same time. It is weird, but I guess that is just how I am wired. After about 10 minutes we headed back into the study to continue the interview. We had a lot of territory to cover and we needed to conclude the day's work early so Sharron could attend her daughter's activity.

"Okay," I said. "Let's continue."

THE FIFTH INTERVIEW 1950-1980

It is now 1950 and the United States has transitioned from a war time economy to a peace time economy. World War II has been over for five years. The 150 million Americans living in the country are happy and doing well in the booming economy. We are still occupying Japan and Germany as those nations transition into democracies. It is easier for the Germans to change than it is for the Japanese. With our guidance and influence, the people of Japan will experience their first representative government instead of an Imperial ruler. Soldiers have returned from fighting the war and are using their G. I. Bill of Rights to attend school or learn a trade. Life in America is good.

Japan is not the only nation we are overseeing as they transition into democracies. The United States is allowing civilian leadership the control of their nations. We are trying to get out of the occupying foreign lands business. At the end of World War II, the Korean Peninsula was split into two sections along the 38th Parallel. The Soviet Union would oversee North of Korea and the Americans would oversee the South of Korea. In 1949 we turned over all control of the South to the civilian leadership and departed. This was a mistake. North Korea had been turned into a

Communist dictatorship by the Soviet Union and was loyal
to Moscow. Our departure caused a vacuum, and nature
hates a vacuum. The Soviet backed North Korean Army
marched south and claimed the entire peninsula as theirs.
Another war would now begin.

It may be hard to believe, but in 1950 we started sending
military and political advisors to South Vietnam to help
their government. The seeds of another war were being
sown. The idea of another war between two superpowers
was fathomable, but unlikely. Instead both the Soviets and
the Americans would fight proxy wars against each other
in foreign lands. Both sides would gather other nations
to their cause and sign mutual defense treaties to protect
them from an attack by the other side. The lines of mutual
defense were being drawn all over the globe. This would
continue for decades.

To the point made just a moment ago, in 1951 the
Australia, New Zealand, and the United States Treaty
or A.N.Z.U.S. would be signed and ratified between our
nations. This mutual cooperation and protection treaty
would prove invaluable for Australia and New Zealand
so they would be left unmolested by the expanding
Communist threat. Those two South Pacific Nations would
prove to be some of our greatest allies in the future. In
the end, both of those nations would pay dearly for their
loyalty to us.

In this same year the *22nd* Amendment was added
to our Constitution. Former President F.D. Roosevelt
had motivated much of the nation into never allowing

a President to serve more than two terms. We had not escaped a monarchy in 1776 only to endorse an Imperial Presidency. All Presidents prior to Teddy and Franklin Roosevelt knew this and accepted this tradition. Both Republicans and Democrats never wanted the other side to have another four term President. Had either side been truly concerned about our nation and not their power, Congress would have applied term limits to themselves as well as the President. They believed eight years as President was more than enough, but 20, 30, or 40 years in Congress was perfectly acceptable. If the people wanted term limits on their Representatives, they already had one. It is called the ballot box. It was a dishonest argument. They all knew an incumbent Congressman is almost impossible to defeat in an election.

We would usher in 1952 with another Presidential overreach. In a move reminiscent of dictatorships, President Truman seized American steel mills and placed them under government control and management. He did this to block union strikes and slowdowns from occurring because contract negotiations and agreements were at a loggerhead. The Supreme Court overturned this un-Constitutional action six months later.

Besides the Korean War dragging on, there were two other very important events in 1952. The first event was the detonation of the first hydrogen bomb in the Pacific Ocean. Unlike the atomic bombs dropped on Hiroshima and Nagasaki, which were 10 kilo-ton devices, the first hydrogen bomb yielded over 10 mega-tons worth of destructive force. There is a huge difference between a 10 kilo ton weapon with 22 thousand tons of explosive force, and a 10 megaton weapon with 22 million tons of explosive power. The second event was that this was another Presidential election year.

The next President would be the former Supreme Commander of Allied Forces during World War II. Dwight David Eisenhower would prove to be as much of a formidable Commander in Chief as he was a general leading the European war effort. Although I believe he would have preferred the sting of battle to the slings and arrows of the Presidency. Unlike politics, in war you know who your enemies are.

One of the greatest discoveries in science took place in 1953. The double helix deoxyribonucleic acid or D.N.A. strand was discovered. It would take decades to discover and catalogue the building blocks of life and how we became unique individuals. Every great quest must start somewhere and the future was right before our eyes. When perfected, D.N.A. science would help in medicine, law enforcement and all other genetic sciences. Now the question was if we would try and manipulate D.N.A. science for inappropriate reasons.

Three years of war would end this year and both sides would take up positions on both sides of the De-militarized Zone or D.M.Z. along the 38th Parallel. This is where they had been three years earlier and the only thing that had changed was the amount of blood spilled for no real victory. It was also during this year that the official start of the Cold War began between the Soviet Union and America.

The Central Intelligence Agency or C.I.A. was staying busy this year. They had orchestrated the overthrow of the government of Iran and installed a Shah who was friendly to the U.S. 1953 had been a very colorful year and now we could watch these events on our color television sets.

We kept signing treaties with other nations around the world in order to contain the Communist threat from the Soviet Union and to a far lesser degree, China. The Southeast Treaty Organization was ratified in 1954 by the United States, Britain, Australia, New Zealand, France, the Philippines, Pakistan, and Thailand. The nations of Southeast Asia and the South Pacific were now under the umbrella of aid and protection from America and Western Europe.

In movies and books, the 1950's are always pictured as being so cool and as a great time in America. This is true in many aspects. I think those years produced some of the best cars and experimental aircraft we have ever known. With the Korean War now over, it was time to enjoy our peace. Or was it? In 1955 the Vietnam situation was continuing to escalate. Our advisors have been ordered to train the South Vietnamese army so they could better defend themselves from North Vietnam. I am not sure if we were slowly boiling the frog or if we were the frog slowly being boiled into another conflict.

In that year the Supreme Court of the United States or S.C.O.T.U.S. ordered all schools and school districts in the nation to de-segregate. Immediately, Southern Democratic Congressmen called for resistance to the court's ruling. It had been 90 years since the Democrats lost the Civil War and slaves had been given equal rights, but they just could not let go of their racist heritage. That same year was when Rosa Parks, a Black American woman, refused to give her seat up on a bus to a white man. She was arrested and Black Americans boycotted the busses as a protest. This single act of defiance helped spark the Civil Rights Movement.

Just as a point of interest, Disneyland opened its doors in 1955. The Magic Kingdom was called the happiest place on earth. It is, however, the earthquakes that occurred during the cleansing of America leveled almost all of Disneyland. Perhaps there will be another Magic Kingdom restoring the happiest place on earth for families to enjoy.

Organized labor or unions were at their peak of influence and their highest percentage of the labor force during the 1950's. In 1955 the American Federation of Labor or A.F.L., and the Congress of Industrial Organizations or C.I.O. merged and became the overlords of the organized labor movement. Organized labor would lose ground from this point forward as a percentage of the labor force. In the end, very few private sector unions operated in America. The largest numbers of union members are government workers unions and that is where the fall began. *Their future actions ended those organizations.*

The only noteworthy event of 1956 was the re-election of President Eisenhower. His health would decline rapidly during his final term in office leaving his Vice President, Richard M. Nixon, also a Republican to handle much of the day to day necessities of the office. This inability to discharge the duties of the office due to health problems would be the catalyst for the *25th* Amendment to our Constitution.

The 1957 Civil Rights Act is passed in Congress with almost all Republicans supporting it and almost every Democrat opposing it. Once again the Democratic Party is on the wrong side of history by opposing God given rights and human dignity. It has been two years since the S.C.O.T.U.S. ordered all schools and school districts in America to de-segregate. Southern Democratic Party controlled schools either ignored the ruling or stood in vocal and physical defiance of the ruling.

Commercial air travel received a huge upgrade in 1958. Propeller powered air travel would quickly give way to jet propulsion. Air travel times to all parts of the world would be cut in half. Everything in our nation and the world was moving faster.

We had to re-design and re-make all of our national flags in 1959 when Alaska joined the Union and became our 49th State. This was also the year when the National Aeronautical and Space Administration or N.A.S.A. began the Mercury Seven Space Program. We had officially begun the research and development into manned space travel.

It has been 15 years since World War II ended and a baby boom had taken over the nation. In 1960 there are 180 million people living in and enjoying life in America. It is a Presidential election year and President Eisenhower wants to finish his tenure on a high note. He has asked for meetings with the Soviet Union's Premiere to discuss nuclear arms proliferation and reductions. The Soviets have been complaining about the C.I.A. and their spy planes flying over their nation. Eisenhower denies any such flights are taking place. The Cold War will get a lot colder when the truth is presented to the world. Gary Powers had been shot down in his U2 spy plane over Russia and the Soviets parade him before the world as evidence to their claims. The Soviets then cancel all arms talks and will wait for the next President, John F. Kennedy to be inaugurated before they will discuss any other issues.

President Kennedy would be tested very early in his first year on the international scene. Cuba had fallen to the Communists led by Fidel Castro a few years earlier. The Cuban freedom fighters fled to America for sanctuary and to regroup. They wanted to return to their homeland well armed and supported by the U.S. to take their nation back from the Communists. The agreement was for them to go ashore at the Bay of Pigs and they would do the ground fighting and America would supply them with weapons and air support. With American support and air power, it was thought they would accomplish their goal in a short time. As the people joined their cause, the pace of victory and the overthrow of tyranny would steamroll forward. It would not be so.

On the day of the landings, the Cuban freedom fighters went ashore and were quickly cut to pieces, captured, imprisoned and executed. What had happened? At the last minute, the U.S. stood down and withheld air power fearing an escalation and wider conflict in our hemisphere. Fidel Castro now had obtained total control and power thanks to his Soviet Union sponsors and friends. Our failure to follow through with our commitment in the Bay of Pigs was seen as a sign of weakness and resolve by the

Soviets. The Soviets would take advantage of our perceived weakness immediately and would do so for the next 20 plus years. We had learned nothing from World War II. Evil must be confronted immediately or it will grow and it will cost more 'blood and treasure' to defeat. Every action or inaction has consequences.

In that year America finally placed a man in orbit around our planet. The space race was on and running fast. We were behind the Soviet Union for almost the entire race, but we caught up quickly and passed them by on our way to the moon.

One of those consequences I spoke of earlier took place later in 1961 in Berlin. We had shown weakness in Cuba and the Soviets were going to take advantage of it. If we recall, at the end of World War II, Berlin was divided among the victorious allies into zones of influence and control. There was always a great deal of tension between the Soviets and America and our allies. The one thing we all had in common was the use of the German currency called the Reichsmark. America and our allies decided to change the currency into a West Germany based and controlled currency called the Deutschmark. East Germany and Soviet occupied Berlin now had a currency, (the Reichsmark) that had no value in the west. This may have been the final straw that broke the camel's back.

The Soviets had had enough. They decided to isolate East Germany from the rest of the world and then build a wall to divide their territory in Berlin from the west. They also gave their soldiers orders to shoot to kill any person trying to flee to the West and escape *their Socialist Utopia.* The consequences of inaction and the failure to confront evil would last for almost 30 more years.

I was born in the Year of Our Lord 1962. It sounds like it was a long time ago but for me it seems like just yesterday. In that year we were still in Vietnam as advisors and training the South Vietnamese Army. We had already been there for 11 years and in all that time we were not allowed to engage the enemy. This changed when President Kennedy authorized the troops to fire back if fired upon. The escalation was continuing and it seemed like no one would be happy until we were in another war.

Photos taken by American spy planes over Cuba revealed the Soviets were building nuclear missile sites. This brought the world to the brink of a nuclear showdown between our nations. President Kennedy demanded the sites be dismantled and removed from the island. If this was not done, then he would order military action against those sites. The Soviets may have thought he was bluffing because they had seen his weakness with the Bay of Pigs fiasco. They might have thought he would back down again, so they decided to test him to see how he would react. He then ordered a naval blockade of the island. Any ship attempting to break the blockade was to be stopped by any means necessary. Now this was a real poker game.

As ships sailed from Soviet ports towards Cuba both countries had their fingers on the triggers of their arsenals. One wrong move could have turned this situation into a naval war with massive losses on both sides or at worst, a full blown nuclear exchange might take place. Luckily, cooler heads prevailed and a negotiated end to the conflict took place. The Soviets turned their ships around, dismantled the sites, and removed the remaining missiles from the island. In return for the Soviet actions, America removed our missile sites from Turkey. Both sides had stepped back from the abyss.

There are many things an individual can do to offend God. Can a nation offend God? I believe the answer to this question is yes. If a nation received 'Divine Intervention' for its founding, is given inspiration for its Constitution, its first President dedicates the nation to the Lord, and then turns its back on their Creator, would that not be an insult and an offense towards God? In 1963, America did just this.

Nine exalted lawyers in black robes decided to reinterpret the Constitution and tell God he was no longer needed or wanted in our public school system. The Supreme Court decided to side with Agnostics and Atheists in removing God from the public arena. They should have sided with our Founding Fathers who had no problem with Bibles being required reading in class along with school prayer. They did not have a problem with official State religions either. Their only concern was to not have an official national religion such as a Church of England. For 170 years of our history and much of the lives of our Founding Fathers, there had been Bibles or prayers throughout the nation's public arenas of learning and thought. Suddenly, nine judges are far more enlightened than our founders. This could be counted as our first insult to God.

During this year, Martin Luther King Jr. took his Civil Rights marches out of the South and into the heart of national power. His gathering on the steps of the Lincoln Memorial in Washington D.C. gave America one of the greatest speeches in our history. His "I Have a Dream" set the standard for how all Americans of every color, national origin, religious affiliation, or political beliefs should be treated. It would be another year before the fruits of this labor paid off.

Two more tragedies took place before the year would end. The first tragedy happened in Dallas, Texas. Another President of the United States was assassinated. There are plenty of conspiracy theories surrounding his death such as who really killed Kennedy and why? I have never believed the official findings of the government to be true. My belief is President Kennedy was killed because he was a believer in American sovereignty and would not bend to the globalists and their designs. One day the truth will be known regarding why he was killed and by whom.

Americans have been fixated on the Kennedy Administration and Camelot for decades. We should remember he was a flawed human being and not grant him Sainthood. Besides his abhorrent personal behavior, he had learned to use the Internal Revenue Service or I.R.S. against his political enemies. He had learned the method of changing people's viewpoints and impacting legislation from Franklin D. Roosevelt. His brother Robert would do the same thing while he was in the halls of power.

The second tragedy to occur during 1963 was Lyndon B. Johnson, a Democrat, was sworn in as President upon the death of President Kennedy. He was far more pliable for the Globalists and the United Nations. He would speed up the implementation of the *Progressive Agenda* with his *'Great Society'* programs. The Federal Government was about to grow again. With such growth, a decline in freedom will follow.

It is 1964 and 'Beatlemania' has swept the nation! The British invasion of music began with John, Paul, George, and Ringo. It would be an amazing decade in music and counter culture.

The Civil Rights Act of 1964 was long overdue legislation. Even though President Johnson was a racist himself and had blocked the passage of the 1957 Civil Rights Act while he was in the Senate, he was smart enough to see the writing on the wall. Civil Rights were solidifying Black Americans to the Republican Party. He knew if he was to get them to ever vote Democratic he would need to be seen leading the cause of Civil Rights Legislation. He had full support from Republican lawmakers because it was the right thing to do regardless of party affiliation. He needed to twist the arms of many Democrats in Congress to pass the legislation, and twist he did.

The quagmire that truly was Vietnam would officially begin in 1964. Congress never declared war on Vietnam; instead, they authorized the use of force to fight Communist North Vietnam. It may be splitting hairs but if you are sending troops into harm's way, the entire nation should know it is a war and get fully behind it just like World War II. We should never call war an 'authorized use of force' or 'a police action.' We should only call it what it is: war.

1964 is a Presidential election year. President Johnson will win his election after having finished President Kennedy's final year in office. From this point forward the agenda he will pursue will be his own and not that of President Kennedy's. When President Kennedy said, "Ask not what your country can do for you but ask what you can do for your country," the meaning of this statement was lost on President Johnson. To his very core, he was a Progressive ideologue and believer in an all powerful Federal Government. The final pieces of our destructive puzzle were about to be put in place. Once this was accomplished it would only be a matter of time for OUR FALL to occur.

From this time forward President Johnson is 100% owner of the Vietnam War. He can order his generals to win the war in the most effective manner or he can take control of the day to day operations and target selections. He did the latter. Targets to be destroyed and objectives to be reached were run through the White house instead of the Pentagon. This was a huge mistake. You either release the dogs of war or keep them kenneled. President Johnson ordered the bombing of North Vietnam to begin in 1965. Like it or not, we are now committed to his war.

At home in this year, Congress passed the Voters Rights Act. If you couple this law with the Civil Rights Act of 1964, the Democrats will now face federal prosecution for violating the Constitutional Rights of Black Americans. These laws did not end racism and discrimination. They have always existed and will continue to do so regardless of any law man makes. What these laws did was give federal law enforcement the tools they needed to prosecute Civil Rights violations.

One of the most important inventions for law enforcement and other safety measures was created during this year: Kevlar. It is used in bullet proof vests, helmets, and a variety of products for law enforcement and the military. Any commodity that saves lives is a miracle product. Kevlar is one of those miracle products.

Another major violation of the Constitution took place in 1966. President F.D. Roosevelt placed all elderly Americans on a federal retirement system and *'Ponzi Scheme'* called Social Security 30 years earlier. Now, President Johnson would place those same elderly Americans on a *'federal healthcare system'* and a second *'Ponzi Scheme'* called Medicare. Promises of *improved access* and *affordability* were made to secure its passage into law. These were lies. The reality is the costs went through the roof and access had to be controlled and restricted. The future cost projections out to 1990 were *9 billion* dollars a year. The real cost by 1990 was over *90 billion* dollars per year.

Our Federal Government's entry into the health care industry would distort the market and cause supply and demand issues all across the nation. This was of no concern to the President or his fellow Progressives. Their main objective was to create a system to keep Americans dependent on the Federal Government. This was done in order to ensure political power and maintain control over the citizen's lives. President Johnson was not through with his agenda of generational dependency and destruction.

The Supreme Court's ruling was that the Medicare program was Constitutional. It was not. Nowhere in the

Constitution will you find the authority to implement a federal retirement program or a federal healthcare program. They do not exist and under the 10th Amendment, they should have never existed. At the end prior to the fall, Social Security and Medicare were bankrupt. When you added the debt service to this mess, all tax revenues were used to sustain these three obligations leaving nothing to pay for other programs. The only option was to borrow and spend to try and keep the ship from sinking. It did not work.

Before we go any further, perhaps a review of President Johnson's 'Great Society' is called for here. In the end before OUR FALL, there were over 10,000 people retiring daily. With only 11,000 births daily, it was impossible to fund the program at these ratios. A one to one ratio equals collapse. A thirty to one ratio is sustainable. It does not take a genius to figure out what the end result would be. Johnson's Medicare was another Progressive failure.

Another situation which added to the collapse of Social Security and Medicare was the people who worked for cash under the table. They paid little to nothing into Social Security and Medicare yet demanded the most of these benefits. I find it laughable that these same people often criticized the system and demanded that the wealthy pay more in taxes.

The expansion of the federal welfare system, started during F.D.R.'s Presidency in 1935, ballooned with the creation of the food stamp and public housing programs during L.B.J.'s Presidency. These programs would have their greatest destructive impact on Black American Families. The culmination of these programs removed husbands and fathers from the household and the family unit by subsidizing out of wedlock babies. The Black American family unit was the most stable family unit of any race up until this time period. They had the lowest divorce and out of wedlock birthrate in the nation. The Democratic Party and other Progressives intentionally dismantled the most stable family unit in order to create a permanent underclass, expand government dependency, and secure a permanent voting base.

The evidence or should we say the outcome of such an ideology from the Democrats and Progressives has been the explosion of youth gangs and young black males being imprisoned at twice the rate of other races. The lesson here is this: Remove the father from the home and relieve him of any responsibilities to his offspring and you will have generations of wild and un-disciplined young males roaming the streets and getting into serious trouble. This is the true legacy of the Democratic Party.

I want to remind you the Democratic Party Legacy also embraced segregation, slavery, the denying of citizenship to freed slaves, promoting Jim Crow Laws, the Ku Klux Klan, and the denial of voting rights of Black Americans and all women who were citizens. Furthermore, let us not diminish the intent of Margaret Sanger and Planned Parenthood placing of 80% of abortion clinics in predominantly Black American neighborhoods to practice and encourage the ideology of Eugenics veiled as birth control or reproductive rights. This is a soft genocide of those deemed inferior.

These ideas and practices are evil. This is the Legacy of the Democratic Party.

Now let us get back to 1967.

The war in Vietnam was still raging in 1967 and thousands of Americans have already died or have been wounded. There is no end in sight for this conflict. Life goes on here at home even with a war raging half a world away. This year would be the first championship football game to be held called the Superbowl. The game was between the Kansas City Chiefs and the Green Bay Packers. The Packers would win this inaugural event. If I remember correctly, it was played in Los Angeles, California.

On the international scene, Israel was in a fight for their very existence when Egypt, Jordan, and Syria attacked them. The war lasted a mere six days and Israel upon being victorious took possession of the West Bank, the Golan Heights, the Gaza Strip, East Jerusalem, and the Sinai Peninsula. We would continue to support and arm Israel while the Soviet Union did the same for Egypt, Syria, and Jordan.

The following year was a whirlwind of events. President Johnson made it known he would not seek or accept the nomination from the Democratic Party for his re-election. This opened the door for Richard M. Nixon to be elected President. On April 4, 1968 one of America's greatest Civil Rights leaders Martin Luther King Jr. was silenced by a bullet. The civil rights movement would be taken over by others who did not have the same vision and discipline as its founder. Later in the year Robert Kennedy, the younger brother to President Kennedy, was assassinated while he campaigned for his election to the Presidency. To finish off 1968, there were riots at the Democratic Party Convention in Chicago. Anti-war forces, anarchists, and other agenda driven groups clashed with each other and the police. America had seen enough of the violence from the left. Nixon won the election quite easily.

Three topics come to mind in 1969.

First, President Nixon starts downsizing American forces in Vietnam. He wants the South Vietnamese Army and politicians to take over the war effort. We should look at this war and learn the lessons from it. If we support a corrupt government and commit our troops to combat missions on behalf of that regime, we should not be surprised when support for a war is lost at home and abroad. Also, we should never commit our soldiers to any conflict if we are not fully committed to winning the war.

The second event that comes to my mind is a walk on the moon. Man finally accomplished the impossible. Two American astronauts landed on the moon and walked around for a brief time then returned home safely. The seemingly impossible goal President Kennedy had given America before his death was completed. Five more missions would land on the moon and then we would not go back. We left the moon for others to explore. For thousands of years man has looked at the moon and desired to travel there. In less than 100 years Americans had gone from horses and buggies to walking on the moon.

What could we accomplish in another 100 years?

My third and final event or milestone that happened in 1969 was an invention which would not be used to its full potential for decades in the future. The invention was the internet. It was originally created as an information sharing system between universities and government agencies. During the 1990's the true potential of this system was realized and it has expanded into a system we could not live without or so it seems. After more than 50 years, this creation is still growing and expanding in its abilities.

Before we move on to 1970, I would like to discuss another aspect of L.B.J.

It is incumbent on me to inform you of President Johnson's corruption and abuse of power while he held office. He would weaponize government agencies against his political enemies like few had done before him. He used the I.R.S. to intimidate and financially destroy enemies just like the Kennedys and F.D.R. had done. He also became a multimillionaire as President. He purchased radio and television stations in Texas and then used the Federal Communications Commission or F.C.C. to deny other Americans the licenses they sought for their desired stations.

We are finally at 1970. I was eight years old and was starting to notice the world around me and ask questions concerning this world. I considered myself a curious kid but I was probably more of a nuisance in many ways. I would ask my parents how and why things worked the way they did in this world. My mother was the one who would get the bulk of my questions and she would give me the very best answers she could to all of my queries. In that year, I was but one of 200 million people living in America.

Up until 1970 the U.S. Postal Service or U.S.P.S. had been under direct control and budgetary constraints of the Federal Government. This would be the year Congress would change the long history of this service. It was made an independent agency outside of the Federal Government. When I would hear people say this, I would ask if it was true. To me, it is not. The U.S.P.S. still had to have Congressional approval for price increases. They had a self funded pension system placed on them by Congress that no other business had ever been burdened with. So was it really independent?

Proof of President Nixon being a Progressive Republican was shown in 1970. The environment was becoming a big concern throughout the nation. Congress and President Nixon decided to grow government again with yet another un-Constitutional agency. The States were free to set their own environmental standards and work together through their respective legislatures or litigate in the courts for cleaner and healthier air, water, and land. But the Federal Government stepped in and decided to administer and regulate everything and anything that might affect the environment. The Environmental Protection Agency or E.P.A. would override State Laws and Sovereignty. Once again, government grew and liberty contracted.

In 1971 President Nixon finished what President F.D. Roosevelt started. He officially took America off the gold standard. No longer would our currency be backed or valued against any precious metals. The value of our currency would be the full faith and credit of the United States. The dollar was quickly becoming a flat currency and its value would decline greatly over the next several decades.

During 1971 we added another Amendment to our Constitution. The 26th Amendment lowered the voting age from 21 to 18. It was only proper to do so. You could be drafted into the military at 18 and be given the responsibility to defend the Constitution and nation yet you were not old enough to elect those leaders who would send you into combat. This was wrong. If 18 year olds could have voted 20 years earlier, would politics have been affected, especially the Vietnam War?

Another example of President Nixon being a Progressive Republican occurred this year. He, along with Congress violated the Constitution, again. Worker safety is very important. The States could have formed their own individual State worker safety agencies or formed a coalition to promote a general standard for all States. This is what should have been done. All that was needed was a federal agency to be an information clearing house. This is where the Federal Government overstepped its authority. They created the Occupational Safety and Health Administration or O.S.H.A. and imposed their standards on all the States. Prior to the fall all States had their own Worker Safety Agencies. Did they still need a Federal O.S.H.A.?

President Nixon wants the war in Vietnam to end soon. It is not his war and he never supported it. The nation is split into three camps concerning the war. Some want it to end immediately and leave Vietnam without a victory. Others want us to win the war and stay until we do. Still others have no real opinion on the war as long it does not impact their lives. President Nixon had asked for the North Vietnamese to negotiate in good faith an end to the war. They ignored his request. He then orders the bombing of the North to continue. The North responds to him in favor of peace talks. Sometimes you have to use a club on some people to achieve peace.

President Nixon flew to China for an official State visit in 1972. He would begin the process of normalization of relations and negotiate trade agreements with Beijing. China would receive a 'most favored nation' status for several decades due to this trip. This would open the doors to American markets for Chinese products other nations had achieved little access to without tariffs. Perhaps instead of bolstering the Chinese government while it was dying, we should have isolated them like we did the Soviet Union and Cuba and then aided the freedom fighters to overthrow the Communist regime. It is just a thought.

President Nixon was not done visiting other nations. His next stop was Moscow. He was the first sitting President to visit the capitol of the Soviet Union. The main topic of conversation was nuclear arms talks. We each had thousands of nuclear weapons pointed at each other and our allies. One bad decision would have worldwide consequences. Progress on this issue was slow and tedious. Neither side wanted to make any concessions. Each side believed they had a position of strength, so why give it up? It would take almost two more decades before any meaningful reductions in nuclear weapons took place.

All of these trips provided President Nixon with a great deal of respect and political clout. And since these trips took place during an election year, it positioned him in a very positive light. President Nixon would be re-elected in a landslide. Everything was going his way, except for a little incident at the Watergate Hotel.

There were three events in 1973 that really stand out and had long term consequences for our nation. The first event would actually be the second slap to the face of our Creator. In a 7-2 ruling, the Supreme Court of the United States declared the 14th Amendment to our Constitution contained a woman's right to abort an unborn child. The Roe vs. Wade case gave State sanctioned pre-birth infanticide freedom to women and doctors who would perform this heinous act.

Under our Declaration of Independence, all men (women, children, and the unborn) are granted certain unalienable rights. Among these are LIFE, liberty, and the pursuit of happiness. Under our Constitution, before a criminal can be executed for a capital crime, he must have a trial and be found worthy of death for his crime. This is called due process. The Supreme Court stripped all these rights and protections from the unborn. With this ruling we took another step in dismantling our humanity and slapped the face of our Creator again.

The second event which took place in 1973 was the Paris Peace Accords. These peace talks and subsequent agreement ended the war in Vietnam. We had lost the war. There is no other way a rational person can look at the situation and not come to the same conclusion. The North Vietnamese did not surrender to us and we left their nation without declaring victory. It was a bitter reminder that no nation is victorious in every war.

Our nation was at a low point both domestically and on the international scene. A nation the size of California had withstood the most powerful military in the world and we had lost over 58,000 men in the process, for what? America wanted to forget about the war and move on. Unfortunately, we also forgot about the soldiers who were sent into combat by politicians. There were no parades for these men when they came home, only disdain and, worst still, they were forgotten. It was a disgrace to treat those who survived in such a manner.

The third event which took place in October of 1973 was the Yom Kippur War. Even though we had no direct activity in the war, President Nixon ordered Henry Kissinger, the Secretary of State, to give Israel everything and anything they needed or wanted from our military storehouses. This was critical in Israel's victory over its enemies from Egypt, Syria, and other Arab nations. Israel was losing the war in the first three days and then events turned in their favor.

Within three weeks, the Israeli Army had advanced to the outskirts of Cairo, Egypt and Damascus, Syria. We were in full support of Israel and its actions until it looked as if the Soviet Union was about to enter the fray on the side of Syria and Egypt who were Soviet client States. President

Nixon called for Israel to halt their actions and return to Israeli lands and territory. Israel complied but kept some of the captured territories as a buffer between them and their Arab neighbors. The full support of Israel after they had been attacked was the right policy by the United States.

It might be 1974 and President Nixon may have won re-election in a landslide, but a break in at the Democratic Party headquarters in the Watergate Hotel in 1972 would trigger an investigation and cover up that would bring down his Presidency. The objective was to spy on the Democratic Party. The crime to accomplish this was to break in to their headquarters. The reason for President Nixon's resignation was his attempt to cover up the whole affair. Vice President Gerald Ford, a Republican would be sworn in as President at the appointed time of his predecessor's resignation. It was another low point for our nation.

One of the reasons President Nixon resigned was he did not want to go through an impeachment process and a Senate trial for removal. He had been involved in trying to cover up the Watergate break in. One of the listed crimes he committed was his use of the I.R.S. against his political enemies. He was guilty of this crime but to a far lesser degree than his predecessors such as F.D.R., J.F.K., R.F.K., and L.B.J. had done. President Nixon would pay the price for getting caught doing what so many other Presidents had done. I still contend had he been a Democrat, his crimes would have never seen the light of day.

Nature hates a vacuum. When the U.S. military departed Vietnam in 1973, the South Vietnamese Army was not equipped to fight off their Northern neighbors. On April 30, 1975 South Vietnam fell to North Vietnam and we closed our embassy there and departed. We basically abandoned the South and created a vacuum the North would fill. This was the year the Communists united the nation of Vietnam under one flag, the Communist flag. Vietnam's neighbors, Cambodia and Laos would fall to Communism shortly after South Vietnam fell. Southeast Asia was now under Communist control and the reeducation, imprisonment and murder of people in those nations would begin. Millions would pay with their lives for resisting Communism.

A nation celebrating its 200th birthday should be a good reason for celebration. This would have been true if not for the events over the previous three years. We had lost a war, some of the President's advisors had been sent to prison, and President Nixon had resigned in disgrace. We were still the most powerful nation in the world, but we had had the wind knocked out of us. Nothing lasts forever but it sure felt like it. It would take some time to dig our way out of this mess.

Our bicentennial year was also an election year. Gerald Ford was now President due to Richard Nixon resigning two years earlier. He wanted to be elected and serve another four years. You did not need to be a fortune teller to know anyone tied to President Nixon was damaged goods and had a snowball's chance in hell of winning the Presidency. Jimmy Carter who was a peanut farmer and Governor from Georgia would win the election. To say it would be an interesting Administration would be an understatement.

An event took place in 1976 that would have a major impact in the future. It might have only been a trademark but in business, trademarks and patents are critical to one's business' success. Computers were about to come of age and the issuing of a trademark to Microsoft set the nation and world on the fast lane of home and personal computer ownership. One of the founders of Microsoft would have the most recognizable names in the world. Bill Gates would eventually hold the title of world's richest man for many years due to the company he founded.

The Vietnam War had ended some three years earlier and during the war there had been more than 10,000 men who dodged the draft and fled to Canada, other parts of the world, [and for those who were less motivated or had vehicles that were unable to make the trip to Canada], they took up residence in Oregon and Washington State. President Carter issued a general pardon for all those men and just like that, their felony warrants were dismissed and their records were expunged.

Was this a good action to take? Perhaps it was. I believe their actions should have had some form of consequences though. I think a pardon for their actions tied with a banning from receiving any form of government employment or benefits other than Social Security and Medicare would have been an appropriate penalty.

On a personal note here; something happened in 1977 that had nothing to do with what led up to our fall and yet I include it because it meant a lot to me. We were taken to a time long ago and to a galaxy far away. In 1977 the first of the Star Wars movies debuted. The struggle between good and evil forces it seemed took place in every galaxy throughout the universe and it was not unique to our own Milky Way Galaxy. Everything in science fiction movies changed from this point forward.

During this year, President Carter and Congress formed a new cabinet level position within the Executive Branch. It had no Constitutional authority to exist but we were at the point of 'what does this matter anymore?' It would not do a thing to solve the problems for which it was created. This is nothing new when it comes to our federal bureaucracy. All it did was place another federal agency between the people and the free market to solve a legitimate concern. The Department of Energy was supposed to fix our energy woes. As lofty as this goal might seem, I can find no evidence to support its validity for having been created. In fact there is more evidence to the contrary showing what it had done was stifle new ideas and increase the cost of one of most needed commodities, energy. *Big government equals bad government every time.*

Why is it there are so many nations that cannot solve their own problems and turn to the United States to do it for them? Then once the problem is solved and they are stabilized and profitable they tell us to get out of their business and leave our creations and money behind for them to enjoy and benefit? This is where we found ourselves in 1978. President Carter had decided to turn over the full operational control of the Panama Canal to the Panamanian Government. We designed it. We built it. We paid for it. We defended it. We operated it for over 60 years and now we were going to give it away. It was another *'not so bright move'* from another 'not so bright President.'

Economically, the nation was not doing particularly well during the President Carter years. In 1979 the Federal Reserve would change its original operational directive and policy from protecting the value of the U.S. dollar. They would now pursue an all encompassing policy for complete control over all money circulating in the economy. No person or government should have this much power and influence, especially an un-Constitutional agency operating outside of Congressional oversight and controls.

The creation of the next cabinet level agency within the Executive Branch by Congress and President Carter was nothing more than a payoff to the A.F.L.-C.I.O., American Federation of Teachers, and the National Education Association to help re-elect President Carter for another term. It was yet another agency without any Constitutional authority to exist. The Federal Government would now expand its reach into every aspect of educating children by setting standards and guidelines for the States and attaching federal tax dollars to those programs. Any resistance to this federal coup was eliminated when the States saw the money pour in. The *Progressive Agenda* and indoctrination would be welcomed by the States as long as there was money accompanying those directives.

Before we go any further, Sharron, I just wanted to apologize for not being as interactive with you during this interview. I had intended for there to be more discussions during these interviews. I wanted to make sure we were done with this time period before you had to go. I did not want anything to interfere with your being able to attend your children's activity. Again, I apologized. She appreciated me being conscientious of the time and of her being able to leave on time. Okay, with that said, let's finish off the 1970's with one last event then we can stop for the day.

One single event in the last couple months of 1979 would end President Carter's chances of a second term as President. He would enter the 1980 Presidential election year in one of the weakest positions an incumbent President could face. Iran had been a friendly regime since we overthrew it decades prior and installed a Shah. Now the Shah would feel the wrath of his people and lose power to a religious leader named Ayatollah Khomeini. The radical students who followed his teachings stormed the U.S. Embassy in Tehran and took 52 of our citizens hostage. It was an embarrassing time for America on the international scene. President Carter had the most powerful military in the world to use on the criminals as punishment or to use as a bargaining chip for their release. But he was paralyzed.

President Carter had other problems going into 1980. He was overseeing an economy in decline, high interest rates choking off borrowing and lending, inflation, a loss of prestige in the world, and a nation needing a boost in its morale. The perfect storm was building for a massive change in our nation.

What time do we want to start tomorrow Sharron? She said nine o'clock would work for her if it was good for me. I told her it would be just fine for me.

As we were concluding our interview I heard a knock at the front door. My wife Linda answered it and I could hear voices talking and laughing. The voices sounded very familiar. As Sharron and I left the study we walked into the front room and three of the best men I know had stopped by to say hello. It was Mike Leander, David Mahonri, and Wesley Dennis. I introduced them to Sharron and told her if she wanted to know more about our fighting the enemies of America during and after the fall, she should interview each of these men. She took their names and contact information and excused herself from the group and left. She had plenty of time to make it to her daughter's activity.

I then joined Linda, Mike, David, and Wesley in the front room. I told them a little about what was going on with my interviews. They were very pleased to know our history and the events of the past several years would not be lost to time. As we talked, Linda offered to make them some dinner and they accepted the offer with enthusiasm. I was not sure if they had come to see me or if they just wanted a free meal. Either way, they were here and it did me a lot of good to see them again. We sat there visiting for a while and then heard those magical words from the kitchen; dinner is ready!

We all went to the dining room and after Linda had taken her seat, we all sat down and I offered the dinner prayer. We ate and talked about their families and how everyone was doing. Life was going well for my sons. I call them my sons because they are every bit my sons as are my own children. They asked me if I was still causing trouble as a delegate of the State for our Constitutional Conventions and Mayor of our little town. I told them I only cause problems for people who do not love our nation, our Constitution, are not Conservatives, and do not agree with me. This caused a little laughter and Mike said, "So nothing has changed since we were all kids then, right?" I told him he was correct.

We spent the next hour enjoying each other's company and catching up on what was happening in their lives and with their families. It was after 7 pm when Mike said he had to get going so he could put his daughters to bed. David and Wesley also needed to get going for similar reasons. When we got to the front door I gave each of them a big hug and told them how much they each meant to me. It was great to see them and we all agreed to get together again for a longer visit. Linda told me how happy she was that they were still around considering what they had all been tasked with during the fall. I know, I said. So many didn't make it, yet some of my special sons had survived the horrors of the cleansings. We did the dishes and I went to my study to make some notes for tomorrow's interview.

It took me about an hour to write down the highlights from 1980-2000. Those two decades were amazing and I am so glad I was alive to experience them. They were the years I solidified my Conservative views and began my investigations into future events and writing about my discoveries. I reflected on my visitors earlier in the evening and began to recall what had happened just a few years ago.

I had known what was coming in the very near future. I had prepared for the inevitable fall of our nation. We had gathered supplies and personnel to surround ourselves and to help our survival chances. Mike, David, and Wesley had been in my Scout Troop when they were teenagers and had a similar view on the future. They were natural fits for my plans and preparations. We had all agreed to meet at our house in the middle of nowhere when the fall began.

When it began, within a couple of days the first of our group showed up and we began to make our final preparations for what was coming. Within a week, all of my children and grandchildren, along with Mike, David, Wesley, their families and other invited friends were all at our compound. There was no real civilian authority to follow so in our area it was more of a tribal organization and civilization.

Each person in our group had unique abilities and skills to use for our overall survival. We set forth on our previously agreed upon line of authority with command and controls. By voice and vote of all in the group, I was given the reins of leadership for our tribe. I first assigned Mike to be in charge of security for the group and made him akin to a sheriff. He would have several other people assigned to him to secure our perimeter out to a mile away from our compound. Everyone in the group carried side arms and high powered rifles within reach of everyone on a moment's notice. Mike, along with everyone in the compound, was the final line of defense for protecting the children and elderly.

I assigned David and four others to use their skills to obtain information necessary for or survival and to obtain more supplies as they came across them. David had lived on the streets for many years and had survived by being street smart and fearless. Those experiences and skills were invaluable for our survival. He would show up from time to time with information and supplies and I would ask him how he got them. He would tell me, "I will tell you about it some other time." I would not seek further information for I knew he had seen something hideous while obtaining the materials.

Wesley was tasked with securing our distant perimeter and intercepting everyone who was entering our valley from the three possible entry points. Sniper nests and barricades kept the job of entering our valley limited to those who should be there or those we felt should be allowed to join our group. His was the largest group of people needed to operate under our rules of engagement.

Even though survival was of a paramount importance to everyone, we had strict rules of engagement so we could remain civilized and keep our hands clean from the blood of innocent lives being taken. Defense was the key word. We would defend ourselves from every foe but we never sought to engage in an offensive action unless it was absolutely necessary.

The four years we survived from the beginning of the fall and through the cleansing of our nation were accomplished by following the rules and laws within our community. No one escaped any ordeals without having to get their hands dirty to protect themselves and their families. Mike, David, Wesley, and I had all been compelled several times to end the lives of other people trying to do harm to our community. It was justified and necessary but it was never easy to do and even harder to live with afterwards.

It was getting late and I had to be up by 7am to be prepared for my next interview. It was uncomfortable to sit and reflect on what had transpired during the fall and the cleansings. I knew the interview for that time period was in the very near future. I also knew I would try to describe what had happened in our nation and to our people in the least graphic manner possible. I was not looking forward to that interview but I knew future generations needed to know what had happened and how we survived. The most important question they needed answers to was why it all happened. For now, those questions would have to wait. It was time for bed.

THE SIXTH INTERVIEW 1980-2000

Today is Friday. It will be the fourth day of interviews. I was looking forward to the weekend so I could relax and re-energize. I had not realized how energy draining being interviewed and preparing for those interviews would be. The 1980-2000 and 2000-2016 time periods would be covered in today's interviews and were vivid in my memory. Having lived through these times as an adult, I was well aware of the political and social aspects of those times. It was during this time I became firmly anchored in my Conservative beliefs.

Standing on my porch, I took several deep breaths of the moisture laden air. It was still overcast and raining from yesterday and I thought back on how I always loved the rain and the smell the rain creates or enhances. It smells and feels like the earth is renewing itself every time, and somehow the change in the ions gives me the same sense of renewal.

Sharron would be here soon and we would discuss 1980 and beyond. To my grandkids, 1980 was ancient history. To me, it was just yesterday. I had written quite a few notes on the next time period but they seemed very sterile compared to my feelings and remembrances of those years. In 1980,

I was an 18 year old senior in high school and about to graduate from Valley High School in Las Vegas. I had several good job prospects and the possibility of attending college was possible but not high on my list of probabilities. Regardless of all these side notes, I was looking forward to these next interviews.

The Monday after graduation, I would become a stagehand just like my father and like his father before him. I started out my over 40 year career as an apprentice in the M.G.M. Scenery Studios building Don Arden's stage spectacular 'Hollywood Jubilee.' It was a great job and it paid very well. During this time the Presidential Primaries were taking place and it was quite evident Ronald Reagan, a Republican was the right man for the job as President. It has always been a sense of pride knowing my gut feeling about him was correct. I had cast my first vote as an American for him and have never, ever regretted doing so. I did not know it at the time but my political education had now officially begun.

When I look back on my life from 1980 until now, I can see how I was guided by a higher hand through the tough times and blessed beyond my ability to repay them during the prosperous times. The information I learned and the experiences I had all contributed to the shaping of my political philosophy and beliefs. I had written a book called "Just Thinking" many years ago that had described my beliefs. I still to this day hold firm to almost every part of that book.

Sharron would be here any time now and I still had a few things to tend to prior to her arrival. I made a mental

note to myself to include her more in the interviews.
She had a good mind and had a well grounded belief
in our Constitutional system. I wanted to hear more of
her thought process. I also needed to ask her about her
daughter's school activity last night. I would ask her about
that during lunch.

It was just before 9 a.m. when the neighbor's dog
ventured into the rain long enough to bark at a car
coming down the street. A moment later, Sharron pulled
up in front of our house. She jumped out of the car and
quickly grabbed her bag and dashed for our porch to
minimize her exposure to the rain. Once inside, she set
up her equipment and we prepared to begin the sixth
interview. Before we started, I asked her what year she was
born. She told me it was May of 1987. I told her we would
include that year in today's interview.

1980 began with the Soviet Union attempting to
expand its influence into the Middle East by toppling the
government of Afghanistan and then invading it. They
installed another one of their puppet regimes and moved
on to crush all resistance. Afghanistan has been called 'the
country where empires go to die' for good reason. Every
empire that has tried to conquer the people has failed
miserably and at an extreme cost in 'blood and treasure.'
The Soviets believed they were different. Time and blood
would determine that outcome.

President Carter's response to this aggression was to
impose sanctions on the Kremlin. He would also use the
United Nations to condemn this action but it would not

deter the Soviets from their objective. We also placed an embargo on grain and technology on the Soviets and their satellite states. The Soviets stood firm in their defiance.

The Winter Olympics took place this year and America got a much needed boost to its morale. The 'Miracle on Ice' as it was called occurred when our college hockey team defeated the professional Soviet hockey team in the gold medal round. The 1980 census said there were 226 million people living in America. Here are a few highlights from this year. The U.S.A. boycotted the Summer Olympics in Moscow to protest the invasion of Afghanistan. This gave other nations the opportunity to win some medals. President Carter showed again how inept he was by overriding the military objections to a rescue attempt of our hostages in Iran. The attempt failed and several U.S. servicemen paid the ultimate price. I believe this was President Carter's "Hail Mary" attempt to win re-election. Finally, America got to experience the power of Mother Nature when a 'sleeping' or thought to be dormant volcano in Washington State named Mount Saint Helen erupted.

With all the events of 1980 taking place, it is easy to forget there was also an election for President. Ted Kennedy ran and lost against President Carter for the Democratic nomination. In the end the race between Ronald Reagan and President Carter resulted in one of the most lopsided Electoral College landslides in American history. I do not believe it would have mattered who the Democratic contender was. America had seen enough of Democratic policies and was eager for a change. President Carter would lose the Electoral College vote to Ronald Reagan 489-49.

The nation was about to experience a surge of prosperity and national pride not witnessed since after World War II.

Sharron spoke up at this point and told me she noticed every time I spoke about Ronald Reagan I would smile. Was she right? Probably, no, she was right. I was asked if I would briefly explain why I felt like I did about our 40th President.

It was easy to admire Ronald Reagan. I had heard his famous "Rendezvous with Destiny" speech long before he had become a candidate for President. He whole heartedly believed throughout the entire history of man that America was the greatest nation on earth. He loved being a patriot and had complete confidence in the American people doing what is right. He knew America was man's last and greatest hope for liberty in the world and that Communism was evil and it must be confronted every time it tries to expand in the world.

These are just a few reasons why I admire Reagan. Perhaps the main reason I am a Reaganite was he loved liberty. Sharron seemed satisfied with my answers but said she would have more questions for me later centered on Reagan's Presidency. I thought she had reservations about him but added her dad was a huge Reagan admirer. She was curious if we both respected the same traits in him or if there were differences in our perspectives. She was going to collect information and evaluate it later before coming to any conclusion. She was firmly fixing reason in its place. I continued to be impressed with her critical thinking skills.

The 'Reagan Revolution' would take some time to turn this nation around from the course it was on, but on January 20, 1981 it began. Speaking of that date, on Inauguration Day the 52 American hostages held in Iran for 444 days were released. Iran had no fear of the United States led by President Carter. The same was not true about our new President. He had repeatedly said he would treat Iran like the criminals they are when he became President. A new day had truly dawned in America.

Three interesting events took place during 1981. The first highlight was the maiden flight of the space shuttle Columbia. The second highlight was I.B.M. invented and placed on store shelves the very first personal computer. The home computer revolution had now begun and everything would change. The final event to take place was 205 years in the making. President Reagan nominated the first woman to the Supreme Court of the United States or S.C.O.T.U.S., Sandra Day O'Connor.

Sharron spoke up and informed me I had not mentioned the attempted assassination of the President during 1981. She was right. How could I have forgotten such an event? We almost lost one of our most beloved Presidents in the first few months of his Presidency. This close call seemed to have changed our President. He came back from this attempt on his life with a laser focused determination to throw the Soviet Union and their ideology on the scrapheap of history. The 80's would only get more interesting from this point forward.

At this point I decided to just highlight the events that took place in each of the next few years instead of commenting on them in detail. There were many events taking place but few of them had much bearing on Constitutional matters. I will include what I think is relevant. I will highlight some events to maintain a historical timeline. The focus really needs to be on the growing abandonment of our nation from the Constitution. A trip down memory lane will occur in some years and a detailed commentary will happen in others.

I am sure all true Capitalists would agree monopolies are bad and should not occur. The largest monopoly in the nation, 'Bell Telephone or Ma Bell' was broken up in 1982. Competition was reintroduced into the telephone industry and for a while it was a Wild West *free for all*. Eventually self imposed stability ruled the day and within a few years the cellular phone industry was born. Competition and Capitalism are not always pretty but they are efficient. Innovation is always the driving force for advancements.

In the early 1970's forced bussing was the Progressive solution to de-segregating schools. Black children were bused from their neighborhoods into white schools from 1st grade through 5th grade. White children were bussed into black schools for 6th grade and then Blacks were once again bussed into white schools from 7th through 12th grade. This was considered 'fair' by the self proclaimed masterminds. In 1982 we ended this social justice and experimentation on our kids. The idea had failed just as all Progressive ideas have and will.

The U.S. economy is often referred to as the largest ocean liner in the world. For four years President Carter was steering the ship in the wrong direction and it was nearing a rocky shore. Double digit interest rates were common, inflation was growing, and people were suffering from the economic recession. President Reagan has been in office for one year and repeatedly said this ship would take a little time to turn around. Unemployment hit its highest point in 1982 at 10%. From this point forward it would decline drastically. The ship was turning around.

Also, in 1982 the Vietnam War had been over for almost 10 years. In order to try and heal the wounds of a political failure, a memorial to the more than 58,000 soldiers who paid the ultimate price was constructed. The long black wall had every soldier's name who had died serving in the war engraved on it. It should stand as a witness and guard against sending our best people into harm's way and not allowing them to complete their mission and declare victory.

Negotiating with the Soviet Union on nuclear reduction agreements was always a tough chore. They had numerical superiority in both conventional and nuclear arms. We had technological superiority which reduced much of their numerical superiority to a level playing field. They knew any agreement reducing their numbers meant an increased probability at losing a conflict with America and our allies. President Reagan knew he could start an arms race with the Soviets they could not sustain. Part of this plan was to create a missile defense system that would neutralize the Soviet's numerical superiority.

President Reagan proposed the Strategic Defense Initiative (S.D.I.) in 1982. It was also called the 'Star Wars Defense System.' It was a simple idea: Place an umbrella of anti-missile platforms in space to intercept Soviet ballistic missiles before they entered the atmosphere. President Reagan now had the full attention of the Soviet leadership. Their fear of such a system was the catalyst for advancing peace talks for the next several years.

In 1983 if you asked Americans where the nation of Grenada was, most of them would not have a clue to its whereabouts. Even Sharron said she did not know where it was. This was important for our next topic. The Caribbean nation may have little recognition, but it had a good medical school and many Americans attended it because it was less expensive than American medical schools. Under the direction of their Soviet masters, Cuba and other puppet nations invaded the tiny island to try and establish another Communist nation in our hemisphere. President Reagan would not tolerate any of this nonsense by the Soviets. He sent military forces to the island to rescue the Americans on the island and expel the invaders. Within days, the mission was complete and the Soviets now knew who they were dealing with. It would not be business as usual for them. Things in the world had changed.

I could see Sharron was a little annoyed. I asked her if she was all right. She told me she had never been taught about this military action in school. I told her I was not surprised. Schools, the media, and the Liberals who controlled both of them all hated President Reagan. They also had disdain for our military, patriotism, and our Constitutional Republic.

Any victory for those who they hated was a defeat for them and a setback for their agenda and ideology.

The 1984, the Summer Olympics were held in Los Angeles, California. The Soviet Union decided to boycott the games just as we had done in 1980. This once again gave other athletes the opportunity to win medals in events usually dominated by the Soviets and America. The Soviets used lame excuses why they would not attend, but I think they were worried about mass defections by their athletes to America.

The 1984 Presidential election was in full swing. The Democrats called upon Walter Mondale from Minnesota, former President Carter's Vice President, to try and unseat President Reagan. The economy was roaring along, America had regained our prestige around the world, the military was being rebuilt, and life in America was good again. The writing on the wall was plain to see. President Reagan won 525-13 delegates in the Electoral College. Walter Mondale only won his home State of Minnesota by 3,000 votes over the President. It was almost a 50 State sweep.

It had been six years since a Soviet leader and our President had met face to face. I am sure they were hoping for a Mondale victory but when this did not happen, they knew a meeting was needed as soon as possible. The two leaders met in Geneva, Switzerland and from this meeting a nuclear reduction treaty would move forward.

Also, in 1985 Microsoft Windows landed on store shelves for the first time. Computers and their programs were in a race for domination of the industry.

It had been almost 20 years since he was assassinated but it was time for one of America's greatest civil rights leaders to be honored. In 1986, Dr. Martin Luther King Jr. was memorialized by being given a day as an official Federal Holiday.

This same year the space shuttle program suffered a massive setback when the Challenger Space Shuttle blew up shortly after takeoff. All the astronauts were killed. All space flights were grounded until the re-design of seals and other critical hardware could be completed on remaining shuttles. Space exploration has always been dangerous, but most people in this nation believed it was worth the risks.

It has now been a year since their first meeting in Geneva, Switzerland and the nuclear reduction negotiations are moving forward but at a slow pace.

What President Reagan would later call his greatest mistake took place in 1986. Illegal immigration has been a problem in this nation for many years. President Eisenhower used the military to forcibly remove one million illegal immigrants from America over 25 years earlier. There was an estimated two million illegal aliens living here in 1986. To solve this problem, President Reagan signed the Immigration and Amnesty Act allowing the two million lawbreakers this one time opportunity to stay here legally and seek citizenship.

In return for his signature on the law there was supposed to be enhanced enforcement of existing immigration laws and a border wall built to stop easy entry into our country.

Neither of these things happened. Before our nation's fall,
there were over 30 million illegal aliens living here. All the
law did was signal to every lawbreaker in the world that it
was okay to come here. Once their numbers were sufficiently
large enough, there would be calls for 'comprehensive
immigration reform. Those who called for such a fix had
no love for our nation or our sovereignty. It was a ploy to
grow another permanent underclass of people for political
benefit. The only solution was to build an impenetrable
wall, immediate deportations of illegal aliens, stiff fines and
imprisonment of employers of illegal alien workers, and
absolutely no government benefits to illegal aliens.

In 1987, when you were born, Sharron, President Reagan
nominated Robert Bork to the Supreme Court. He was
one of the staunchest Constitutional judges America had
on the Federal Bench. The Democrats could not allow a
firm Constitutionalist on the Supreme Court. They blocked
his nomination and America lost a voice of liberty and
Democrats celebrated their victory. This shows you who the
Democrats truly are.

It had taken two years but negotiations between the
Soviet Union and America finally paid off. The two sides
both agreed to eliminate an entire classification of ballistic
missiles. All missiles with a range of 300-3,000 miles were
to be removed from all over the world and destroyed. Both
sides were stepping back from a world ending nuclear
conflict and now the world could breathe a little easier. It
shows tough negotiations from a position of strength pay off.

When 1988 came around, it was sad to know President
Reagan would be leaving office in a year. Who would take

over and continue his revolution? George H. W. Bush, also a Republican had been Reagan's Vice President for eight years and was chosen to continue Reagan's policies. He would easily win the Presidency in the general election.

Several years earlier, President Reagan traveled to Berlin and stood at the Berlin Wall and called for Soviet Chairman Gorbachev to *'Tear down this wall.'* In 1989 what was once thought of as only a dream, came true. The Berlin Wall was opened to free access and would soon be torn down. Other events were taking place within the Soviet Union and it signaled a change within their empire was at hand.

1990 was an amazing year. The census said there were now 248 million people living in America. They have been prospering like no other people on earth.

What had started out at the Berlin Wall the previous year was spreading all over the Soviet Union. The empire Lenin started some 70 years earlier and Stalin expanded 45 years ago collapsed overnight. Communism has never and will never succeed as long as man has even a spark of freedom in his bosom. There is not just a single event you can point to and declare it was the reason for the collapse. I believe the one thing that was the final straw was an airplane.

While President Reagan was negotiating nuclear arms reductions with the Soviet Union, he was building the most powerful conventional fighting force the world has ever known. To combat this buildup, the Soviets had just spent billions of dollars upgrading their air defense system to intercept U.S. bombers. The money they spent was money they could not afford to spend but they believed they had no choice. Their entire expenditure of those funds was made irrelevant when the B-2 Bomber was unveiled by the U.S. Air Force. Reagan was right again. The Soviets could not keep up with the industrial and technology might of America.

Even with freedom breaking out all over Europe and Asia from the collapse of the Soviet Union, the Middle East would flair up into crisis when Iraq invaded its neighbor Kuwait. It would prove to be the biggest mistake Saddam Hussein ever made. The United Nations ordered Iraq out of Kuwait but Saddam stood in defiance. To ensure the free flow of oil, Congress authorized the use of force to be used against Iraq if they did not leave Kuwait. The United Nations also authorized the use of force if Iraq did not comply by a certain date. The military buildup in Saudi Arabia began.

As forces gathered in the deserts of Saudi Arabia the deadline drew ever closer. At a certain point there would be no turning back. Diplomats worked overtime to try and solve this issue peacefully but it was becoming apparent there was little chance of a peaceful solution. Iraq had one of the largest militaries in the world. Previously they had been at war with their neighbor Iran for eight years. A long drawn our war was not going to be repeated by U.S. forces and our allies.

The military Ronald Reagan had built would destroy the Iraqi military in just 100 days. When the air campaign began, the world watched the most advanced stealth air planes destroy targets with ease. Cruise missile struck their targets with accuracy never known before in modern warfare and with impunity. When the ground forces were unleashed on the Iraqi army some 96 days after the air campaign began, it took a mere 4 days for the war to be over. Our enemies and the world were placed on notice. America was back on the world stage and we were more powerful than ever before.

The only event taking place in 1991 of interest was a mild recession starting within our economy. It would cause President Bush to go back on his word of "no new taxes." The soft underbelly of the President was now exposed. He would not hold to his word in tough times. It does not help your case if you are known as a Liberal Republican by the nation concerning your political views. This did not bode well for the upcoming Presidential election year.

When 1992 came around, President Bush would not be re-elected. He had shown his true colors to the Conservatives within the Republican Party and his support waned. The lies from the media concerning the economy did not help his hope to be returned to office. In the end, a Democrat, Bill Clinton, the Governor of Arkansas, won the election and became the 42nd President.

The first attempt to collapse the World Trade Center Towers occurred in 1993. A massive truck bomb was placed in the underground parking lot beneath the two towers by Muslim terrorists. When the bomb went off, it caused a lot of damage but the towers stood firm. Muslim terrorism had finally come to our shore. Were we going to take it seriously and confront it?

The heavy hand of government power fell on a Christian Fundamentalist group in Waco, Texas during Bill Clinton's first year as President. The standoff turned into a shootout when Federal Agents from the F.B.I. and A.T.F. tried to storm the compound; 51 days later, every man, woman, and child in the compound was dead. It was proven that the reason given for this federal action was based on lies. However, no one within the Justice Department was held responsible for this crime.

Our Constitutional Rights are always under assault by national, state and local governments. The Democrats have led the charge on almost every assault on liberty, especially the 2nd Amendment. President Clinton signed into law the Brady Bill which was named after President Reagan's spokesman who was also shot at the attempt on Reagan's life in 1981. A year later the Democrat controlled Congress passed another infringement on the 2nd Amendment. This time they called it the assault weapons ban. Please take note, when Democrats are in power the law abiding citizens lose their money, their guns, and their liberties.

The 1994 midterm elections would be a revolt by the law abiding citizen against the Democratic Party. The overreach by the Democrats for the past two years would be stopped by the Republicans when they took back the Senate and took back the House after 40 years of Democratic control. President Clinton would have to triangulate his position and move to the center if he wanted to get anything accomplished in his Presidency. I know he did not make this move willingly.

When a nation is about to implode, one of the first things that happens is the value of its currency plummets, and over the course of time, it becomes worth less and less until it becomes worthless. This is what happened in 1995 to Mexico. The Mexican peso has never been strong against the U.S. dollar. Congress decided to take action and infused 20 billion dollars into the value of the peso. It seemed to have worked, but I am not sure it was the right thing to do with American taxpayer funds. However, it did stop what may have been millions of economic refugees from flooding across our border in mass.

Two more events took place in 1995. Two homegrown terrorists, or more appropriately, two anarchists, used a car bomb to destroy the federal building in Oklahoma City, Oklahoma. Many were killed and injured in this inhumane event. The culprits were caught, tried, and paid the price for their actions. Lastly, the forgotten war known as the Korean War had a memorial dedicated to those who served their nation in that conflict. At this time there was still no World War II Memorial in the nation.

It was not hard to predict the outcome of the 1996 Presidential election. President Clinton would easily defeat his challenger Bob Dole for another term in the White House. Even though Bob Dole was a World War II hero and the Majority Leader in the Senate, he had little appeal among many Republicans and even less appeal throughout the nation.

Sharron asked how Bill Clinton could succeed with all the various scandals surrounding him. I knew what she was thinking and as best as I could tell her it was because the media was liberal and supported the Democrats. They refused to scrutinize President Clinton like they would if he were a Republican. Also, if you run a weak Republican against any Democrat, the Democrat will win. You have to have a strong, dynamic, Conservative Republican to defeat a Liberal Democrat. A Liberal Republican will almost always lose.

Only six years after the collapse of the Soviet Union, N.A.T.O. expanded its membership in 1997 to include the Czech Republic, Hungary, and Poland. If another Soviet Union type empire tried to form again, the members of N.A.T.O. would be obligated to intervene. More nations were considering membership in the organization. There were others who had sought membership and were waiting for acceptance.

1998 was the first year the American people heard the name Osama Bin Laden. Unfortunately, it would not be the last year or last time. His newly formed terrorist organization called 'Al Qaeda' or 'The Base' would start their terrorist activities in Africa. They would bomb embassies on the continent killing 224 people and wounding even more than they murdered. Their tactics and body counts would increase over the next few years.

1999 would usher in the end of individual European nations. The European Union or E.U. was formed to compete as a consolidated economy against American and Asian markets. For the 'privilege' of joining the union all member nations gave up their currencies and sovereignty.

Bureaucrats would determine rights, laws, immigration policies, and commerce for the entire continent. Members would have little say regarding their own nations on these topics. I will say it again, Europe is different.

President Clinton was impeached by the House of Representatives in 1999 for perjury, obstruction of justice and abuse of power. The Senate refused to have a trial for conviction and removal from office. He would complete his second term in office but would have the cliff note of impeachment by his name.

It was time for some lunch before we moved on to the next interview and time period. Linda prepared some chicken strips and fries with ranch dressing and fry sauce. We sat around enjoying the food and conversation. I asked Sharron about how her children's activity went at school last night. She told me her two daughter's middle school had an award ceremony and musical presentation. Her two oldest daughters, Helena and Leah were recognized for their academic, athletic, and musical excellence. It was obvious she was very proud of her girls.

Her two youngest children, Logan and Emma, were also given awards at their elementary school. Her husband Evan had been out of town on business and arrived just in time to see their children receive their awards. This made me think back on how many special events and similar activities I had missed because of work. Linda had gone to them and reported to me on what had transpired. It was not the same as being there but it was the life I led. There is no way to fix the past. I am reminded of the words; you can always make more money, but you cannot make more time.

I told Sharron how wonderful it was to see her and Evan make sure they are at activities like the one last night. It is so important for their kids to see them there. Lunch was now over and we were ready for the next interview.

THE SEVENTH INTERVIEW 2000-2020

Back in the study, we took our usual places and began.

Now the year is 2000. A new century and a new millennium have been ushered in. The census said there were 281 million people calling America home. The first group of Pilgrims came to this nation less than 500 years ago and now here we are with nearly 300 million people living here. If you stop and think about it, this is an amazing amount of population growth.

The 2000 Presidential election was one of the most divisive in American history. The Democrats would nominate Al Gore, the Vice President to Bill Clinton, as their standard bearer. The Republicans would nominate George W. Bush, the son of George H. W. Bush, our 41st President. In the end G.W. Bush won the Electoral College 271-266. Al Gore had won the popular vote, but according to our Constitution, this point is irrelevant. The Democrats claimed Bush was an illegitimate President because he was selected by the Supreme Court and not elected by the people. Once again, the Constitution was followed and it was in direct opposition to the Liberal agenda; therefore, it must be demeaned and defamed.

On January 20, 2001, George W. Bush was sworn in as our 43rd President. Within eight months, our nation would be hurled into another war that would last for decades.

The morning of Tuesday, September 11, 2001 started like any other work day. It would end with the largest terrorist attack on American soil. Four planes took off from Logan International Airport in Boston, Massachusetts. On board there were 19 terrorists prepared to die in the name of Islam. The first two planes flew into the World Trade Center Towers. The third plane flew into the Pentagon. The fourth plane crashed in a field in Stony Creek Township, Pennsylvania because the passengers fought the terrorists for control of the plane. Everything anyone needed to know about Islam should have been learned on that morning. When the day ended, the two towers in New York had collapsed, military personnel had died in the Pentagon, and all on board the crashed plane in Pennsylvania perished as patriots. As the Muslim world celebrated a victory against the 'Great Satan,' Americans got angry. Someone somewhere was going to pay for this attack.

What happened next should have been put on a slow track and had further contemplation attached to it. It was only proper we should retaliate against those who attacked us. With more than 6,000 injured and 2,996 dead on that day, it could not go unanswered. The contemplation should have been how far and for how long do we pursue justice. I fully supported a massive air campaign for months or even years against all terrorist states. This would have been an appropriate response. I did not support an extended ground conflict in a nation that has been known to defeat empires from all over the world.

It would only take six weeks for our Civil Rights and Constitutional liberties to be infringed upon. We as Americans will often allow our government to wrap laws that diminish our rights in patriotic jargon. Congress ran, no, they trampled over each other to be supportive of the Patriot Act. Once it was signed into law, a secret court could issue warrants, government agencies conducted illegal electronic surveillance on communications, Americans would be treated like criminals at airports, indefinite detention was allowed for suspected terrorists, and other civil liberties went by the wayside. The cry went out across the land to give us safety and we will surrender liberty for it. We deserved neither.

The war in Afghanistan would begin within weeks and last for many years.

Ten years earlier, the Gulf War ended with the defeat of Iraq. Since then, Iraq and Saddam Hussein had continued to be bad actors on the international stage. Saddam was a despot in his own nation and had used chemical weapons on his own people. He was also suspected of trying to obtain nuclear weapon materials from other nations. It looked as if war and regime change was in the air for 2002.

Congress authorized the use of force against Iraq if they did not give up their chemical weapons and abandon their nuclear intentions. Saddam stood in defiance against the world. The clock started counting down as coalition forces began once again building up their forces, this time in Kuwait. The United Nations continued to demonstrate how useless it is as an organization to promote peace.

Zero hour for Iraq arrived in the spring of 2003. The defeat of Iraq would take only weeks to accomplish. Saddam Hussein fled Baghdad and went into hiding. The people of Iraq were now free from a murderous dictator and his regime. Winning the war was easy. Winning the peace and changing Iraq into a democratically elected government would prove to be difficult.

In 2004, President Bush won re-election over John Kerry, a Senator from Massachusetts. Unfortunately, 2005 was another year for the war on terror especially in Iraq and Afghanistan. In 2006, the Democrats took back both houses of Congress. Nancy Pelosi was elected to be the first female Speaker of the House.

Continuing in 2007 was yet another year of the war on terror. 'Blood and treasure' were being poured on the ground in Iraq and Afghanistan with no end in sight. During this time, the U.S. real estate market has been on fire. This house of cards was on the verge of collapse and when it did, trillions of dollars in wealth would be lost.

Sharron asked what the causes of the 2008 real estate and stock market collapse were. I had not planned on going into depth on this subject but when a question is asked, it must be investigated deeper and answers must be found.

The origins of the 2008 real estate collapse are rooted in the 1977 Community Reinvestment Act {C.R.E.}, during the Carter Presidency. If I remember correctly, the purpose of this law was to create a banking and government partnership to loan more money in urban neighborhoods. The law also gave heavy incentives for high risk inner-city loans. The law also guaranteed loans to be red flagged for the poorest areas mainly inhabited by Black Americans. This was just another piece of social engineering gone wrong by the Democratic Party.

For most of its life, the C.R.E. remained in the background and was inert in the U.S. real estate markets. This changed drastically during the Clinton Administration. Attorney General Janet Reno and her Justice Department crony Andrew Cuomo gave the big banks an ultimatum. If they had desires to merge, expand, cross State lines or anything else to profit their companies, they would need to comply with some new rules. Regardless of a loan applicant's ability to repay a loan, the banks must approve all high risk loans to minorities and any other person seeking a loan. The whole concept of getting money from a bank and not having to repay it, is nothing more than thievery. Bank robbery is a Federal crime. But not now according to Janet Reno and Andrew Cuomo.

The real estate market was going to get even crazier. The banks started making no money down loans, 125% of house value loans, easy home equity loans, no documentation loans, and high risk speculation loans became common in the mid 2000's.

Greed was a disease and everyone was infected. It is easy to blame this disease on the banks but this would not be accurate. The banks, Wall Street, real estate agents, and millions of average citizens were flipping houses left and right. Each time a house flipped, the value of the house went up and everyone in the real estate food line got fed. The banks would bundle their real estate loans as collateral against other loans. Everything was overvalued and one hiccup would cause the wheels to come off this car.

A fool and his money are soon parted.' Whoever came up with this quote was a genius. By the time the real estate and stock market collapse bottomed out, only us fools were left wondering what had just happened.

The fallout from this crisis was as follows: Investment/brokerage companies went belly up. Banks tried dumping their toxic assets. Foreign investors demanded being made whole for the bundled mortgages. The value of homes plummeted. The stock market was in a free fall. Gold soared and the price of oil spiked to $140.00 a barrel. Thus, 2008 was an economic nightmare.

Too big to fail was the quote of the year in 2008. Banks ran to Washington D.C. with their hands out for help. They walked away with almost $800 billion to help stop the bleeding. I do not know why we have taxes. I mean, I know taxes are the main source of funding the Federal Government. All I am saying is since Congress was able to create $800 billion out of thin air and not have any method to repay it, then why did they need to rob the U.S. taxpayer? President Bush said he had to abandon the free market system in order to save it. This sounded a lot like Adolf Hitler's 'we must give up freedom to be free' speech. *Weird.* Right?

I thought it only appropriate to ask Sharron how she thought the government should have handled the meltdown. She paused for a moment and then answered the question. "If the government actually ordered or threatened the banks to give loans to un-qualified borrowers, then I believe there was an obligation for the government to make the banks whole."

It was an excellent answer, but now I wanted to press her further. "Okay," I said, "Let me change the scenario a little. If there was no government mandate or interference, how should the government have handled the meltdown?"

Simple," she said, "government should stay out of the fray and let the Capitalist system purge itself. It would be messy but it would be efficient. In fact, if government had stayed out of the mess, it may have made the situation worse for a short time but it is like ripping off a bandage fast or slow. The only role in this for government is the use of bankruptcy laws and courts."

I said, "I can tell you understand the proper role of government whether it was from your parents or from your in depth study of history. Either way it is great to hear your thoughts. Have we covered the 2008 meltdown enough you think?"

"Definitely" she replied.

The insanity of 2008 continued into the Presidential election. The Democrats nominated Barack Obama and the Republicans nominated John McCain. Both of them were a disaster from my perspective. That year I voted for the Libertarian candidate. Barack Obama won the election easily and became our 44th President. America had finally elected a Black American to the highest office in the land. The week before his inauguration, he declared we were five days from the fundamental transformation of America. I knew right there and then our nation was in peril.

On January 20, 2009 Barack Obama was sworn in as President. The nation was still in the grips of a deep recession and unemployment was over 10%. President Obama's solution to this problem was to expand government and its programs. Also, he wanted a $700 billion stimulus package from Congress. The money was not for the creation of jobs in the private sector. It was used to bail out State and local government employees and their pensions. President Bush was the Herbert Hoover of the depression and President Obama was the Franklin D. Roosevelt of those times.

The Democrats now held all the reins of power. There was a believer of *Marxism* who was also a Muslim sympathizer living in the White House. The House of Representatives was filled with far left radicals and the Senate had a filibuster proof majority of *'Leftists'* and Progressives. One of the scariest things concerning this group of ideological radicals was their devotion to the writings and ideas of Saul Alinsky. They had one other thing in common: They were going to force feed their un-American and un-Constitutional ideology down the throats of all Americans. The Constitution and our rights were now in serious jeopardy.

In 2010, there were 308 million people living in America. For Liberals that means there are 308 million people in need of controlling and regulating. In order to have a truly free and fair society, every aspect of their lives must be directed by government masterminds. One part of their *Marxist Ideology* would be fulfilled in 2010.

Even though there is no Constitutional authority for it, and even though the American people by a majority of 65% to 35% wanted no part of it, and even though the entire law was a lie forced on Americans by professional liars, the healthcare bill known as Obamacare was force fed to the American people. The law was so good for all Americans the people who passed it exempted themselves and their staffs from it. A roadblock was needed to stop the Democrats while we still had a country and a Constitution left to fight for.

Encouraged by our President, the Arab Spring broke out all over the Middle East. Morocco, Tunisia, Libya, Egypt, Syria, and other Arab nations had an uprising against authority. It would not end with those nations electing a leader by way of the democratic process. Instead, they would end up in civil wars for decades with each faction trying to assume power. It was just a year into his Presidency and Barack Obama was lighting the world on fire, literally.

On April 15, 2010 the roadblock to the Democrats took shape. It was called 'The Tea Party.' Through their actions and efforts, the Republicans took back the House and Senate. *The real question was this: Now that they hold a check on the President's ability to destroy our nation, will they stop him or will they go along to get along?*

The uprising in Libya was different from the other Arab Spring uprisings. I believe it was a calculated move to remove Muammar Gaddafi from power and promote chaos in that nation. He had been a sponsor of terrorism for many years but had changed his ways and now disclaimed terrorism. He even compensated victim's families for his crimes. He wanted to join the world and participate in the global economy. In fact, he wanted to make Libya the center of all African trade and commerce. He also wanted to base his currency (I believe it was called the dinar) on gold and silver. This would make his currency the strongest currency in the world. All the nations of Africa who signed onto this pact would benefit greatly from this economic transformation and they would become less dependent on the U.S., United Nations, and other nations for aid. Before the end of 2011, Gaddafi would be dead and the talk of an African currency more powerful than the U.S. Dollar or Euro would die with him. Coincidence? I think not.

One of the longest manhunts ended in 2011. After 10 years, Osama Bin Laden, the leader of Al Qaeda who had planned the September 11, 2001 attacks, was tracked to a compound in Pakistan. Special Forces raided the compound killing him and taking his body back to American jurisdiction for positive identification. Also the computers and records found in the compound were taken back for evaluation and intelligence gathering. His reign of terror may have ended but others would take his place. You can kill a person but a belief is much, much harder to kill.

Over the past ten years the leadership of Al Qaeda has been either killed or imprisoned at Guantanamo Bay military base. The problem with this is you can chop off the head of this snake and another one grows back in its place. We would hunt down terrorists all over the world right up until our fall.

The 2012 Presidential election would demonstrate how important a Democratic Party Press {i.e. CNN, MSNBC, ABC, NBC, CBS, Washington Post, and the N.Y. Times} is to *covering the tracks* and the *ineptitude* of one of *their ideological soul mates.* President Obama had accomplished nothing of real value for America. His authorization of the killing of Osama Bin Laden was the highlight of his accomplishments. The economy was still in recession {1% growth}. Unemployment was still high {8.1%}. Labor participation was at record lows 61%. Welfare and food stamp roles had exploded. By all accounts, his first term was a huge failure. Had he been a Republican with this track record, the media would have been screaming for his defeat. But just like F.D.R., he would get re-elected to another term.

On September 11, 2012 a terrorist attack in Benghazi, Libya took the lives of four Americans including the Ambassador to Libya. The calls for help went unheeded by the Obama Administration. Help from Italy, just across the

Mediterranean Sea could have been there within an hour or two. The C.I.A. security force and their operatives were left to defend themselves against heavily armed insurgents for 13 hours. This dereliction of duty should have cost President Obama his re-election, and ultimately his immediate removal from the Oval Office. Sharron, in my opinion, he was one of the worst Presidents we have ever had.

Even with the press in his back pocket, President Obama should have been a one term President. It should have been a slam dunk to replace him except for the two words that would derail such an idea. The two words were Mitt Romney. Republicans could not understand how their candidate could lose to such an inept President. I knew why. Mitt Romney is a Progressive Republican which means he has the same basic beliefs as Barack Obama.

Here is truth. If you run a Progressive Republican against a Socialist Democrat the Democrat will win. The Conservative base of the G.O.P. will not support a Progressive Candidate in a general election. If a Progressive is chosen, the base will vote 3rd party. The failure of the *Progressive Ideology* must be tied to the Democrats and not to the G.O.P. I think after all this time, the Republican Party leadership has never come to understand this simple formula.

The other negative that came out of the 2012 general election was the Democrats took back control of the Senate.

Islamic terrorism raised its head again in 2013 during the Boston Marathon. Two bombs exploded in the crowd where people had gathered to cheer on the runners. Several people died and many were injured. The manhunt for the bombers ensued and Constitutional Rights were once again violated by the police.

Sharron spoke up and asked, "I remember the bombing very well. You stated there were Constitutional violations during the manhunt. I think I know what you are going to say, but would you go into detail concerning this topic?"

"I will be glad to explain myself," I said.

Nobody argues with the necessity of finding the Islamic terrorists before they could harm others or escape to an Islamic sanctuary nation. As the police searched for the suspects, they would at times forcibly enter homes without a search warrant. The people of Boston seemed to accept such a violation of their rights because of an emergency. I will never understand such *capitulation of rights. Police state tactics* are common in many parts of the world. As Americans we should *never accept* such activity from any *government agency.*

"So Sharron, do you agree with my explanation?" I asked.

"Yes," she answered. "Although, there are times when I lean towards safety being the highest priority, yet I do know we should err on the side of '*Constitutional Rights*' regardless of the circumstances."

She was absolutely correct in her thinking. I wanted to move on to another violation of our rights by the Federal Government.

President Obama was not the only person to violate the Constitution on a regular basis. He did, however, weaponize the Internal Revenue Service (I.R.S.) to attack his political adversaries. Tea Party groups were routinely denied their desired 501c3 on nonprofit status. When the scandal came to light, the head of this division was called before Congress where she read a statement and then claimed her 5th Amendment rights and refused to answer any questions. She then retired and the whole scandal was swept under the Democratic rug. President Obama appeared to have won this battle but the next election would unleash the wrath of the Tea Party and Conservatives on Congress.

In 2014 we learned a new word: I.S.I.S. It stands for the Islamic State of Iraq and Syria. As President Obama withdrew our forces from Iraq, it created a vacuum and as we all know *nature hates a vacuum*. I.S.I.S. then moved in and filled the vacuum. Their method of operation was simple. Invade a town and kill everyone who opposes them. If you are Christian, you could convert to Islam, or be put to death. They would enforce their interpretation of Sharia Law in all their territories. As further proof of their depravity, all captured children 2 years of age and older were sold as sex slaves.

If we would have had a President who was not a Muslim sympathizer, he would have recognized I.S.I.S. for the threat they truly were. A few thousand troops with planes, helicopters and tanks could have wiped out this terrorist group in no time at all. All President Obama did is give speeches and bring Muslim refugees to the U.S. He left the Christian refugees, who were the true victims of persecution, to their fate.

The 2014 midterm elections saw another shift in the power base. The Republicans took the Senate back. The final two years of the President's term would be one of Republicans blocking his agenda. Nothing else would be accomplished. President Obama responded to the obstruction of his agenda by issuing Executive Orders in violation of the Constitution. By way of example the Constitution authorizes Congress to establish immigration laws. President Obama implemented by executive order his own immigration law, Deferred Action for Childhood Arrivals Program or D.A.C.A. This is a direct violation of the Constitution. The separation of powers in our Constitution was instituted so tyranny, whether by a President, or Congress, or a Supreme Court could be stopped by the other branches of government.

Communism is evil in any form and in any amount. As a nation we should have one foreign policy when it comes to diplomatic relations and trade. We should only trade or have diplomatic relations with nations who have democratically elected governments. To do otherwise would be to support dictators and tyrants. I make this point for a very specific reason.

President Obama decided to normalize relationships with Cuba in 2015. This gave the Communist dictatorship exactly what they needed: cash. What he should have done is place further sanctions on the regime to break the back of the government. This may have sparked a revolution.

With a little help from their neighbors to the north, freedom might have taken hold in the nation.

The year 2016 had arrived and the Presidential election promised to be interesting. The Democrats would nominate Hillary Clinton to continue President Obama's legacy. She would try to expand the *Progressive Agenda* under her tutelage. The Republicans nominated Donald Trump to take back the White House. The press and odds makers gave Hillary a 98% chance of winning the election. Somehow I knew Donald Trump would win and here is why.

Americans had had enough of low economic growth, low labor participation levels, record high welfare and food stamp recipients, and an unemployment level at recession levels for eight years. Change was in the air and a continuation of the Obama legacy by Hillary was not desired. My gut told me Trump would win decisively. I did not vote for him because I aligned my beliefs closer with the Libertarian Party. Besides, I was not sure just who Donald Trump was and what he believed in. However, on election night it was a delight to see the entire Democratic Party go into meltdown mode when Donald Trump won the election.

The Democrats, including President Obama's Administration, committed crimes during the campaign to help Hillary win. When her election to President did not happen, they had to act fast to cover their tracks. They made claims about Russia interfering in our election and helping Trump. Of course none of this was true but they had to keep pounding this nail because if anyone investigated the role of Obama's Administration in these crimes, there would be jail time for some people. It is easy to tell what crimes Democrats have committed. If you follow the teachings of Saul Alinsky, like the Democrats do, then you know you should look in the mirror and whatever you see, claim your opponent is that very thing.

Just a side note here, Hilary Clinton was a student and devotee of Saul Alinsky. His Book, 'Rules for Radicals' outlined how to overturn our Nations' Democracy. Also, his book was dedicated to Satan. This is who and what Hilary Clinton believed.

On January 20, 2017, Donald J. Trump was inaugurated as our 45th President. He would immediately begin to erase the Obama legacy. When North Korea fired a missile like they had during previous Presidents, our new President told them to stop the provocative behavior and if they ever threatened America he would wipe them off the map. The third world bully now knew he had someone to fear in the White House. When you have the most powerful military in the world, you can use rhetoric to make your point.

In his first year President Donald Trump did what he said he would do. Presidents before him had said they would move the U.S. Embassy from Tel Aviv to the Capitol of Israel, Jerusalem. But they got cold feet in doing so and did not follow through. On December 6, 2017 President Trump announced the moving of our Embassy. On May 14, 2018 or Embassy opened in the Capitol of Israel. It had taken 70 years since the rebirth of Israel and a President willing to keep his promise to show the Arab world he was serious about peach in the middle east.

Throughout President Obama's Presidency, he had issued several Executive Orders that were in violation of our Constitution. Logic dictates and legal opinion would agree: If an illegal Executive Order can be created to address an issue, then another President can issue a legal Executive Order to overturn said order. This enraged the left. The Democrats never complained when Obama violated the Constitution by implementing his Radical Agenda, but when President Trump corrected Obama's Constitution violations, they had massive temper tantrums. Several Obama-appointed Federal Judges ruled President Trump's actions as illegal. As these judges' rulings were overturned by the Supreme Court, time had been lost in correcting the damage of Obama's overreach.

One of President Trump's biggest campaign promises was to build the wall on our southern border and stop the illegal alien invasion into our nation. The Democrats vowed to oppose the wall because it is immoral and said they would never approve one dollar to build it. This declaration was in stark contrast to their position only a few years earlier. During the 90's, both Democrats and Republicans worked together to secure our southern border. They approved 50 billion dollars to build a wall and improve electronic surveillance. Somehow the money was spent, yet the wall was never built.

Sharron could not keep quiet at this point. She said, "I really despised the Democrats for not only destroying this nation, but for the open arms they gave to illegal immigrants. I disagree with the free healthcare, free education, welfare, food stamps, free housing, amnesty, sanctuary cities and States, and a slew of other benefits that should have only been for citizens and legal residents. The thing I really detested them for was their attitude towards American citizens. They acted as if we were obligated to pay for these benefits and if you spoke out against it, the Democrats went to their favorite play book and called you a racist. It still annoys me to this day even though it has been years since the Democratic Party was destroyed."

"Do you know why the Democratic Party had such contempt for the American citizen and bent over backwards for the illegal aliens?" I asked.

She said, "Sure I do. A one word answer sums it all up: VOTES. The Democrats were losing the black vote in America with the guidance of President Trump. They, the Democrats, needed a new permanent underclass to be dependent on them. In return for benefits, the illegals would keep voting for Democrats even though an illegal alien voting was illegal." She was right again.

Let's quickly finish 2018. President Trump met with the President of North Korea, Kim Jung-un face to face in Singapore. No agreements were reached but the first meeting of a U.S. President and the North Korean leader broke the ice. For two years President Trump had to fight the media, Democrats, Liberal Judges and several Progressive Republicans at every turn. His own party had been vacant and feckless during this time and had not supported him against the relentless onslaught. The Republicans would surrender the House to Nancy Pelosi because they were exactly what I said a moment ago:

feckless, and fearful, and they refused to stand firm with their Party Leader.

In order to get other nations to the negotiation table, President Trump threatened and placed tariffs on many goods from other nations. It is a fine line between using tariffs as a threat and those tariffs starting a trade war that could cripple the world economy. I am against most tariffs. With this said, I will tell you I was in complete agreement with President Trump's tariffs on China. No other President had stood up to China and their bad behavior. China had stolen intellectual property, forced technology transfers to their military, and become aggressive in the South China Sea. They needed to be confronted and President Trump was the right man at the right time to do this.

In 2019, the richest and most powerful companies in the world decided to end free speech in coordination with the Democratic Party. Facebook, Twitter, YouTube, Google, and Apple decided to join forces with the Democrats to make Donald Trump a one term President. Conservatives were *shadow banned* or removed from most of the social media sites. Add to this the mainstream media/Democrat Party Press, constantly lying about President Trump and his Conservative base and the 2020 elections were shaping up to be a literal fight to the death for our nation.

I think we should spend some extra time here in 2019 and early 2020.

In March of 2019, Special Counsel Robert Mueller presented his report on the so called Russian-Trump collusion to Attorney General William Barr. The Democrats had pinned their hopes to remove President Trump on this report. They were gravely disappointed when the report found no evidence of any collusion between the President and Russia during the 2016 election. They now had to switch tactics and look for anything else the President had done in order to start an impeachment investigation and hearings.

The President and the nation had been put through a two year witch-hunt by the media and the Democratic Party. The truly evil part of this whole spectacle was the main players involved with this investigation knew there was no valid basis for the investigation yet they pushed for it on the basis of politics. With the investigation concluded and the report submitted, we as a nation would be forced by the Democrats to endure another violation of our Constitution. The President would be forced to endure a violation of his due process rights.

On December 18, 2019, the House of Representatives formally voted to impeach President Trump on the charges of 'abuse of power' and 'obstruction of Congress.' The House had spent the last three months having secret interviews with undisclosed witnesses trying to find enough evidence to warrant an impeachment vote. House Republicans were not allowed to call any witnesses nor was the President's legal team allowed to cross examine these witnesses. This would be a one sided investigation in a *kangaroo court.*

When the official vote for impeachment took place, there was not one single Republican vote in favor of the motion. This was now an official Democratic Party vs.

the President affair. The Democratic Party has always been a party of division and with this vote they had now divided the country into two camps. The two camps were not Democrat vs. Republican; it was tyranny vs. the Constitution and the rule of law.

The U.S. Constitution is very specific regarding the grounds under which a sitting President can be removed. It states treason, bribery, and high crimes and misdemeanors as the only reasons this drastic action should take place. I believe we all can agree that if a President commits bribery or treason, he or she should forfeit the highest office in the land. The debate many so called Constitutional experts have is on what constitutes high crimes and misdemeanors.

If we look back to our founding and understood English Common Law, we would discover this phrase means crimes that are as serious as treason and bribery are also worthy of removing a President from office. 'Abuse of power' and 'obstruction of Congress' are not listed as just cause for impeachment. They do not rise to the level of seriousness as treason and bribery.

The Democratic Party did what they have always done; they ignored the Constitution and pushed to overturn the 2016 election. Had they been successful and this occurred, they would have disenfranchised 63 million voters. They did not care about this simple truth. For the Democrats, it is always about the Party and politics, not the good of the nation or the rule of law.

Their reasoning for pursuing an illegitimate impeachment was obvious. The candidates running for President on the Democratic ticket were lackluster to say the least. The Party faithful and establishment knew if they ran any of those candidates seeking the Presidency, it would be an Electoral College landslide for President Trump. The party knew they could not win running openly Socialist, Marxist Progressive, and Communist candidates. But this describes, in one way or another, every single person vying for the Presidency on the Democratic ticket.

I often called the Democratic Party evil. This impeachment charade was brought to us by a Soviet Union style trial and court system in the House of Representatives by Democrats only. I believe this proves my declaration of their party being evil as accurate. Only those who are blinded by hate and embrace the ideology of *Marxism* would want such a *miscarriage of justice* to continue but they did.

In January of 2020 the Senate evidentiary hearing took place. The House prosecutors presented what they believed was evidence of crimes worthy of removing President Trump from office. The President's legal team rebutted this so called evidence with surgical precision. After two weeks of hearings, the Senate had heard enough. They voted to acquit the President on all charges. There was only one Republican vote in favor of removing President Trump from office. This vote came from a former Presidential candidate named Mitt Romney.

Had the government, and for that matter, our nation been paying better attention to what was going on in the world instead of being all consumed in an *illegitimate impeachment,* we might have seen the economic time bomb that was about to go off in Wuhan, China.

In December 2019, the Chinese Communist Party, (the only political party and official government of China) knew they had a serious problem in their nation. Instead of warning the world of the situation and working to isolate the problem, they denied the truth at every turn and continuously covered up the seriousness of this event. Had they done what any truly civilized nation should have done the spread of the Coronavirus or COVID 19 could have been isolated to a small part of China where world health agencies could have concentrated their efforts.

Instead, the lies and deceit from the Chinese Communist Party created a global pandemic. Once the full truth of the virus was revealed in February of 2020, almost every nation on earth had the virus within their borders. In response, most nations closed their airports to international flights. Some nations even closed their borders to deal with the virus by isolating their nations from the rest of the world.

Here in America the Governors of some States took action into their own hands. They forbid gatherings of more than 100 people, closed restaurants except for takeout orders, closed bank lobbies, and even limited grocery stores on the number of customers permitted in their stores at one time. In my home state of Nevada, the Governor ordered all non-essential businesses to close for 30 days. I saw things for the first time in my life I thought I would never see in Las Vegas: casinos and hotels closing their doors to the public. It was surreal. Basically, the nation was going into quarantine in order to stop the spread of this virus.

Fear and panic gripped many in the nation. The hoarding of bottled water, toilet paper, paper products, baby supplies, canned food, and other items both essential and non-essential began in earnest. It was amazing to watch what people placed the most importance on and valued the highest concerning their future. I still contend it was a completely exaggerated reaction to a very real, but mild crisis.

Sharron asked. "Can you explain why you believe this Coronavirus crisis was overblown?"

"I will be glad to explain myself," I said.

I believe by looking back on this issue, it was clear to all those who investigated it, that the Wuhan, China Corona virus epidemic was either intentionally or accidentally released into the general population by a biological research lab. It was used by the various moving parts within what some might call the Globalists Agenda and *perpetuated* by their media outlets to bring economic turmoil and destruction. If we look at the largest corporations of that time, we can see how they were fully vested in the Chinese Communist Party form of government and desired all governments, especially the U.S., to follow the Chinese design.

Apple, Google, Facebook, Twitter, YouTube, big pharmaceuticals, news/media companies, entertainment companies and many others were convinced the Chinese form of central planning and control over every aspect of every person's life was the future of all governments. During the years Obama was President, this nation was well on the way to this very form of government. The revolt of Britain from the European Union and the election of President Trump threw a wrench in the globalist's plan to implement central control over all world economies.

This did not stop them from looking for alternatives with which to implement their ideology. The hyped up Corona virus pandemic was their next attempt to take down President Trump and the U.S. economy. When one crisis ended, they had another one waiting in the wings at all times to end liberty.

In response to this crisis, the Congress and the Federal Reserve created trillions of dollars in stimulus payments and guarantees out of thin air. Never letting a crisis go to waste, the Democrats placed billions of dollars of special interest spending and *Progressive Ideology* language in the bills. By the time the spending was over, our kids and grandkids were over 10 trillion dollars deeper in debt.

Nevertheless, it was a great warning to all who had eyes and ears on what a true crisis could entail. Some people used this time as a lesson and prepared for a potential large scale crisis. Others went on their merry way once it was over. They acted like nothing had ever happened and the good times would soon be upon them. When the collapse of America did occur, those people were among the first to suffer for their lack of vision.

With the highly publicized deaths of some Black Americans at the hands of the police, a wave of protests and riots spread across our nation. Leading the way was an organization called *'Black Lives Matter or B.L.M.'*. As people rallied around this mantra and corporations and celebrities donated millions of dollars to them, nobody in the press investigated this group or where the money was going. It is important to discuss this group and their ideology.

Though their name sounds appealing and logical because Black lives do matter {just as all lives matter}, this group is a Marxist/anarchist organization. Their objective from the rioting, looting, and tearing down of historical monuments and statues was to overthrow the government and force President Trump to resign. They were anti-America, anti-Constitution, anti-religion, anti-Semites, anti-police, anti-military, and anti-family. This is not me saying this for emphasis, this was in their charter.

They even told reporters they were *trained Marxist*s and the mainstream media did nothing to expose them. So what is a *'trained Marxist'*? Karl Marx preached in order to usher is Socialism and Communism, you must first *destroy society*. You must destroy the status quo. This would mean the civil society. Also included in their destruction were religion, artifacts, statues, memorials, and monuments. A propaganda machine or a media that is in lockstep with your ideology is critical to control the narrative. If anyone gets in their way, they were dealt with by any means necessary to end resistance.

B.L.M. was not the only group of trouble makers and malcontents during 2020. *ANTIFA* or the *Anti-Fascists* organization was supporting B.L.M. and on the streets with their militant anarchists. Socialist indoctrinated college students were deeply involved with the rioting and destruction of our history. This is what our nation gets when we allow Leftists to dominate universities, media, entertainment and all other aspects of American life.

Sorry about that Sharron. I guess I got on my soap box again.

Before I could continue she asked me if I believed the Democrats supported the rioters and anarchists. I told her I believed they were 100% behind those groups. The Democrats need their Black voters to be angry in order to keep them on the *'plantation.'* The Democrats never condemned the *rioters* or their *violence.* To not condemn something such as *rioting, looting, and violence* is to support it. She agreed with my premise.

Now, where was I? Oh, that's right.

Turmoil in our nation would continue through the 2020 elections. The escalation of anger between the Democrats, Socialists, Fascists, Marxists, Communists, Globalists, and their rivals the Republicans, Conservatives, and Libertarians would continue well after the elections. We were heading for a violent showdown with those who wanted to overthrow the Constitution and we were not about to let that happen. Then, gasoline was thrown on the fire. We will discuss this on Monday.

One more thing of great importance took place in September of 2020 as we neared the election. The Muslim Nations of Bahrain and the United Arab Emirates both normalized relations with Israel as a result of three years of work invested by President Trump. Also, the nation of Kosovo, a Muslim Nation announced they would be normalizing relation with Israel. Following America's lead, Serbia announced they would be moving their Embassy from Tel Aviv, to Jerusalem. For a change, peace was breaking out between Israel and Arab Nations.

Sharron asked me, "before we call it a day and also a week is there anything else you would like to discuss about this time period"?

I thought for a second and said, "yes, there are two or three more things worthy of my getting back on my soap box again. I will keep each of them short and to the point"

My first comment is this: True change does not come from or by destroying statues and or history. Change comes from teaching our true history, both good and bad. The good in our history should make us all very proud. The bad in our history should make us angry and vow to never let it happen again. If you destroy our history then where should we stand as a nation?

The second point is this: Concerning the rioters and revolutionaries of this time period, none of them understood the way to have true change that would benefit the entire nation was to have a revolution that would break the iron grip of the Democratic Party on every level of government, education, the media, entertainment, and all other aspects of American life.

The third and final point is this: If the media or mainstream news organizations were truly fair, balanced, and reported the truth instead of being a propaganda machine for the Democratic Party, I believe Democrats would have never won a Presidential race from 1900 to 2020. This was the power of the bias media in America during those years.

I said, "Okay Sharron that should conclude our week. The next two time periods should really be interesting." We agreed to meet again on Monday at 9 am. After she left I felt as though I had worked a job from my past. I was ready for some rest and relaxation.

THE EIGHTH INTERVIEW-
THE FALL BEGINS

I woke up, as usual, before the alarm went off. It was 6 a.m. and I was looking forward to today's interviews. I had very much enjoyed the weekend. The rest I had made me feel quite energized this morning. I figured I would lay here for another hour and contemplate the events over the last few years. Today's interview would focus on the time period just prior to our fall. I had made a few notes concerning the key events. Laying here for the hour made me confident what I had planned for today was sufficient in scope to describe the times without being too graphic.

It was now 7a.m. and it was time to get going on the day's tasks. A few chores, breakfast and a shower filled the remaining hour and a half. I went out on the porch and enjoyed the morning air. The rain had subsided and it was a clear day. The neighbor's dog had barked at several cars driving on our street as people went to work and took their kids to school. It was now a few minutes before 9a.m. and the dog started barking. Sharron pulled up in front of our house a moment later.

She got out of her car and started walking towards our house. We gave each other the usual good morning greetings accompanied with the how each other's weekend was. Some more casual dialogue transpired between us as she set up her gear and we assumed our usual positions. The first of today's interview could now begin. I started with a simple statement.

When your nation and economy is debt driven, it does not take much to push it over the edge into insolvency. The end was near.

"If you were God and your children all over the world would not listen to your Prophet's call for everyone to repent and return to the Lord, how would you humble them so they would do as they are commanded?" I asked Sharron.

She replied, "I would use natural disasters on an escalating scale to bring them to a remembrance of their God. If a nation still refused to turn away from wickedness, I would unleash plagues and even wars on that nation until they either repented or had their fate sealed." At first, she may have sounded a little harsh, but Biblical history shows her to be accurate.

I then asked her, "If a nation does repent of their evils, do you believe God will put an end to its suffering and destruction? Perhaps a better way of asking this question is. If each humbling event is a domino that falls over and topples the next one, will God place His hand between those dominos and stop them from toppling over if they repent?"

Sharron answered, "Absolutely. If a nation turns away from evil and back to the Lord, why would a loving Father continue punishing His children?"

I told her I agreed with her answers.

The hand of Almighty God had been active in our nation and throughout the world for many years calling His children to repent and return to Him. Our nation was on the verge of collapse and there were few who could see it coming. As the years went by, the eyes and ears of the wicked continued to remain closed to the Spirit of the Lord.

In ancient times, natural disasters were thought to be punishments placed on man due to God's or the gods' displeasure with man. We were too advanced to believe in such superstitions now. We believed in science or pseudoscience to explain all of nature's workings. As an example, the cause of climate change was known to be man's use of so called 'fossil fuels' to power our lives. It was a ridiculous claim. To believe that man had the ability to change the climate over the entire world is bewildering. But man's arrogance, hubris, and belief in his power over the world knew no bounds.

So how did the fall or collapse of America begin?

The failure of insurance companies could have a cascading effect on our economy if it happened. Flooding in the Midwest and Great Plains States caused billions of dollars in crop failures and damage. Record rain fall in the South, hurricanes on the South and East Coast, tornadoes in the Midwest, and wildfires in the West put an enormous amount of strain on insurance companies. The failures started with smaller companies and then the run began. The insurance companies sought cash from every source they had at their disposal in order to pay their claims but it was not enough. Banks and Wall Street supported the insurance companies at first but their support was short lived. The insurance companies eventually ran to Washington D.C. to seek help in the form of a bailout.

Over the past few years the insurance companies had found it necessary to borrow vast amounts of cash in order to cover their growing list of claims. They had been using the dividends from their holdings in the stock market to pay back their loans and basic expenses. Now the well was dry. Banks were being very cautious loaning them any more money due to so much red ink on the balance sheets. As the claims surpassed their ability to pay, they began selling their stock portfolios and real estate holdings in order to raise cash. This boulder thrown in the pond started large ripples throughout the entire economy.

It was amazing to see how few safeguards American corporations had in place to protect themselves from a firm gut punch to the stock market like the one that was occurring from the insurance industry. Nervousness streaked though the economy but it had not turned into panic, yet. As the stock markets began to fall C.E.O.'s did what they have done for years. They went further into debt by trying to borrow money from the banks and issue corporate bonds backed by their stock and corporate value. Banks declined the loan request and expanded lines of credit. You cannot blame the banks; they were now trying to protect their interests. It would not take much time for the corporate bonds to become worthless. When this happened, the real destruction would follow.

International economies had been struggling for several years due to the weight of their social welfare programs. The tariffs placed on them by America had not helped. They retaliated with their own tariffs and, as a result, American companies had less access to foreign markets. This now put even more pressure on the stock market. Nervousness was subsiding regarding the U.S. economy and stock market and it was being replaced with tepid panic.

Between the tariffs on foreign resources and goods along with shrinking access to foreign markets, it all added to the corporate debt. A large percentage of America's fortune 500 companies were becoming insolvent and heading towards bankruptcy or possibly shutting their doors. Over the past several days the stock market had been falling 2-4% on a daily basis. With this news, it was about to get worse.

Throughout the nation, self preservation was beginning to take hold of the American people. They began withdrawing their savings from the banks. It was not a full financial panic or run on the banks, yet. That was just a day or two away. The banks were struggling to find the cash to give their customers. In order to protect themselves, they had recently refused to extend credit and loans to corporate America. It was too little, too late. Regardless of the Federal Reserve printing money 24 hours a day, seven days a week, they could not keep up with the demand from the banks. Any further downward pressure on the economy would collapse the banks.

The worst bloodletting within the stock market so far was in the hedge funds. They had been making fortunes over the past years placing orders on stocks and only putting up a small percentage of their purchase in cash for collateral. The rest of the purchase was on credit. These funds 'hedged' their bet the stock would go up and when it did they would take the profits of their purchase as if they had placed the full amount of cash up as collateral. They would then pay back the small amount of interest on their credit and take the rest of the money for profit. With the fall of the stock market, margin calls were happening every day for full payment and the hedge funds did not have the cash to cover their debts. It was almost over.

We used to complain about the $23 trillion in national debt and the $220 trillion in unfunded liabilities the American government had on its books. That was chump change when compared to the derivative markets. No one was able to give an exact number on this debt but it was to be north of $1.5 quadrillion. This market epitomizes greed. This market would buy debt for let's say $100,000. Then they would sell it for $125,000 to someone else and take the $25,000 profit. This process would continue up the line until the original $100,000 was now a $1,000,000 or more debt. Yet, the value of the debt was still only $100,000. Even a blind man can see where this type of manipulation will take him.

With the failing of the stock market, banks, and hedge funds taking place, the next failure would seal the fate of the U.S. economy. The derivative markets started calling in their debts. It meant nothing as far having a slight possibility of being made whole but it was the final nail in the coffin.

Now it was time to panic.

Too big to fail banks were beginning to do just that: fail. Bank holidays were being called every other day to stop the run on them and give them time to restock their vaults with cash from the Federal Reserve. On a good day, the stock market would only lose 7% of its value. On a typical day, it would lose 10% and the triggers would be pulled to stop all trading until the next day. Everyone was looking for cash, including businesses and governments. It became a mad dash to do so.

With everyone looking for cash to plug the leaks in the banks, stock market, and political sacred cows, the Federal Reserve did not have enough printing presses to keep up with panicked demand for currency. This situation was made worse due to the printing of so much money. You might think everyone getting the cash they needed would solve this problem. It does not. Such a vast quantity of cash flooding the market was causing the devaluation of our currency. The dollar was doing the dance of death. Within a few days, the nations of the world refused to use the American dollar as the world reserve currency. This caused the value of our dollar to plummet even further. It is now close to a fiat or worthless currency.

Over the past few decades, smart people and nations bought all the gold and silver they could afford. They had insulated themselves from inflation and were safe from the strain of only having worthless cash. In some ways, they were now very wealthy as gold heads north and surpass $3,000 an ounce. Within the month, it will pass $5,000 an ounce heading towards $10,000. It used to be said in America, 'cash is king.' Now, cash is a lowly peasant.

In the past, the U.S. bond market would sell individuals and foreign nations our debt in the form of Treasury Notes. The promise on these notes was to pay back the principal and interest in U.S. dollars at a specified time in the future. In March or April of 2020 the Federal Reserve in cooperation with the U.S. Treasury began buying back our Treasury Bills or national debt. They would also buy State, county, city, and municipal bond debt in America. They were not finished. They then moved on to buy junk bonds from corporations and finished with the purchase of toxic real estate debt from the banks. This made the Federal Reserve the nation's largest holder of debt. It also made them the largest land owner besides the Federal Government in the nation.

How was this done? Easy. They printed money out of thin air and paid for these debts to the tune of $650 billion a week. By November of 2020 our national debt was paid off in paper currency. Foreign governments were livid in receiving worthless cash as payment. They demanded gold, silver, precious stones, land, and mineral rights instead of cash. We refused their demands. We did not know it then but armed conflict was just over the horizon. After the fall, the cleansing, and restoration of our nation, America would never sell federal bonds again.

The only casualties in a collapsing economy are not just banks, the stock market, or businesses. People lose jobs, savings, and hard earned assets as economies plummet.

The economic collapse occurred so quickly there was no method to accurately report what percentage of people were being let go from their jobs. The State's unemployment insurance roles were exploding with new claims and the claims were lasting for long periods of time. Federal welfare and food stamp programs were being deluged with claims. What little money people were getting from unemployment was being used to purchase the necessities of life. They were not using this money to pay their consumer loans. At a certain point none of this would matter.

People not paying their credit card, car, boat, and other consumer loans were not the only loans not being paid back. The real estate mortgage industry collapsed as most Americans opted to use what little money they had to buy food and not pay their mortgages. The 2008 economic meltdown was a walk in the park compared to this total collapse.

The amount of financial strain being placed on government relief agencies was enormous. The States would run out of unemployment insurance benefits within weeks. The Federal Government would end its ability to feed people and give them financial aid within months. Social safety nets would fail and the burden for self preservation was shifted to the individual. There was not much more that could possibly go wrong in our nation, or so people thought.

As the nation's conditions worsen, desperation grows within the public. People tell themselves it is not the fault of government policies or corporate greed or individual demands for benefits which caused this collapse, it is the (fill in blank's) fault for all our misery. This is when a nation turns on its self. Foreigners that are here legally or illegally are harassed and assaulted by mob mentality groups. The nation started to see a mass exodus of those who do not 'look' like they belong here. Fear had turned into anger and now anger has turned into hate. With an increase in violence occurring all over the nation it will not take long for bloodlust to begin.

"Okay Sharron, I know this part of our interviews went by fairly quick. The next time period will be longer and more involved. I know it is a little early but how about a little lunch?"

She replied, "That sounds great. I missed breakfast this morning so I'm quite hungry."

I replied, "Great, let's see what Linda has going on in the kitchen."

After lunch we would return to the study. This next interview was the one I was not looking forward to.

THE NINTH INTERVIEW-THE FALL

Sharron, you know I have been around for a fairly long time. I have seen a great deal of worldly living from my past career in the entertainment industry. I have witnessed a great deal of man's inhumanity to man but also witnessed the best of what man can be. This interview will take the remainder of the day and I should point out the topics in this have caused me a great deal of anxiety over the weekend.

After Mike, David, and Wesley stopped by the other day, it caused me to think back to a time when our survival was never guaranteed. Even though I was overjoyed having seen them again, it did trigger some memories which were terrible and I had hoped to forget. Other memories highlighted the greatness and tender mercy of the Lord.

What we will now talk about was known to me and probably a good number of people before it actually happened.

The 2nd American Civil War

The final collapse of America only took a few months. *Over a hundred years of 'Progressive Ideology' indoctrination*

implemented incrementally led us to the point of no return.
In the past when we had strayed from the straight and
narrow path, the Lord had given us reminders to turn back
to Him. *The past reminders always brought us back to the
proper course. Until now.*

In 2020, the one person who tried to stop the globalists
and the government machine from destroying our
nation was worn out by the deep state. The President had
given everything he had to fix America but no man is
greater than the nation he leads. Four years of frivolous
investigations and having to fight the Democrats on
every issue had taken a toll on him. Their agendas were
different. The President wanted to see America restored
to her greatness with prosperity for all citizens. The
Democrats and Progressive Republicans were hell bent
on enslaving America under the banner of Socialism. The
Globalists' ideal model was the Orwellian Chinese form of
government for all people in every nation.

What would happen if President Trump was unable
to finish his second term? A new and even more
Constitutional Conservative leader would need to be found
to run as Vice President and finish the President's work.

The Democrats staked out their position for the
Presidency and the direction in which they wanted the
nation to proceed. The Republican Party had different
problems. They had never really obstructed the President's
agenda, but they had also never really embraced it or
worked to support him. They had a choice to make here.
The establishment Republicans or R.I.N.O.'s (Republican

in name only) wanted another establishment or Liberal Republican to be the Party's candidate. The lessons of the past are slow to learn.

A candidate like Mitt Romney was their preference over our sitting President. The only true path to victory was for the President to choose a staunch Constitutional Conservative with Libertarian roots. This is exactly what he did. The President would win the Republican Party nomination and a true Conservative/Libertarian would be his running mate. The stage was set for a showdown on political beliefs and ideologies like no other time in our history.

In October of 2020 the value of the U.S. dollar began to fall. The consequences of printing money backed only by a printing press was about to take place. It wasn't well known, but as I stated earlier, in April of 2020 through November, the Federal Reserve began printing money in order to buy back all U.S. Treasury Bonds throughout the world. They also bought corporate junk bonds, toxic real estate assets, and State and local municipal bonds. They were buying back these debts at a rate of 650 billion dollars a week. This action flooded the world with useless currency.

With only a month until the election, this became the focal point of which candidate and Party could fix this inflationary mess. The Democrats saw their chance to push their *Socialist Utopian* dream in America across the finish line. They proposed the government take total control of the economy and guarantee food, housing, education, and income for all people living in America. This meant everyone living in the United States including illegal aliens. They were convinced the time was right to fully implement President F.D. Roosevelt's 2nd Bill of Rights. They overplayed their hand.

The President wanted Congress to fulfill their Article One duties in the Constitution to set the value of the dollar even though the Federal Reserve had paid off the national debt. There were still over 200 trillion dollars in unfunded liabilities that were not even being discussed. It was not known at this time but the unfunded mandates and liabilities would erase themselves after the 2nd Civil War.

The President's question to the American people was this: Who should set the value of the American dollar, Congress as it is stated in the Constitution or an un-elected group of bankers known as the Federal Reserve Board? This question was asked because he wanted to abolish the Federal Reserve System and Bank. He extolled the virtues of placing America back on the gold standard and ensuring Congress would exercise its Constitutional authority by valuing the dollar. This plan would bring balance to the Federal Government, but the States and cities were under different stresses. There would be a great deal of pain if America chose the President's plan but there was a future of freedom on the other side of the mountain.

The question on many American's minds was: Had we as a nation gone over the cliff or was there something we could do to rescue our Republic? The past had shown us and proven to the world that we were able to come back from just about any economic failure and we usually came back stronger. Was this downturn a reflection of the past or would it be something different and far worse?

Americans were scared. Everything they had worked for could be demolished with the President's plan. But there were enough people who looked into the future and refused to kick the can of debt down the road for future generations to suffer from. It was true everything they worked for could be at risk by re-electing the President, but the same was true if they voted for the Democrat. The real difference this time would be what the country would look like if they chose un-wisely.

Do they vote for a great deal of pain now and work for a better future for their posterity? Do they go through the same pain and place generations of people yet to be born under Socialism with all of its evils? This choice for many was easy. Too many of our fellow Americans wanted free stuff. Too many of our fellow Americans wanted a free ride. The election was a split result. The Democrats won the popular vote by a fairly wide margin but this has little bearing on who wins the Electoral College.

A few weeks after he won re-election and Conservative Republicans secured both Houses of Congress, the bottom fell out of the dollar. The Presidential Inauguration was still a month away but the fall of the dollar had its greatest impact on States where public employee union salaries and benefits are guaranteed under their State Constitutions. Illinois was the first State to fail. It was followed by California, Michigan, New York, Minnesota, and the other Northeastern States. Chicago would be the match that lit the fire of riots and eventually the 2nd American Civil War.

The 1st American Civil War was fought over State secession and ending slavery. The 2nd Civil War would be fought over State employee wages and benefits and who should pay them. Federal Bankruptcy laws can apply to cities, towns, and counties. There is nothing in the U.S. Constitution which allows bankruptcy for States. The States were set up under the 10th Amendment to operate with sovereignty. This objective would hopefully keep them from becoming dependent on the Federal Government when any crisis raised its head. It was further thought that such exemptions from bankruptcy would aid in controlling their spending with balanced budgets. In theory it should have worked perfectly. In practice though, when the States found they could borrow money or sell bonds for any purpose as long as it was allowed under State law and their Constitutional restrictions, many States went on a spending and borrowing binge just like the Federal Government.

If you were one of the lucky people to have a job during this time period, you would receive a paycheck for your usual amount. The problem with a devalued dollar is what you can purchase this week will be even more expensive next week when you are paid again. Discontent was growing. Everyone knew Third World nations went through this type of inflation every once in a while but not us here in America. Protests were popping up everywhere. People were demanding something to be done. Isn't it amazing that whenever there is a problem, people look first to government for solutions to solve their problems? The indoctrination and brainwashing of Americans has been a success by governmental masterminds.

The loudest voices of protest and disobedience came from the public sector unions. They wanted special treatment from their neighbors and taxpayers in the form of cost of living adjustments to compensate for the falling value of the dollar. Prior to the fall of our dollar, many States did not have enough money to pay their public employee's paychecks, pensions, and benefits. Where would the States find even more money in order to keep up with hyperinflation just to appease and quiet the unions now?

Overnight, the system collapsed. In a coordinated action, public employees in many States walked off their jobs to strike for cost of living increases. In most of the Northeastern States there were no teachers, police, firemen, hospital workers, garbage pickup, water or sanitation workers, and more. Community organizers like our former President Barack Obama were working feverishly to hold these groups together in Solidarity. They felt their numbers were sufficient to bend the State Governments and the people living there to their will. In the past, the Solidarity movement worked favorably for the unions. This time would be different. As cities, counties, and States collapsed under the weight of public sector employee's wages, retirement systems, healthcare, and other entitlements, it quickly became self evident there was no turning back to the good old days. That is when the real enemy struck with everything it had. *Fear is the true enemy of man for it will quickly turn into anger and then into hate.*

Which city would be first to revolt and riot? Because I am a student of history and knowing this day was coming, I had thought the riots would begin in one of four cities. The top of my list for these events was Oakland, California; Chicago, Illinois; Los Angeles, California; and New York

City. The winner of this title went to Chicago, Illinois. It only took a little nudge to push the protesters from walking a picket line in peace to rioting in the streets. Community organizers, anarchists, Communists, and other Democratic Party loyalists wanted real change. They did not accept the re-election of our President. This was not new. They had not accepted his election four years earlier either. The Democratic Party has always been the Party of violence. It has been through violence and force that all Socialist or Communist regimes have come to power. Now, it was their (the Democratic Party's) turn to seize power. They would use force and violence to change the United States of America into a Socialist Republic.

It was now mob rule in most of the large cities. The exception to this was the South. Conditions were different in most of the Southern States. Even though most of the large cities in the South are run by Democrats, they are surrounded in the rural areas by armed citizens who are ready to put down any insurrection. When some of the larger cities had rioting, the citizens of those States put the rioters in their place rather quickly. The rioters who could not produce anarchy in the Southern States departed for the Northeastern States to join the cause of forced National Socialism and to participate in the mayhem. As mobs, gangs, and other groups became more organized, a common theme ran through all those groups: If you did not support their cause, believe as they did, and were not willing to join their movement, you were their enemy. They would run you out of town, beat you into submission, or eliminate you.

If you lived in the Northeastern States and you believed in Constitutional law and were one of the lucky ones, you could escape to the Southern States and find refuge and freedom. Violence and death were everywhere in the Northeastern States. Mobs took what they needed and wanted from everyone. If you opposed them, they committed whatever violent act on you they desired. Many husbands and fathers perished trying to defend their families. Wives, mothers, and women were abused in the most horrific ways by the mobs. Even children were abused for their entertainment. The trauma and shock from these experiences along with the feeling of hopelessness caused many to take their own lives. Some who survived the violent attacks were mentally and emotionally scarred and devastated. It might seem impossible for mothers to do so, but many of them abandoned their children to fend for themselves.

In order to maintain control and keep the mobs focused on what the 'leaders' of the revolt wanted them to do, they constantly needed a new group to persecute. Conservatives and Constitutionalists had been the first groups to be targeted for expulsion and termination by the Socialists. But once the Northeastern States had run out of these groups, then what? Hate is an emotion that must be continually fed.

Once the cleansing of the Northeastern States of any Conservatives or Constitutionalists had been accomplished, the leaders would direct their followers to turn their focus and hate on anyone or group that was different. The term 'different' was completely objective and was applied to anyone the mobs did not like. Foreigners were the first victims of the new purge. Hispanics, Asians, Africans, Middle Easterners, and Muslims were all to be driven out of the Northeastern States or they would be eliminated. Many of them flooded across our northern border into Canada and across our southern border into Mexico seeking safety and asylum.

As word of the atrocities spread in the Southern States from the refugees, it was apparent the next wave of purging could head south. The President, Vice President, many members of his administration, and several Congressmen had abandoned Washington D.C. and headed to the Southern States when the riots started. They, along with most of the Governors of the Southern States had gathered to formulate a plan for mutual protection and economic cooperation. The Governors all agreed to call out their National Guard units and militias and send them to the front lines to confront any Northern States aggression. They would join forces with the U.S. Military which was still under the civilian control of the President.

The line of defense chosen was on the south side of the Ohio River. The Mississippi River would be the skirmish line in the West. The Appalachian Mountains would be the buffer zone in the East. North Carolina's northern border with Virginia into the Appalachian Mountains would be their East Coast defensive line. With their defensive lines established, all they needed to do now was to wait and prepare for what was assuredly coming.

It may have seemed like there would be an endless amount of food and resources in the Northeastern States for the mobs to live on but eventually everything would soon run out. Farmers were not planting crops, warehouses were emptying of their food stockpiles quickly and store shelves were bare. Starvation was not uncommon in the mob controlled areas unless you were a member of the mob. But now, even they could see there was little food and resources in their areas to sustain them. As fellow Socialists and anarchists from the Southern States joined with the mobs, they told the leaders that the Southern States had plenty of food and resources for everyone living there. All they had to do is head south and take it. Along the way, they could kill all the Constitutionalists they wanted. The Northeastern Rebels now had a new plan and they headed south.

The first of the mob scouting parties were turned back or destroyed rather quickly by the military and militias. This did not deter the Rebel's ambitions. Everyone on the line knew the real invasion would come soon once the mobs found a weakness in the defensive lines. In a military conflict, you want to choose the terrain, time, and all other conditions for every battle. Unknown to the Rebels, multiple traps and ambushes had been set along the line. When the Rebels saw only the militias, they chose to attack those positions supposing they were the weakest of the fighting forces aligned against them.

The militias let the Rebels see exactly what they wanted: intentionally engineered weak spots all along their lines to give the Rebels a place to attack and invade the South. This was nothing more than an ambush. The Rebels would be met by National Guard and regular military units. Once the Rebels encountered the ambush, they were not allowed out alive. The order from the President and the Governors was very clear: All Rebels invading the South were to be exterminated. This may sound inhumane, but this is what the Rebels were planning for the South.

Not to be outdone by the regular military units, the militias and citizens were also armed to the teeth and ready for just about whatever the Rebels could throw at them. The ranks of the Rebels had swollen to tens of millions of like minded Socialists and Anarchists. The Southern States sent even more armed citizens than the Rebels had to the front line. Regardless of who would win this 2nd American Civil War, in the end, there would be tens of millions of Americans dead and wounded.

For the first several days, the ambushes the Southern States had set up worked just as planned. The slaughter of the Rebels was by the tens of thousands. As stated before, no compassion was given to those who surrendered or were wounded. Very few of the Southerners were killed at this time but this too would change. It was decided by the Rebel leaders, who were safe in their new headquarters in Detroit, Michigan, to try and overwhelm the entire front line with a full offensive using everyone and everything they had. It did not take much to get the Rebels fired up and angry with the Southerners. Rhetoric and reminders of a past conflict gave the Rebels all the motivation they needed to seek death and destruction upon the South. This war of old grudges would bring out the worst of humanity on both sides of the line.

How things had changed since the 1st Civil War ended over a hundred and fifty years prior. The first Civil War was between Southern Democrat slave owners and Northern Abolitionist Republicans. *This war would be a reversal in geography.* This time it would be between Northern Democrat/Socialist Rebels and Southern Republicans/Conservatives. The years, conditions, reasons, political influences, objectives, and outcome may have changed but the color of blood spilled is always the same. Before it ended, this war would last for only five months but it cost over 60 million lives. This means 20% of the population of America perished and this war would end in a flash.

Concerning the Rebels, every likeminded person from every State in the Union had chosen a side in the conflict. Those who wanted destruction decided to join the revolt and end Capitalism and Constitutional Conservatism in America once and for all. The leaders of this revolution were all former Democratic members of Congress, leaders in the Socialist, Communist, and other far left Parties. Their ranks had been filled and led by hate groups such as *ANTIFA, Black Lives Matter,* and *Occupy Wall Street*, just to list a few. Students that had been well indoctrinated at almost every college and university joined to help the revolution just as their *Socialist Professors* had taught them. The mobs and *Rebels* were the new *Democratic Socialist Party*. The leaders of this revolution would never put themselves in harm's way. Their indoctrinated minions were on the front line to fight. They preferred to direct the mayhem and work of death from their headquarters in Detroit.

The Rebel's overthrow of our Constitution and their implementation of the *Marxist Ideology* upon all Americans was not going as easy as the leaders thought it would. Their mob forces were being defeated and slaughtered by the Southern forces. The order went out from the President and the Southern State Governors to take no prisoners in this war. All mob soldiers were traitors to the Republic and should die a traitor's death. There are some who might believe this was a very Draconian penalty to exercise against our fellow Americans. It was not. Those who sought to destroy the Republic were a cancer and all cancers must be cut out or killed, or it will grow back one day.

The Democrats/Socialist Rebels had forced a Civil War on the nation and the Conservatives/Constitutionalists had responded with everything they had to defend their liberty. The Rebels could see their hopes fading away with every passing day and with every defeat. Just when the Rebel leaders thought it could not get any worse, their worries ended. In a flash of light, the entire city of Detroit was destroyed with several nuclear bombs. The head of the snake had been cut off. The revolution now had no official leaders and every Rebel participant was being killed and hunted down for execution. There would be no mercy given to the mobs.

The leaders of the Northeastern Rebels had made a massive mistake in judging their rival's desire for victory. The Rebel's leaders had a willing group of members from hate groups, anarchists, anti-American and a host of other groups willing to kill or enslave their fellow Americans. These groups were united in their basic desire for a fundamental transformation of this nation through bloodshed. What they truly wanted was to usher in a

Socialist/Communist government and eliminate individual rights and liberties.

For decades the Liberals/Socialists had promoted gun control laws that were nothing more than a ruse for gun confiscation. Having failed at this, they quickly wanted to arm themselves with the same 'evil' guns the Conservatives had. When the fall occurred, these groups raided the gun stores in their areas and had even raided the armories of the local military bases. They now had many of the same weapons as the Southerners and the military. One of the things the Rebels did not have was the main portion of the military on their side or the training the military had. There was one other thing the Rebels did not have. The President was with the South.

The President was still the Commander in Chief of all military forces. He had at his disposal almost the entire defense force of the U.S. There were very few defectors from the military who had joined the rebels. It was with immense pride to witness how many current and former military personnel took their oath to defend the Constitution seriously and rallied to its defense. Once the Rebels had drawn first blood on the South, then all consequences heaped on them were justified. The North wanted bloodshed, destruction and enslavement. The South wanted liberty and freedom. The Rebels never realized it, but this war was over before the first shot from the North was fired.

Once the Northerners flooded into the South, the full weight of the U.S. military along with our citizen army was unleashed on them. The work of death commenced and the fighting was intense and merciless. The North was losing this fight from the very start and within days they were being pushed back into their Northern lands and especially into the large cities. This was not done by accident. Once the *Rebels* had been encircled in their cities, this is when the nuclear weapons were used on them. Detroit was the first to be vaporized but other cities suffered the same fate. After the nuclear weapons were used and the Rebels were encircled, it was time to lay siege to their areas. There was little need to hunt down the remaining *Rebels*. They were trapped in their cities and territories. They would now turn on each other like caged animals and eliminate themselves over the next few months. Those that tried to escape or fight their way through the lines were eliminated.

The 2nd American Civil War was over. The five months of war had exacted a huge price with over 60 million dead and a nation in almost total collapse and ruin. For all intents and purposes there was not a Democratic Party in this nation. Even though California, Oregon, and Washington were 2,000+ miles from the war, they had encouraged millions of their most radical Socialist/Democrat Party members to fight in the revolution. There was only a token amount of Party loyalists left in the Pacific Coast States. They had been left there to look out for their States until the *Rebel* victors returned. Almost every person who joined the rebellion was never seen again. Even though the war was over, conditions in many parts of the nation were about to get worse, much worse in fact.

During this time of a political party disappearing from the American landscape, a new political party would arise. The American Independent Party or Constitutional Party as it is known in some States, filled the void or vacuum. It is very conservative, Libertarian, and focused on the Constitution in its original form and intent. There would never be a Democratic Party in this nation again. The Republican Party would still exist, but it was considered too Liberal by many in the American Independent Party to join or support. True Constitutional Conservatives and Libertarians were the only people welcomed into America's newest Party. The President, Vice President, many members of Congress, and most of the remaining State Governors joined America's newest Party. Changing America back to our original foundation was taking place if America could only survive future events.

While the war was raging in the South, some of the most radical Socialists and Anarchists stayed behind in the Pacific Coast States. They were determined to take advantage of the national crisis and cause mayhem in their own States. In California the so called 'evil corporations' were targeted for destruction. It is amazing what a couple hundred people armed with basic weapons and gasoline can destroy in a very short time. The mob's target was Silicon Valley. The nation's technology and innovation center would never be rebuilt there again after its destruction by the Anarchists. The new Silicon Valley would be re-located in Utah and would remain there from this time forward.

I asked Sharron how much she pays for a gallon of gasoline.

She said, "Between 6 and eight cents a gallon."

"Do you remember how much it was during the 2nd Civil War and during the three years of tribulations?" She answered she did but before she could answer, I told her I wanted to discuss this subject now.

Since we were speaking of gasoline being used for destruction by the mobs, I should point out at this time gasoline cost $8-10 a gallon due to our dollar's devaluation and internal conflicts. I also wanted to make a note here concerning Utah. It is obvious the Church of Jesus Christ of Latter-day Saints is headquartered in Salt Lake City. During the 2nd Civil War, the church stood with the Southern States and their actions to maintain the Constitution. Many members in the church felt strongly they should have stayed neutral in the conflict. Others felt they should have stood with the Democrats and revolutionaries. Suffice it to say about half of the membership in Utah left the church and *apostatized*. There is nothing like conflict and tumult to test your convictions and faith.

In our past, one of the best places to live in America was San Diego, California. The violence of the 2nd Civil War was felt all the way to the border of California and Mexico. When the mobs of California began their purge of 'different' people, they began with the Conservatives. In order to protect their personnel and secure their military assets, the Navy abandoned their base and took position off shore. They would sit this part of the insurrection out due to their location on the West Coast. The mobs then went after the foreigners and that is where it got very nasty. The Mexican gangs and others from Central and South America like MS13 fought back. By the time the 2nd Civil War had ended, there was little if anything left of San Diego. Grudges and blood vendettas were now the norm in that once beautiful city.

Now that the war was over, the nation would experience something it had not witnessed in over a century. The government was a very Conservative/Libertarian one and every law and statute the new government passed was done so through the lenses of liberty. We were no longer in a position to police the world. So, even our military was scaled back to a defensive force that would always be on the ready to combat aggressors. Federal Emergency Management Agency (F.E.M.A.) camps had been set up in parts of the nation to deal with the disasters and refugees from the war. There had been horrible mismanagement and in some camps atrocities committed against refugees. By Executive Order the President shut down the camps and shut down F.E.M.A. We would never see F.E.M.A. camps again in this nation. Soon, all federal welfare programs and safety nets would end. State and local governments would manage their crises and allow the citizens and charities to shoulder their fellow man's burdens.

NATURAL DISASTERS

The 2nd American Civil War was over and there were only pockets of civil unrest still going on. Americans thought they could finally get back to solving their economic problems and rebuilding their nation. Surely, the worst was behind them now, or so they thought. The 2nd Civil War had lasted five months and everyone believed they had learned the lessons the Lord wished them to learn. The Lord apparently had other ideas regarding what was sufficient for repentance.

The January after the Civil War concluded began three months of the worst natural disasters mankind has ever known. Seismologists had been predicting an earthquake in New York City for many years. A 7.0 magnitude quake happens about every 3,400 years. They had always claimed a higher magnitude earthquake such as a 9.0 would never happen. They were wrong. At first, people did not know what was happening to them. By the time they realized it was an earthquake, it was too late for most of them to escape.

New York City had been spared the immediate destruction of a nuclear attack. The mobs and civilian warfare had caused a great deal of destruction, but now it would escalate. I am a firm believer in *omnipotent retribution*. I believe the Lord had been patient enough in calling His children to repentance and being ignored. The State and city of New York had cleaved themselves from the Lord for many years choosing to follow the dictates and the desires of their hearts. They had pushed themselves as far from the Lord as possible by placing in their laws every so called right any person or group could conceive. In following a *Humanist's Agenda* they wanted the citizenry to follow every desire playing in their minds. They then persecuted those who did not agree with this agenda.

One of the final nails in the coffin for the city and State was people cheered and applauded as the Governor signed into law the right for women to murder their unborn children right up to and during the time of giving birth. As evil as this was, *Democratic/Socialist Politicians* were not through attacking The Civil Society.

Both the Governor of the State and the Mayor of the city made it clear that anyone who did not agree with the agenda the State was pursuing, especially Christians and Conservatives were not welcome in their State and should seek a life in another part of the country. These leaders were pandering to their base and knew not what they were sealing upon themselves.

All throughout the Bible, we can read stories of the righteous being driven out of evil nations and once this happens there is no need for the Lord to spare that nation. They were ripe with iniquity and ripe for destruction. Their fate was now sealed and they had no idea of what the wrath of God meant. They would quickly be educated.

It was 10a.m. in New York City when the 8.8 magnitude earthquake struck. The shaking would go on for over four minutes. When the shaking did stop there were very few buildings standing. Most of the city's tallest buildings snapped like toothpicks and fell to the ground burying everyone still living there after the war. Fires broke out all over the city as gas mains and electrical lines snapped and sparked an inferno. New York City was dead. Neighboring States such as New Jersey, Pennsylvania, and Massachusetts would also feel the wrath of this quake and have severe damage to buildings.

The fires that were burning in many of the cities near the coast would not burn for long. The earthquake generated a massive 150 foot Tsunami. Boston was submerged under a wall of water drowning everybody not killed by the quake. The island of Manhattan suffered the same final fate. The Northeastern Atlantic coastline cities were being submerged by tidal waves and storm surges. Millions of people died from these 'acts of God.'

Albany, the capitol of New York State, had been bombed by the U.S. Military with an enormous amount of both smart and dumb bombs. What the U.S. Air Force did not destroy was later burned to the ground. Fires were set by arsonists and within an hour the entire city was engulfed in a firestorm. The war had been lost so the mobs set fire to everything just for pleasure. The riots and revolution had failed to usher in the fundamental transformation and change the *Socialists/ Democrats* desired. They would never be given another opportunity in this nation to try again. The Big Apple and Empire State would never rise again to their former grandeur from the ashes. The South was not free from these acts of God. Dallas, Texas was almost completely destroyed by the riots and revolution prior to the war. Nature or the Lord would complete the job.

Chicago was at the center of the riots and birthplace of the 2nd Civil War. It now stood mostly desolate and uninhabitable. Most of the American Midwest was barren land and desolate from the war. Nature was ready for her time on stage. The New Madrid Fault runs from the northwest corner of Mississippi heading north northeast through Tennessee, Kentucky, Missouri, Indiana, and into

Illinois. The last New Madrid earthquake happened in 1968. It was a prelude to what was coming in the future. The 8.2 tremor that struck after the war caused the Mississippi River to run backwards from south to north for a few hours. Suffice it to say the natural calamities and war caused much of the Midwest to be practically void of people.

In most of the nation at this time it was very difficult to obtain any news concerning current events. Atlanta and New York City were the main news hubs for the East Coast and much of the nation. They were in ruin now and did not look as if they would be restored any time soon. Any news you did get was often times wrong and was more gossip, rumors, and lies, than truth.

I want to return to my comments on Dallas, TX. Giant storm clouds grew over the city. These were not rain clouds, they were hailstorm clouds. For almost three hours the city was pummeled from hail ranging from goofball size to basketballs. Everything was destroyed and anyone living there was killed. Hail of this size, duration, and magnitude was thought to be impossible but nothing in nature is impossible. The hailstorm in Dallas was a precursor to what was coming to Florida and Georgia.

A category five hurricane slammed into the Florida and Georgia coast in March. There had been almost no warning from any government agency due to the war and its destruction. Most coastal cities along the hurricane's path were destroyed by winds and flooding. The death toll would end up in the millions. Atlanta, Georgia was torn apart by the winds and the people still living there were drowned by the rain and floods. The cleansing of America was not yet complete. There was more to come.

The West Coast and Southwest also had plenty of turmoil and destruction to deal with. The Great Southwest Fire burned everything and everyone to the ground from Phoenix, Arizona west to Los Angeles, California and south into Mexico. San Diego had been in a blood feud between mobs and foreign gangs but was now nothing but ashes. At this point it didn't matter whose land it was. Next, the Cascadia Fault line had its turn on center stage and had a major convulsion. From Canada through Washington State and into Oregon, the earth would shake violently for over an hour. There would be aftershocks at slightly less magnitudes as the original event for several days. This caused volcanoes in the region to erupt and fill the air with ash clouds. Further south, it triggered the San Andreas Fault to rupture and shake the remaining West Coast down to Mexico. What happened next was even worse than the preceding quakes.

These earthquakes would rip a seam in the United States from the Gulf of California, near Mexicali, Mexico north following the Colorado River through Lake Havasu, up to Lake Meade and ending near the end of the Grand Canyon. This rip in the earth's surface is some 80 miles wide where it started in Mexicali, Mexico and extends dozens of miles wide on each side of what used to be the Colorado River. Riverside cities and towns along the Colorado River were all swallowed by the sea as it rushed in to fill the void. Even Boulder City which was near Hoover Dam and only about 20 miles from where I used to live is now submerged under 1,000 feet of ocean water. The Baja Peninsula was now separated from the main landmass of Mexico. Travel between these two areas was by boat, plane, or driving a thousand mile detour through America.

The earthquakes did what they do best near any large body of water; they cause giant tidal waves or Tsunamis. All of the American West Coast was getting hammered by massive waves. The Pacific Ocean off the West Coast of America has several named fracture zones and as each of these responded to the earthquakes inland, they too wrenched in sympathetic convulsions causing even more tidal waves to lash out at America's coastline and across the ocean.

San Francisco is no stranger to earthquakes. Some of the most horrific damage and destruction were heaped upon that city during this time. Between the buildings being leveled by massive earthquakes, the firestorms caused by the quakes, and the several enormous Tsunamis burying the lower parts of the city under water, the city and surrounding areas were dead. Lest we forget; there were an enormous number of Socialists/Democrat zealots who went to join the revolution and were never heard from again. Their fellow zealots who stayed behind to 'hold down the fort' would suffer the same fate as those who went to fight. There were very few survivors left in that once beautiful city by the bay.

California, Oregon, Washington State, and other devastated States were no longer hospitable to man and his continued existence. Millions fled from those States looking for basic humanitarian needs. Surrounding States closed their borders to anyone who did not have a home, family, or friends willing to help support them. Too many desperate people seeking too few resources would cause waves of people to break like waves on the mountain passes of the Rocky Mountain States. Most, if not all of these people would perish from starvation, exposure to the elements, and at the hands of other stranded people.

With all the destruction happening in this nation, it is quite amazing how the Rocky Mountains had stayed relatively safe and free from destruction. Members of the Church of Jesus Christ of Latter-day Saints had been given instructions by their Prophet several months earlier to leave the coastal areas and cities and make their way to the Rocky Mountains for their safety. Those that heeded their Prophet were now relatively safe. Those who did not heed the Prophet had most likely perished.

Now that the new technology center of the nation was in Utah and there was no Federal Government to interfere and inhibit ideas and inventions, a new wave of technologies bloomed like flowers from the Utah deserts. New clean electrical generation, water purification, building materials, electronics, and a host of other incredible technologies appeared for man's benefit. Of highest importance were the new advances in building materials. There was a housing shortage due to the migration of people seeking refuge. The rapid manufacturing and assembly of houses was done in a factory on an assembly line. Everything was shipped to the site and quickly assembled on the house pad. From digging the footings and foundation to moving in took less than a month. Also, the cost of these houses was much cheaper than in the past.

The end of the natural disasters was coming to a close. Businesses from all over the world decided to move to the United States and set up their factories and operations. America was once again open for business and Capitalism was king. Many of the countries around the world did not like so many of their companies coming to America. This and their displeasure at having been paid back the money they invested in our Treasury Bills or debt in devalued dollars caused them to become openly hostile towards us.

All appeared to be getting back to normal but appearances can be very deceiving.

First Year of Tribulation

The 2nd Civil War was over. The natural disasters that had destroyed much of the East, West, and Midwest cities had subsided. The Southwest Firestorm had finally burned itself out. Few refugees from the devastated lands had found sanctuary in other States. The Angel of Death had taken his toll on the land with over half of our population heaped upon the land and unburied. But the work of this Angel was far from over. The Lord had declared in previous revelations He would one day cleanse this land of all wickedness when the inhabitants turned from Him. The Lord never lies.

The first year of the second term of our President's administration had proven to be the most turbulent and destructive of all past Presidencies. Over half of the nation was dead or dying from the calamities that had already occurred. The other half of the nation was holding on to life looking to the future with fear but also hope. Our President had proven he was what he has always claimed to be: A Constitutional Conservative or Libertarian in his use of Federal Government authority and power.

He had used the U.S. Military to defeat the revolting Socialists/Democrats, and had even ordered the use of nuclear weapons on American soil to destroy Detroit, the insurrectionist's headquarters, and other strategic targets. This would have been a tough decision for any President, but it was the right decision at the right time. The President, what was left of Congress, and the Supreme Court had been flying from city to city on government planes using Southern State Capitols as temporary administration headquarters. Washington D. C. was in ruin from the war and riots. There was no point in trying to convene and administer the Federal Government from that city. A new national capitol would eventually be built but this time it would be in the center of the lower 48 States.

During a national crisis, the Constitution gives the President vast powers to exercise in maintaining the Republic. An evil or corrupt President would use these situations to expand and consolidate power into his office. A President turning into a dictator is a real possibility during a national emergency or crisis. This was not true of our President. In fact, he used these turbulent times to roll back and eliminate departments and cabinet positions not found within our Constitution. He knew one day in the future we would come back from this crisis and when we did the same Federal Government leviathan needed to be non-existent. If a rollback of federal power was not done then what would we have learned from our trials?

It was now the December after the war and a message from the Prophet of the Church of Jesus Christ of Latter-day Saints in Salt Lake City went out to all members still alive. They were to gather at their respective Wards or church buildings with their food storage and survival equipment on the following Monday morning. From there they would be escorted to pre-established tent cities to dwell for an unspecified amount of time. The method in which the call out happened and the conditions placed on those who would be called out was of some real interest. We should go into further detail on this subject.

Word went out from Salt Lake City there were two letters to be read at the next congregational services. These letters were sent to the Stake Presidents, (a Stake President is a leader over several Wards or local congregations), and were given to each Ward's Bishop. The first letter instructed every member of the Ward that had a full year's food storage for every member of their family and survival gear to meet in a designated room after church services had concluded. There they would be given further instruction.

It was a great disappointment to see only about 10% of each Ward or about 20 people gather for the meeting. The second letter basically read that because of their faithfulness in obeying the Lord in keeping their lamp oil full, they were instructed to bring their food storage and survival gear to the church the next day and travel to areas of refuge. When they arrived at their assigned destinations, they would dwell in tent cities before the next tribulations began. There they would find safety and shelter from the world. They were instructed when the meeting concluded, to not discuss what transpired in the meeting with those who had not prepared. For some members in the meeting this was information too important not to share with best friends. There would be a great deal of discussion, contemplation, prayer, and soul searching on this night. Sometime in everyone's life a test of obedience will be given and some will fail miserably.

The next morning in the parking lot of every church around the world, families gathered to make the trek the Lord had asked of them. Several families that had attended the second meeting on Sunday did not show up. After much discussion the night before, they had decided to stay in place and try to survive with family and friends gathered nearby. Other members of the Ward who had not attended the meeting but had heard what the topic and instructions were, gathered in the parking lot to see who would leave. Some of the unprepared tried to convince their friends to stay and work together to survive. More of those who had attended the second meeting gave in to peer pressure and decided to stay. Now only half of those who attended the meeting would drive away into the unknown.

All over the world, less than a million of the Church's 17 million would follow instructions from the Prophet given by the Lord. When the faithful members arrived at their new homes for the next undetermined period of time, they would discover there were many other people from other religions gathering into the tent cities. Because the Lord loves all of His children, they had been given the same instructions through their church leaders and would journey to the tent city sanctuaries on condition of following instructions given by the Prophet. Everyone there was free to worship God according to the dictates of his heart, but a form of order and compliance was expected of everyone.

To bolster the ranks of the faithful, the nearly 100,000 missionaries from all over the world were called home. They would be sent to the tent cities to join their families or they would go by themselves if family members declined the invitation. Most were obedient to the Lord and made their way to the camps. Regardless of church affiliation, the tent cities were now filled with the most faithful people on the earth who loved God with all their hearts. Their faith would soon be put to the test.

It was now the second year of destruction of American cities by mobs and gangs. What the war and natural disasters had not destroyed, rampaging gangs would leave in rubble from territorial and resource disputes. The first year of people living in tent cities began with a great deal of adjustment when compared to previous lifestyles. These safe cities or zones were set up all over the Rocky Mountains from Canada to Mexico. The camps were not built for creature comforts. They were built for survival, and they were safe from the evils of the outside world.

In the outside world, the United States had paid off the national debt with promised American currency. As stated before, the devaluation of a nation's currency is a two edged sword. Promises made to pay our debts in American dollars would be fulfilled but the dollar had become such a worthless currency that those who held our debt saw a negative return on their investment. They were outraged.

In the U.S., those who held Treasury Notes saw the same negative return. The difference was there were few of those people left in America. The war and natural disasters had cleansed America of half its population. Congress and the President decided to retire the remaining debt held by Americans. It was a symbolic measure more than anything else because there were bigger problems for Americans to worry about on the horizon.

DEATH FROM THE SKY

For over a century, scientists have debated the origins of man. Some of them believe life began in the sea and over billions of years evolved into man and all other creatures roaming our planet. Other scientists believe meteors likely brought primitive bacteria to earth and from there life evolved. It was a common belief that those same comets or meteors could also bring death. Meteors several miles wide impacting the earth are planet killers. This is how the dinosaurs ended their reign on earth or so it is believed. But what would happen if a killer bacterium that man has no immunity against came to our world on the back of a meteor? What would be the results?

We do not have to speculate on this possibility because of what happened during the first year the tent cities were established. On one of those spring nights when the sky was clear and the heavens showed their magnificence, a meteor shower took place in the sky. I have always enjoyed watching meteorites fall to earth and see them streak across the sky. To now know one of those fireballs streaking across the sky brought the first post 2nd Civil War plague to the entire planet is disheartening to the soul of man. By the time the plague ran its course, another 15% of the population of the world, including the United States, would be dead.

The symptoms started out like any other viral infection. It was at first thought another influenza epidemic had broken out all over the world. When the blue dots started appearing on the bodies of the infected, it quickly became evident this was something straight out of a science fiction novel. Once the blue dots appeared, the victims were dead within 48 hours. The only positive attribute of this virus was it had a very short lifespan. By the time summer arrived, the plague was over, but the damage was done. Over 20 million more Americans were now dead and the tribulations would continue.

It was from the middle of June through the end of July when life seemed to be returning to normal. It would not be so. August arrived with more death from a second plague. How and where this one formed or came from is still a mystery today. Some speculation has been made it was a genetic mutation from the first blue dot plague that found its growth medium in water. Others speculated it was a biological/chemical agent placed in the water by our enemies after we had paid them in worthless currency for the debt they held on our nation. It matters not at this point. All we know is another 15 million Americans died at the hands of this plague. Thank Heaven this was another short term plague. By December it had vanished.

Up to this point the people living in the tent cities for the past year were free to leave anytime they desired to do so. But once someone left, he was not allowed to return into the camps. This helped in keeping most infections and diseases from entering the camps. It was now December and the first year of tent cities was nearing its anniversary. Word came from the Prophet that the camps were to be opened for three weeks for the purpose of replenishing supplies. It is safe to say that the camps were points of light filled with the righteous. The Lord had seen fit to allow his followers to 'restock the shelves' with the promise all would be well when the gatherers returned. After three weeks, the camps would once again be sealed from entrance by the outside world.

Reciprocity

It had been two years since the riots and 2nd Civil War had begun. It had been a year since the tent cities were established. One might think the worst was behind us, and it was time for our nation to heal itself and continue this grand experiment called America. You would probably desire a return to normalcy as many Americans did, but it was not to be. Tribulations and the cleansing of America would continue.

There was not much of the city left from the war, natural calamities, and mob and gang destruction, but it was still our nation's capitol. Washington D. C. had been invaded and burned once before by a foreign army when the British tried one last time to bring us back under their control in 1812. Once again, the British returned home in defeat. We rebuilt the city of Washington, and it would be the center of power for the most prosperous people in the history of the world. Three bright flashes of light would end the necessity of this city for all time.

Even though the city was in ruins and the leadership of our nation was in another State, the Kremlin wanted to send a message and make a point. Russia used their nuclear weapons for the first time on a foreign nation. Washington D. C. was removed from the map and would be a topic in history classes from that day forward. They had had enough of America constantly interfering with their designs and desires. The price of launching a first strike was calculated and deemed worth the risk. They and China had spent the past two years moving their critical assets into secure areas while we were dealing with a Civil War and plagues. America would retaliate and tens of millions of Russians would die in a counter strike but this cost was already factored into their actions. It was thought by the Russian and Chinese governments that America was now weak enough to invade, conquer, and occupy.

Russian airplanes, troop ships, cargo ships, and military ships headed for the East Coast of America and Alaska. China sent its troops and ships to the West Coast of America. They would avoid Los Angeles because prior to their ships landing here, they used several of their nuclear weapons to eliminate the City of Angels and soften up the resistance of Americans. China had 1.5 billion people in its nation and the government was willing to lose hundreds of millions of their people in a nuclear exchange with America if it meant we would be conquered. We unleashed much of our nuclear arsenal on China in retaliation. Their estimations of their casualties were correct. Even though we had used hundreds of nuclear warheads on them, both China and Russia refrained from using any more nuclear weapons on us for the simple reason they believed a conventional war could win their war quickly. They also did not want to contaminate America's natural resources. China had decided to support Russia in this war and retrieve some of their wealth not in worthless paper currency, but in land and resources.

Prior to being attacked and invaded by Russia and China, the tent cities were opened for resupplying. The Lord gave the righteous one last chance to seek safety in His tent cities. Tens of thousands of people heeded the call this time after having fought for their survival on the outside of the camps. The tent city entrances were shut just as the nuclear weapons rained down on Washington D. C. and Los Angeles. The righteous and pure in heart were no longer in any city in America. The Lord would now send down His judgment upon our nation and finish the cleansing of America.

The Lord now withdrew His Spirit from the nation outside the tent cities. The Devil had full control over the hearts of man throughout the land. Where the Lord would fill the hearts of man with love, Satan filled those hearts with fear, anger, and hate. City after city fell to the gangs and mobs. Some of these cities had withstood the first two years of civil unrest but once the righteous left, they fell into chaos and mob rule overnight. Bloodlust was in the hearts of all man as gangs killed each other for the thrill of killing another human being. Salt Lake City had been relatively quiet during the past two years but once the records and leadership of the Church of Jesus Christ of Latter-day Saints left the city, mobs claimed the city as theirs and blood flowed in the streets all around Temple Square.

Even while the mobs and gangs were at constant war with each other, the Lord released another plague on the land. So man would always know these plagues were released on man by the Lord, His next one would be different than any plague known to man. It was called the white dot plague because when you were infected, white pustules appeared all over your body. It had a similar appearance to the worst case of acne any teenager could imagine but this acne would kill you. It also had a hemorrhagic fever element to it. Tens of millions of mob and gang members succumbed to this awful death.

The next plague released on America would be giant locusts. We had been relatively free of locust swarms for almost our entire history. The rest of the world knew much about locusts and their destruction. We would now know that experience. The scarce crops or food that had survived the upheaval would now fill the bellies of locusts. Starvation would quickly ensue on the remaining populace. Starvation claimed the lives tens of millions in our nation.

In the tent cities, the Lord saw to it that all the needed water was delivered to them by plentiful rain. Many of the camps had gardens and fields for crops to feed both humans and animals. There were times when the Lord would feed His children and their animals with manna from Heaven. The opportunity to experience this same miracle as the Children of Israel did in the wilderness was both humbling and priceless. The Lord was merciful to His righteous followers and blessed them with abundance while He delivered His judgments and punishments on the rest of the land.

Thirteen months of war now began between the Russian/ Chinese Coalition and America or what was left of our once great nation. World War III had officially begun. Russian and Chinese troops started landing on American soil at the end of February and first of March. They were confronted by a remnant of our military. The Civil War had depleted our armaments and we had not been given enough time to replenish our stockpiles. We were outgunned and overwhelmed in numbers by the enemy. We would fight a defensive war trying to stall the advance of foreign soldiers while we waited for our allies to come to our aid. That aid would never come. We were left to our own devices and probable destruction. For those who had not realized before this, our fate was now completely in the Lord's hands.

The goal of Russia and China was simple: destroy America and eliminate all Americans. The tactics were also simple: kill every civilian and soldier in America and take no prisoners. There is a word for this: genocide. In the cities where mobs and gangs controlled the streets, there was a truce among the factions so they could unite and fight a new enemy. The gangs were very effective inflicting heavy losses on our enemies. There was a great deal of death on both sides as mercy was not shown to any person by either side.

THE 13 MONTH WAR ENDS

The war continued on the East and West Coasts. Each city the Russians and Chinese conquered cost them many lives and casualties. The mobs and gangs were losing more of their so called soldiers than the Russians and Chinese, but all parties were completely engulfed in a bloodlust and hate for each other. I had been taught early in my youth that the Lord uses and allows the wicked to punish the wicked. The truthfulness of this teaching was being played out right before our eyes. Each side went to battle each day believing they would not see tomorrow. Yet they went with their fellow warriors to fight another battle hoping it would be their last.

How is it possible for a people who were so highly favored of the Lord to descend into such inhuman life forms? Each day is filled with a desire for blood and destruction and praise from others who are like minded in their debauchery. Is there any doubt the Lord has exercised His righteous judgments against this nation for our disobedience? This land has witnessed a cleansing twice before, and I pray this will be the last time it will happen.

Sorry about that Sharron. I guess I needed to get that off my chest and out of my mind. This chapter in our interview has brought up a lot of old feelings and thoughts. We should get back to the topic at hand now. Where was I? Oh yes.

Our European Allies had decided to sit this war out for the time being. Two World Wars in a hundred years dampened the desire for another one on their continent. Russia had also made it clear that anyone who did help the Americans would be dealt with after they conquered America. That coupled with Muslim uprisings all over the continent kept them focused on their own survival. The only nation to try and help was Great Britain. They would attack the convoys from Russia to America by ship and plane. Their punishment for trying to help us was a sustained bombing campaign reminiscent of World War II.

In the Pacific, Australia was doing all they could to help their friends and allies. China wanted Australia's natural resources and knew they would support America to the very end, so China sent a massive force to the Northern Territory. The one million strong Chinese army regulars were bolstered by almost the same number of North Korean soldiers. The plan was simple. Half of the force would head west to Port Hedland and then turn south to Geraldton and on to Perth. Once the West Coast was secure and all Australians had been eradicated, they would board ships in Bunbury and head east to Adelaide. They then headed east on land eliminating any and all Australians in their path.

The other half of the force after landing in Darwin would head east through Queensland and then turn south to Sydney and Canberra and would meet up with the other half of their invasion force around Melbourne. Even though they were bolstered by the New Zealand Military, the Australian Military was completely overwhelmed. Ships and planes heading to New Zealand or any other nation were filled to capacity with refugees. Those who could not leave were swept out of this life with no regard or compassion. It took less than nine months to empty Australia of human life. It was completely devastated. Most of the Chinese and North Korean soldiers in Australia were now sent to the Pacific Northwest United States to help in that campaign. Things were not going as well for them in America as was expected and they were about to get worse.

The Chinese and North Korean Armies could have been sent to San Diego or Los Angeles if they had been needed there. But there was nothing left except ashes from the Southwest firestorm and earthquakes the previous year. What had not been burned or leveled by nature had been vaporized by Chinese nukes. They would be sent where they were needed: northern California, Oregon, and Washington State. The advance into the Rocky Mountains had stalled because of very tough resistance by militias and regular army units. In the major cities, the mobs continued to deliver death to their new enemies. The bulk of the newly arrived troops would be needed in Washington State. The same tactics would be used in America that had been used successfully in Australia. China and North Korea had committed over 4 million troops to conquering America. A massive force would push east through Washington into Idaho, and Montana then they would head south wiping out any and all resistance.

The northern California and Oregon forces would head east into Nevada and turn south to Arizona and then east to New Mexico. They would finish their encirclement by heading north and linking up with the bulk of the force and would tighten the noose around the Rocky Mountains moving inward removing any and all Americans permanently from their nation. It was an ambitious plan but it worked in Australia with few flaws. Surely it would work again here in the Rocky Mountains.

They would never get to advance or implement their final solution for America.

By the time the Chinese forces saw this new threat approaching them it was too late. A massive 10 million strong force was moving south along the Canadian West Coast heading to Washington State. No one knew who or where this force came from and why they were headed to America. One thing was evident though; they were heading towards the Chinese Army looking for a confrontation. Any and all Chinese or North Korean troops who confronted this army were eliminated with little effort.

The Chinese generals called every soldier they had on the West Coast to rapidly deploy to Washington. They would use every weapon and soldier they had to try and stop this 10 million person juggernaut. It was all in vain. The combined Chinese and North Korean militaries were completely overwhelmed and destroyed.

What little forces did survive were called back to their respective nations to help quell their own uprisings. The new army of 10 million people kept heading south after they destroyed our enemies until they reached Oregon. They then turned east and headed for Missouri. The East Coast invasion by Russia had been going fairly well but it now came to a halt.

Russia had, at this point, sacrificed over a million soldiers to accomplish their goal thus far. They had wiped clean the East Coast from Maine to Florida and had pushed their way west into Texas. Ohio and West through the Great Plains was free of Americans. They had stopped at the base of the Rocky Mountains waiting for their Chinese counterparts to begin their final push though the Rockies. They would then join forces and finish the job of cleansing America of Americans. As word reached them about the fate of their Chinese Comrades, their hearts sank. Then they realized this new army was heading straight for them.

It was at this point the Russian leadership in Moscow realized their quest was lost. America was too large of a nation to conquer and occupy without their Chinese counterparts. Moscow did not want to lose their army to the new army that had wiped out the Chinese military in just weeks. The battle hardened Russian soldiers were needed at home. Insurrections by angry mobs and revolutionaries were taking place all over the Motherland. The Russian generals were ordered to gather their forces and leave America and head home as soon as possible. World War III had ended. The cleansing of America was complete.

There had been three years of tribulation and only the righteous had survived the Refiner's Fire. When the count was finally taken, there were only 12 million Americans left in the United States from a previous population of 330 million only four years earlier. It was discovered that the 10 million person army which had defeated the Chinese Army were the lost Ten Tribes of Israel. The Lord had sent them on a Holy Mission to defeat all armies standing before them as they made their way to Independence, Missouri. They would be guided to their final destination by a Prophet and when they arrived there, they would be given further instructions on their mission.

"I think we can stop here for the day," I said. "We have covered a lot of topics and I am pretty sure we could both use a night to recover from this extended interview." Sharron agreed. I asked if she wanted to continue tomorrow or take a day off to fully re-energize for the next session. I told her I would be ready to go tomorrow and it was actually good to speak about these last two time periods. It was kind of like getting it off my chest and releasing my memories out to the universe. "How about we continue at 9:30 tomorrow morning?" I asked.

She replied, "That would be great," and picked up her gear and left to go home. It had been a long day for me but I felt relieved and was now looking forward to dinner and a quiet night. Tomorrow's interviews would be a positive experience and I looked forward to speaking about them.

THE TENTH INTERVIEW- OUR PRESENT AND FUTURE

This morning started out like other mornings. The neighbor's dog barked at every car and when it was almost 9:30, the four legged squawk box fulfilled its purpose for being created. I knew Sharron would be here soon and we would begin our interview. Today's session would focus on what happened after the cleansing of America had been completed. I was really looking forward to this interview. I was also a bit sad to know today would most likely be the last day of interviews with Sharron. I have really enjoyed her company and could see why she was one of the few Americans to have survived the cleansing.

The neighbor's dog started barking again, and within a few minutes Sharron was in the study, set up, and ready to begin our last interview. I began with a simple observation.

"Sharron I am not sure where you were during the three years of tribulation, but what happened after that time period was truly glorious. Today before we move on to the restoration of America, I would like to discuss the present conditions in this nation and the world, as I see them. I will start with the world," I said.

252 | AFTER OUR FALL

It has been over 10 years since the fall of our nation. Our prideful ways have been cleansed from this land by the Lord. We have come back from the abyss a humbled people. Throughout the world, we are growing in power and influence. Across the planet the same cannot be said of many nations. Not every nation experienced a cleansing like America. For some nations it was worse, for others it was better. All were being called on to change their ways; some would listen while others embraced pride and covered their ears. Around the globe, for those filled with deaf pride, turmoil and political unrest would run rampant.

Our enemies of World War III, Russia and China have been going through their own revolutions and uprisings. The war with America had cost them dearly in 'blood and treasure.' Tens of millions had been killed and their conquest had failed. Their people had had enough of *tyranny*. They would understand firsthand what Thomas Jefferson had meant by saying, "The tree of liberty must be watered from time to time with both the blood of tyrants and patriots."

Israel is stable and thriving. Much of the Muslim world still hates the tiny Jewish State but even with a 150-1 advantage in people, the anti-Semitic nations are afraid to attack Israel. They saw what happened in America during World War III and wanted nothing to do with our rescuers. America has also warned the world that any attack on Israel is an attack on America and we will respond alongside Israel to any aggression.

I think some highlight of where we are is warranted here.

The nation we live in today is very much like the nation was in *1791*. We are living the most liberty endowed lives ever seen since our founding. I will only mention the restoration of America at this point. The new Constitution was ratified and shortly thereafter we added ten new Amendments to our Constitution called the Bill of Rights. The new government we created was expressly formed to protect our rights and freedom.

It is important to note here that when we do get to the final interview, 'The Restoration,' our rights were *never* taken from us. *We gave them away for perceived security and entitlements.* In 1789 our Founding Fathers told the new nation that our Constitution was created for a righteous and moral people. It is wholly unsuited for any other. We had proven them to be prophetic in their thinking.

When we do discuss the re-establishing of our National and State Constitutions, I hope and pray everyone will understand why we did what we did. I further pray what we did will stand the test of time for generations yet to come.

I only hope it is enough.

The people of this Republic are free again. You are free to do as you please as long as you remember that where your rights end is where other people's rights begin. This is called exercising maximum freedom coupled with maximum responsibility. The only true duty of governments is to protect the citizen. By this I mean, they are to protect our rights above all other functions they are tasked with.

Economically, we are enjoying a level of prosperity in this nation not seen for over 100 years. It is amazing what the American people can do when we remove government taxation and interference from their lives.

Life in America today is the best it has ever been.

So what do you see the future to hold for our nation?" asked Sharron.

"Yoda said the future is difficult to see because it is always in motion. I find it difficult to argue this point with a Muppet, but I will give it my best shot based on my highest hopes and desires," I replied.

My time here on earth is quickly coming to an end. I have done my best to secure the blessings of liberty for many generations still unborn. Our duty is to remain vigilant in our opposition to tyranny and protect our rights. *Freedom has never been free.* Liberty in our nation today was re-secured at the cost of over 300 million lives.

I foresee a future filled with economic freedom coupled with prosperity, scientific discoveries, technological advancements, medical cures, and most importantly, spiritual growth. It is critical for us to understand that all facets of our nation's prosperity are directly tied to our obedience to the Lord's Commandments.

I foresee much turbulence even after the cleansing of vast parts of the world has occurred. Those countries that have stiff necks and refuse to accept the Gospel of Jesus

Christ will never enjoy true peace. This is a tragedy for their people as they witness the benefits of strict obedience to His teachings. Some parts of the world had seen the cleansing America had to endure. One might expect those nations to take notice and learn from our mistakes and embrace a better way. Perhaps it is a reality of life: We must all go through trials and tribulations to fully understand and appreciate surviving them.

"Sharron, I don't have much more to say about the present or our future. Is there anything else you want to ask me about or wish me to discuss before we move on to the restoration of America?"

"Yes," she said. "Before we cover the restoration of America, I would like to express to you how very much I have enjoyed getting to know you through these interviews. I have learned so much in such a brief time and sincerely feel a great kinship having shared so much of your life experience. Not many people can truly say they have been part of changing the world and spoke of it so matter *of factly* concerning their part in it.

Your love for this 'great nation of ours' is quite evident. You speak of it so genuinely throughout your meticulous rebuilding and retelling of such intricate details. Even with all of these facts, I'm not sure I can convey the entirety of who you are from only your point of view. Even in the thick of it with such deeply focused interactions, your subtle humor shines through tempering the weighty magnitude of all you and *your circle* have been through.

In that light, and with an air of levity in mind, I would like to follow your lead and call our next interview *'Loose Ends.'* She smiled and continued., "I am planning to interview a few other people who had direct contact with you during all of these events. I am very interested in their perspective which I would like to include in the overall interview with you.

For now I would like you to tell me a little about your wife and what she did during all you have shared with me already. I would also like to know about those who were closest too you, in the trenches, as it were: *Michael Leander, David Mahonri, Wesley Dennis and anyone else who was crucial to your journey through all that you have come to know now, as 'After Our Fall.'*

I replied, "Certainly! I would most certainly enjoy sharing with you a few details of those very integral people, without whom, I could not have survived. I would have never made it without their input, companionship, and the council of those I feel have been crucial to my life and vital to our country and our survival."

THE ELEVENTH INTERVIEW-
LOOSE ENDS

LINDA

My having to leave while the cleansing of America was taking place was not easy. However, I have heard it said, 'A crisis brings out the best and worst in people.' Linda has brought about the best in me.

In the fight for our Constitution, these activities and their demands took me away from home during a very uncertain and tumultuous time. A lesser woman would have withered from the weight of these labors while she was left at home alone, very literally holding down the fort. My wife, Linda, did not falter. I cannot overemphasize the danger I have repeatedly put her in due to the nature of the activities in the support of our country. My wife never fails to answer the call to service.

Our future together began in our hometown of Las Vegas, NV in 1992 when I crashed a party she was attending. I soon learned she was a Special Education teacher living with her mother while working and saving to buy her own house. Our ages are not of any consequence to this story but suffice it to say she is five years older than I. Even though she wanted to marry and have children of her own one day, it was not at the forefront of her every thought. She was, and still is, a very independent woman. We were unaware at the time, but this would be a great benefit to us both as the years passed. This was not an easy life for her but it was the life we chose, together.

My avid and active support of our Constitution and my denouncing the active deterioration of our National Foundations 'as a whole' was a call to service that we both agreed was our duty to stand for liberty no matter the consequences. This was the life we accepted and embraced for the sake of our nation and posterity. Liberty exacts a price and it was a price we were willing to pay.

I will discuss these missions in greater detail when we get to the particulars of David Mahonri but when I speak of my *excursions* and those *dangerous situations* I want to make it clear I was not involved in any top-secret government missions. I was traveling to other encampments and networking with the other leaders of those communities.

I do not want you to think all Linda did was stay at home and bake tasty treats. She was heavily involved. She helped home school our grandchildren, worked with special needs children's education throughout the community, and was the head of our house while I was away. There were times when everyone in our valley was called upon to defend our area. Linda never hesitated to grab her side arms and head to the front lines. Truth be told, she is a better shot than I am. Fortunately she was spared the trauma of having to end another person's life. I wish this could have been said for all of us.

Prior to the collapse of America, we had weathered many storms. We raised 4 children together and are blessed to have 8 grandchildren at this point in time. We have lived the best lives possible and tried to be productive citizens who support our communities. Looking at where we are today, it is obvious our faith in the Lord and our willingness to serve Him to restore this land was worth the cost. I am home now and barring a call to serve our government or our church, I am looking forward to spending what time I have left at home in quiet anonymity. That being said, a word of advice to younger men is this; never be afraid of a strong woman, she will be a 'help meet' to you if you let her. I know the term *'help meet'* is a curious use of words but it simply means a person who is important or critical to you. Do you hear me men?

So Sharron, does it matter to you who I tell you about next?" I asked.

She replied, "No, it is totally up to you."

I decided to begin with Mike Leander since I have known him the longest. He would be followed by Wesley Dennis and then David Mahonri. Before we talk about those three men, I think I should briefly describe the area we live in so you can understand why we took the course of action we did in our efforts to secure this valley.

The valley we live in was home to about 2,000 people prior to the fall or collapse of America. When the cleansing began and the call went out for righteous people to seek refuge in these designated tent city areas, our valley's population swelled to more than 25,000 souls. The elevation here is 5,300 feet above sea level and we are surrounded by mountains on all sides. There are three main access roads into the valley from three larger cities 40-60 miles away. In many ways this valley is and was an ideal location to be transformed into a fort.

With this said, let us talk about those three men you met last week. What you might not have been aware of is that they were all former members of my Boy Scout Troop back in Las Vegas. Now I consider all of the Scouts in my Troop to be like sons to me. But these three are special. They had similar beliefs on the coming collapse of America. I wanted to have like minded people I trusted around me when that time arrived. I invited the three of them and their families to join me and my family when all of this occurred.

MICHAEL LEANDER - *'Ninja'*

Michael is the oldest of the three men you met a few days ago. He is about 22 years younger than I am. He looks very much like his father, poor guy. I have known his father all my life and I can say this with 100% accuracy, *Mike is a much better father to his children than his father was with him.* When the fall began, he came to our house, just as planned, with his wife Devin and their daughters StoryAnn, Roxy, Navy, and Indy. Our house was filling up with little ones again and this was wonderful. Others would soon join us and fill our house with life and new sounds. Once he and his family were settled in, it was time to put Michael's talents to work in our community.

Even though this valley was being filled with the more righteous and law abiding people in our nation, it is still very necessary to have a system of law and order to maintain a civil society. It does not matter how many good and honest people are placed together. The stress of a crumbling nation coupled with a cleansing of the wicked will cause a rise in stress for everyone. Our city council placed Michael in charge of internal security for the valley. This position was much like a Sheriff or Chief of Police. For the most part, Mike and his group of Deputies were there to promote a sense of safety. They would also give people someone to talk with when they were overwhelmed, stressed or in despair. At their height, there were almost 100 members of his 'police force.'

Their main directive was to be on patrol and watch over the people in the tent city like a shepherd would watch over and protect his flock. With Michael and his officers always on patrol, there were very few instances requiring aggressive force. When Wesley's group would detain a suspicious person in the outer perimeter or if someone unknown arrived in town without an escort from Wesley's group, these people were detained and questioned to ascertain their motives. Michael's officers operated a detention facility for those who needed a closer look or for those who committed a crime in the community.

There were a few times when a group of 'infiltrators' slipped past Wesley's external security force and made it to town. Some of these people were found to be those just trying to escape the horrors outside the valley. Others were people who believed it was permissible to cause mayhem where ever they went. This type of behavior was swiftly dealt with. The 100 officers Michael was in charge of took the lead in violent confrontations but were bolstered by every armed citizen in the valley. It was a clear policy that whenever gun shots were fired in the valley, everyone was to grab their guns and head towards the gunshots to shore up the security force if needed. This only happened a few times.

Neither Michael nor any of his officers were required to exercise judgment on any detainee. If a disturbance or crime was committed, Michael's Deputies would conduct the investigation and present the facts to the judges. A panel or tribunal of three judges was appointed with the task of reviewing the facts and conducting any further investigation they believed necessary. At the conclusion of these investigations they would render verdicts. Discernment was the main requirement for these judges. All judgments by the tribunal had to be unanimous. It is critical, even during times of *tumult* and destruction, to have an established form of law and order. The rule of law must be adhered to or the civil society will completely implode.

Michael and his internal security forces were for the most part, more psychologists and friends to those in need of someone to help with the stress of very trying times and situations. The key to everything operating smoothly in the valley was keeping un-necessary tensions and problems to a minimum. Michael and his officers did a very commendable job of this task.

Michael served in the position of Head of Internal Security for over three years until the tent city was pretty much empty. He then left the valley to live in another town with his wife and daughters. Our house is once again empty and quiet. We miss them.

WESLEY DENNIS - *'Hoops'*

Wesley is the youngest of the three. He earned his Eagle Scout rank when he was 12 years old, which is phenomenal.

By age 13 he had earned his Black Belt in Tang Soo Do Karate. His devotion to the Constitution is enviable. He was the perfect choice for the assignment he would be given.

The city council placed him in charge of external security outside the valley. His people would secure the distant perimeter leading into the valley. The three main entrances into the community needed layered blockade deterrent systems to control those who could travel to our town. Access to our valley was preliminarily granted to people who could demonstrate they would be a benefit to the community. *'Burdens to society'* and *'trouble makers'* were turned away immediately. The job given to Wesley and his defense force was very difficult and dangerous. The plan they followed was to have three barricaded checkpoints on the three main roads at different distances from town. They also needed to patrol the areas between the main checkpoints looking for infiltrators. Wesley's group was very effective at the job they were assigned to do. There were only a few times when people slipped past the exterior defense force and made into town. When this happened, they were ultimately discovered by citizens or Michael's Deputies.

During the cleansing when desperate people or criminal gangs tried to ram through the blockades and push their way into our valley, every able bodied person armed themselves and went to the defense of the community to repel *the-would be invaders*. It was never a pleasant scenario, but when deadly force was used it was always as a last resort. Even so, the loss of life is never an easy thing to live with.

Wanting to learn a little more about the task Wesley was given; Sharron asked if I could go further in to detail on how he operated the blockades and checkpoints.

Wesley had the largest group of men and women in his defense force. There were right around 300 people in his group. This may sound like a lot, but if you went out in the valley and looked at the area they had to patrol you would understand the need for so many people. On the main roads leading into our valley they established a first contact checkpoint and blockade about five miles away from town. There were eight armed people on the roads to intercept travelers and give them an initial contact interview. These eight people were backed up by three concealed sniper teams. If anyone was allowed to proceed towards the valley they were escorted to the next checkpoint and turned over to that group for further vetting and possible escort to the next checkpoint.

That checkpoint was located approximately 2-3 miles away from town. This second checkpoint was manned by 12 armed people just like the first checkpoint. They were also backed up by three concealed sniper teams. If mayhem was your desire, then ramming through the first and second checkpoints would give you exactly what you wanted. You might make it past these two barricades and you might think you were in the clear all the way to town but you would be wrong. There was a final failsafe checkpoint you have to be cleared through before you could gain access to town.

The third and final checkpoint was positioned one mile from town. It was manned by 20 armed people and supported by four concealed sniper teams. The positioning of this final checkpoint only a mile from town was by design. It contained more firepower than the first two checkpoints for two reasons. The first reason was so everyone in town could hear the disturbance and come to the aid of the defense force. The sound of gunfire meant for everyone to grab their guns and run towards the fight. The second reason the final checkpoint was much more heavily armed was to slow down the invaders sufficiently to give the people in town enough time to back them up.

One more comment on the checkpoint system is required here. Everyone who came into town was escorted by members of the previous checkpoints. If you were unescorted and tried to make it to the next barricade you most likely would have been shot on sight. I know this probably sounds a little harsh, but all you had to do to live and possibly be allowed to stay in town was to follow our strict rules while traveling. The safety of our people was of upmost importance to us.

The main roads may have been secured but there was a great deal of land between the checkpoints to monitor. To patrol these areas required a different tactic. Four teams of two people were utilized for this task. These teams were comprised of serious hunters and trackers all riding on horseback. Home owners who lived in those distant areas became the eyes and ears for these mounted patrols. They would also become the first people to back up the Mounted Patrol if a situation arose.

Whenever there was a mounted intercept of an infiltrator trying to sneak into town, they were detained and taken to the internal security detention center and turned over for questioning. There were only three possible outcomes for the detainee after their questioning. They would be welcomed in and enjoy the safety and freedom of the camp, or they could be detained further to address any inconsistencies in their purpose of travel, or they would be taken to the outermost checkpoint and given a small supply of food and water and instructed to leave and not come back. They had now used their one and only *get out of jail for free* card.

Wesley put together a very strong, disciplined group of people. We are eternally grateful for their work keeping us safe and we will always remember those officers who lost their lives defending all of us. The day we were finally able to dismantle the barricades and checkpoints to restore the open flow of travel and commerce in our valley was a *joy beyond words.*

DAVID MAHONRI - *'Buddha'*

David Mahonri was also in my Scout Troop. In fact, he was the first to earn the rank of Eagle Scout while I was the Scout Master. He also received extensive Martial Arts training in his youth. David is probably one of the most Conservative/Libertarian people I know. He enjoyed theater while in high school and is perhaps the most dangerous of the three. His blonde hair, blue eyed, happy go lucky face and attitude disarm people who believe he is an easy target to pick on. They find out quickly how big of a mistake they just made.

He had perhaps the most dangerous of all assignments given out by the city council. He was instructed to find four other like minded individuals who were *street wise* and had *nerves of steel*. They were to infiltrate the areas being cleansed not to create more mayhem but to pass through unobserved and seamlessly avoid detention. I envisioned them more as *Ninja Spies*. Their assignment was to obtain valuable *'intell'* on the outside world for use later in our struggle.

When the tent cities were opened for those three weeks to obtain more supplies for the camp, it was the information David and his group obtained during their missions that directed us to where we would most likely find those supplies. Their information almost always proved to be accurate. The life sustaining skills David had learned while living on the streets in his late teens and early 20's proved to be a blessing to our valley. This affirms one should never *dismiss* or *disparage* the difficult times experienced in life.

Trials and tribulations can mold us into the instrument the Lord intends to utilize later for our benefit and His glory.

One of the most dangerous missions they were sent on was to make contact with other tent cities or camps. There were other encampments dotting the land all over the Rocky Mountains from Canada to Mexico. I wanted to make contact with the camps in our general area to share information and let others know who were going through the cleansing they were not alone. For some reason down deep in the human psyche, we are strengthened knowing others are fighting for survival and have not given up hope.

As David's group would go out on a mission and into harm's way they would send one in their group out front about 200 yards from the three in the center. He would be the scout for the others. The three in the center would split 100 yards left and 100 yards right from the center man. The last man would lag behind the center three about 200 yards and watch the backs of the others. He would make sure they were not being followed by possible hostile forces. Some of the men in this group had been in U.S. Special Forces and would put their skills to use to benefit our camp.

The communication between these men was accomplished at these distances with bird calls, hand signals, and metal clickers like the ones used in other wars like Vietnam. Even though all of the missions David and his group were sent on were dangerous, they were instructed to never take unnecessary risks on their missions. The loss of one of their lives was not worth the objective of the mission. It was better to withdraw from a dangerous situation and try again later when conditions changed for our benefit.

When David and his group arrived at other tent cities, they would split up into three groups and remain concealed in order to observe the camp for a few days. It was important to learn about their activities, security, leadership, and general conditions within their encampment. The group would then huddle up and discuss their findings before planning on any action. Several plans would often be discussed before an agreement on the best way to proceed was finalized.

Once it was decided to make contact with a camp, one of the team members would be sent back towards our valley about a mile away to a place where he could remain concealed and observe the camp and reaction to being contacted. He was the dispatch rider for the camp. If the meeting of the camp went horribly wrong, it was up to him to make his way back to our valley and let us know what had occurred. We could then determine our next course of action.

Once the dispatch rider was in place two of the team members would find a well concealed position to observe the first contact with the camp. If there were problems they could either make an attempt to rescue their fellow team members or they would make their way back to our valley and report on the events. A course of action could then be decided on from that point. This time of first contact was the most dangerous unknown for those team members. They never refused a mission and their participation was completely voluntary.

If first contact went well, I would travel with David and his group to meet with the leaders of the other camps. It could take days or weeks to arrive at our destination. All the while we were traveling we were exposed to multiple threats. It was by following these men's instruction that brought us home after each mission. These missions were always high risk, high reward missions.

I only took these trips after David and his group had made contact with other tent cities and laid the groundwork for me. These trips helped to strengthen our ties to other groups having similar challenges. More than anything else, these trips bolstered the morale of others during a time of great turmoil. Sometimes, all people need to know is that they are not alone.

There were many touch and go situations for David's group but they all survived their missions and returned with valuable intelligence. Every person who survived the cleansing of America did so because they were one of the righteous people and they had a role to play in the large mural of God's eternal plan. We were blessed to have the fearless men in David's team.

Sharron said, "I am looking forward to interviewing each of the men you just spoke about." I told her she would get much more detail and insight when she did. I had only given her some of the highlights of their actions as I could remember them. She then said, "You told me earlier you knew the fall or collapse of America was coming years before it did. Here are some questions for you; how did you know what was coming? Who told you what was on the horizon and to begin preparing? Who was your biggest influence in knowing these truths?"

I will answer these questions in the order they were asked. The first question was: How did I know the fall was going to happen? There were several people who *tutored* me directly and indirectly over the years on what the future of our nation would be. W. Cleon Skousen wrote, 'The Cleansing of America' many years ago. It has been proven to be quite prophetic and accurate. Another great source of inside information came to me from Mark *(last name withheld for the sake of privacy)*. He has been a longtime friend of the family and today he is working on the translation of ancient records found in America and from the Lost 10 Tribes.

I want to say here and now even though the events that took place here in America were foretold by Isaiah several thousand years ago and reiterated by other writers with prophetic insight over the last few decades, the actual timetable was not known to any of us. When the events did take place we were not surprised by them but we were taken back by the magnitude of it all. Reading what will happen and living through the actual events are two entirely different experiences.

Your next question was: Who told me? I guess I answered some of this question a minute ago. The books I read made it obvious the fall of America would take place but plugging events into timetables was difficult. I think if I move on to the next question it will be much more helpful in answering your questions.

Your third question was: Who was my biggest influence concerning these matters? This is an easy one. My mother; Mom was the main influence and sounding board for all the events that took place in this nation. This should not be a shock to anyone though. Men may be on the front lines of war but women do something very well that few men do at all; they listen to the whisperings of the Spirit.

MOM

Over 20 years prior to the fall of our nation, my mother traveled through this valley and felt deep down in her soul it would be a safe place for her family when the coming tribulations began. She immediately began setting up her 2nd home in preparing for what she knew was coming. Several years later my wife was inspired to do the same thing and we immediately did what my mother had done.

By following my mother's lead and then listening to the inspiration given to my wife, we survived the cleansing of America. I have not always listened to the Spirit throughout my life but thankfully I was wise enough to do so this time and act on it properly. My advice to anyone who will listen is this: men, listen to the women in your lives.

"Well Sharron, I could go on for another hour about all the important people in my life that stepped up to and took on the difficult times head on. But I think I have given you plenty of information to work with. Is there anything else I can tell you that would help?" I asked.

She replied. "No, I have plenty to work with and I am really looking forward to interviewing the other men you talked about."

"Sharron, before we discuss the Restoration of America, how about we grab a sandwich. Then we can finish up our interview. If you have any other questions, I will answer them at our conclusion." I said. It was off to the kitchen and dining room we went.

THE TWEFLTH INTERVIEW-
THE RESTORATION

Linda made us some roast beef sandwiches with some of her potato salad. It was very tasty and filling. Once we were through with lunch we returned to the study and began our next interview. If all went well, today would be my last interview.

It had been three years from the time the total economic collapse started, through the riots, into the 2nd Civil War, and transitioned to the invasion and defeat of the Chinese and Russian armies. To many people it seemed much longer but to me it seemed to have passed rather quickly. There were pockets of survivors throughout the nation but the bulk of the surviving population was spread out from Canada to Mexico in the Rocky Mountains living in tent cities.

We have all read about the many miracles found in the Bible especially during the Exodus by Moses. It is now time for us to publicly recognize the Lord's hand in preserving His righteous followers during the second and third year of the tribulations. He had fed, provided water, strengthened the clothing to last for those years, provided needed supplies, and protected the righteous with His mighty arm of power. When the wicked sought to destroy those He had sheltered in the tent cities, He delivered our enemies into our hands for destruction or He destroyed them with a word from His mouth. The Lord truly is a God of love and miracles for those who heed His words. He is also a God of justice and wrath for the wicked.

The time had finally arrived for the camps and tent cities to close. The land had been cleansed of the wicked and it was time for man to reclaim this Promised Land on behalf of the righteous and the Lord. The departure from the camps would be an organized endeavor. All things were to be done with wisdom and in an orderly fashion. The Lord's House is a House of Order and this land must also be. From Idaho east to Montana and Wyoming and south to Arizona and New Mexico 12 million people would begin their trek to spread out across the nation. These people would be much like our ancestors who ventured out West in covered wagons to settle the land over 150 years ago. This time there was an entire country to be reclaimed and repopulated.

It was agreed by the camp leadership council that each group would consist of approximately 500 people. They would be heavily armed in order to gather wild game and in order to defend their group. The groups departed in every direction imaginable and would go until they came across a town. There they would bury the dead and rebuild what dwellings were sound and inhabitable. Members of the group could either stay there and earn a living, or press on to another destination. It was also agreed to by all groups they would not re-settle any major city. Those places were to be used as resources and materials to rebuild small towns and communities. As the towns were reclaimed, a restart of a true free market economy was implemented.

There were two parts to this free market economy mixed in with a Zion mentality. The first part was simple. What you earned, owned, and worked for was yours and no government or other entity such as family, friends, businesses, and especially governments could tell you what to do with it. Your labor, your industry, your property, and your money were yours, period.

The second part of the economy was for the people to align their hearts and minds with a Zion society or a society based on the City of Enoch. This means you follow the example of Enoch and his people by having all things in common. This is not the same as the evil philosophies of *Communism* or *Socialism*. Any time force is used on others in order for them to comply with your desires or a government; it is evil, wrong, and should be strictly prohibited. A change of heart is needed by all people who live in this nation and pursue their happiness. The philosophy of voluntarily aiding their fellow man is now the norm. People help others because they love them and desire them to be happy. This is now the new free market system of America.

The author of this Zion economy is the Lord. He teaches His children what they should do to be a true follower and then He leaves them to obey or ignore His guidance. Rich blessing are bestowed on those who follow Him with exactness. There are no such blessings given to those who disobey. A change of heart and charity, which is the true love of Christ, towards your fellow man, are not uncommon during and since the tribulations and even today. Oh, how we are blessed when we are obedient!

This is the mentality and spiritual roots of those who survived the cleansing and are now leaving the camps. They will assist their fellow man in every way possible so all of them can be successful and stay firm in their faith. Each group will re-enforce the group ahead of them and those who are ahead will aid those coming from behind. This leap frog method of re-settling the land will result in reclaiming the land in a very short time. Within two years most of the West Coast, Rocky Mountain States, Great Plains States, and parts of the South have been reclaimed.

There is an exception to this expansion.

The Great Lakes States and the Northeastern States will remain void of human inhabitation for nearly a decade after the cleansing. Those lands are referred to as the Lands of Desolation for good reasons. The 2nd Civil War, gangs, mobs, natural disasters, plagues and diseases have left the land uninhabitable due to the amount of destruction and sheer quantity of dead bodies covering the land. This is where 200 million of the 300 million Americans perished.

As States and areas within the States were settled, agriculture, energy, fuel, manufacturing, and other vital industries were brought back on line. It had now been five years since the fall began and America was beginning to resemble its once great image and countenance. It would take a few more years for us to get back up to full speed in our economy but we would. This time would be different from our original founding. It would be even better.

"I have a question for you." Sharron said. "What do you have to say concerning the 10 million soldier army that defeated the Chinese in the Pacific Northwest?"

"This is a great question and one I was about to discuss." I replied.

The 10 million person army that helped save America is the "so called" *Lost 10 Tribes of Israel.* In about 70 A.D. the Romans destroyed Jerusalem, tore down the Temple, and took 10 of the 12 Tribes of Israel into the North and they were never heard from again. The Lord through His latter-day Prophets told us the 10 Tribes of Israel are not lost to Him and they are awaiting the time He has appointed for their return to Israel.

To this day, it has not been revealed where the 10 Tribes of Israel were or how they were able to arrive in Canada on the Washington State border without detection by any government or by any enemy military. How does one move 10 million people without detection? This in and of itself should be proof of how great our God is and how His abilities are not limited by man's finite knowledge. All we do know is they arrived at the perfect place at the perfect time and saved our lives and our nation.

There are a few things we do know about them. The term Israel translates as 'Warriors of God.' This is exactly what they are, a warrior people with a total commitment to the Lord. After they defeated the Chinese Army, they headed east to Missouri to dedicate the land that will be used to build 12 Temples surrounding the main Temple in Jackson County. About 9 million people, some of which were their highly skilled craftsmen remained to begin the construction of these temples. A million warriors continued on to the Southeast Coast of America. These warriors were headed to the land of their inheritance or Israel to make that nation whole again. They would also be needed in Israel to support their brothers and sisters against their ancient and modern day enemies.

Let's discuss the 12 Temples and the importance of their layout. The main Temple in the center is the House of the Lord and there is where He dwells and directs His work here on earth. The 12 other Temples are evenly spaced around the main Temple and are like spokes on a wheel. This is a symbolic and literal affirmation of the Lord being at the center of our lives. Each of these Temples was built by the individual Tribes of Israel and is a gift to their Lord. There is much work to be performed within these temples on behalf of the children of God.

After the 10 Tribes of Israel destroyed the Chinese Army and turned east towards Missouri, they headed straight though the Rocky Mountains and crossed paths with many of the people in the tent cities and camps of refuge. Those in the camps were not sure of what they should do about this large military group. Should we fight them or should we embrace them? Tensions grew concerning this group but the group did not seem to have any interest at this time about those in the camps. Their focus was elsewhere.

Word went out from the Prophet to not confront this group or army for they are on a holy mission from the Lord. This is when we discovered this army was the Lost 10 Tribes of Israel. Prophecy was being fulfilled right before our eyes. We were further instructed to not interfere with their progress and if they needed assistance, we were to give them all we could. Official contact would be made with them at a later date.

After the Chinese Army was utterly destroyed by the 10 Tribes of Israel, both China and Russia abandoned their designs on conquering America. Word of this miraculous defeat spread quickly amongst the international community. The nations of the world would now re-evaluate their alliances and treaties with those who were once called superpowers. There was one thing all nations did recognize after this defeat and it was that America is under the direct protection and blessings of the Lord. Since the failed conquering of America took place, we have never been attacked or invaded again.

A few months after the Tribes of Israel arrived in Missouri, the Lord made it known through the Prophet it was time for the official introductions between the leader of the Tribes, the U.S. President and His Prophet. The Prophet and the leader of the Tribes had records and information they were to exchange and translate for their people. The Lord had a request for the President of the United States that He would divulge at the gathering. The Lord gave each group the essential conditions of this initial meeting. Those who would attend this meeting were requested to fast and pray prior to it so their hearts and minds would be in alignment with what would transpire. All obeyed this request.

The 10 Tribes spoke, read, and wrote two languages. The first was the language of their ancient homeland; Aramaic. The second language was the most frequently used by them and was known as the Adamic language or the language of our first father Adam. The Prophet was instructed to search among the survivors to find two people who would help communicate with the Tribes of Israel. The Prophet was told there is a Rabbi and an ancient language professor who speak Aramaic and they were to be brought to this gathering. The Lord promised all who attended this gathering would be touched by the Holy Ghost and would receive the gift of tongues so there could be perfect communication at this marvelous gathering.

On the designated day, the President of the United States, the Vice President, the Speaker of the House of Representatives, and the Majority Leader of the Senate arrived on time in Missouri. The Prophet, his two counselors, the Quorum of the 12 Apostles and the two language specialists arrived earlier in the day to meet with fellow worshipers of the Lord. At the designated time the group of American Ambassadors made their way to the 10 Tribes of Israel's encampment. When they arrived they were greeted by the Prophet of the 10 Tribes and their Leadership Council.

Without a word being spoken the two Prophets shook hands and embraced each other as long lost brothers. Soon the entire group was embracing as the Rabbi and

Professor were doing their best to translate greetings and introductions. This was not a formal meeting such as a visit from a Head of State to the White House; it was a joyous greeting of the righteous on Holy Ground in the Land of Promise. The Spirit of the Lord touched every person at this gathering and then a marvelous event took place.

The air around this group began to glow and intensify. Suddenly the group was encircled by a ring of white fire. To everyone on the outside of this ring it appeared the group had been consumed by fire. They could not see what was actually transpiring within the circle. He who has many names such as: the Lord, the Messiah, the Redeemer, the Creator, the Only Begotten Son of God, or Jesus Christ appeared in the midst of the group.

The Savior's first words to the group were, "Peace be unto you." Immediately every person in the group fell to their knees and lay prostrate before their God. The Lord continued, "I am Jesus Christ, the Only Begotten Son of the Most High God. I am Alpha and Omega. I have cleansed this land so the sins of the people may not come before my face again. This land is a Promised Land, choice above all other lands. All inhabitants of this land will worship the Lord Thy God or they too shall be swept off this land. Inasmuch as you shall keep my commandments you shall prosper in the land. But inasmuch as you shall not keep my commandments, you shall be cut off from my presence."

It was at this moment that every person within the circle of fire knew which direction this nation would pursue in all endeavors. Under the direction of the Lord, America would move to fulfill its destiny as a beacon of liberty and righteousness to the world.

The Savior continued, "Those whom I have spared in this land are the more righteous of this land. I say unto you to cry repentance to all mankind. I say again unto you to repent and come unto me that I might forgive you of your sins and bless you." The Lord then gave instructions to both of His Prophets, the 12 Apostles, and the Leadership Council of the 10 Tribes. He then made a request of the President of the U.S. and our other elected officials.

He instructed the 10 Tribes of Israel to choose 100,000 faithful warriors from each of the Tribes. Once each Tribe had chosen their men this 1,000,000 man army is to be sent to Israel to bolster the defensive force in their Land of Inheritance due to Israel's enemies becoming more aggressive. The selection process was to begin immediately to make that nation whole again.

The Lord instructed the Prophets, Apostles, and Leadership Council to exchange all the records and histories each group had in their possession with their fellow brethren and counterparts. All of these records were to be translated by each group so all may learn of each other and to complete the Scriptures. The Lord also instructed the Prophets to ready a missionary force to go into every nation and preach His Gospel for a season one last time prior to His Second Coming.

Turning to the President and our elected officials, the Lord made a request. He asked for this nation to supply

as many ships and planes as possible to transport the
1,000,000 man army of Israel to the Land of Inheritance. He
promised our leaders if everything humanly possible was
done to fulfill this request, He would ensure the mission
would be completed. He also promised protection from
enemy forces along with abundant fuel and supplies would
be provided for this expeditionary force. The President and
leaders of Congress covenanted with the Lord they would
fulfill His request as quickly as possible.

The Lord commanded all mankind to learn and use a
common language so there would be unity in the world
and less division and confusion. The 10 Tribes were
commanded to teach the Adamic language to the entire
world starting in America and Israel.

The Lord's final words were a blessing on the 10 Tribes
of Israel, upon this nation, and to all the righteous
individuals throughout the world. He then departed from
their presence. As the flames subsided, the people on the
outside of the white fire circle could now see those who
were encompassed by the flames and were astonished to
see none had been injured or consumed. Word went out of
what had taken place and glory was given to the Lord.

There was much work to perform on behalf of the Messiah
and one does not keep the Lord waiting. The first meeting
between brothers and sisters in Christ soon came to a
conclusion. Communication systems were put in place to
ensure quick decision making on overlapping objectives.
Over the next days and weeks there would be many
meetings concerning a variety of subjects and agreements

would be reached on how best to implement those policies. Eventually, everyone would return to their homes and continue working to fulfill the obligations made to the Lord.

The 10 Tribes Leadership Council immediately began their search and selection of their 1,000,000 man army in accordance with the instructions given them by the Lord. It would take a few weeks for them to fill the ranks of their army and prepare for the journey to Israel.

The President requested the remaining military, merchant marines, and civilian population to supply every type of sea worthy vessel and placed them in service. Aircraft of military and commercial designs were also sought for this buildup of forces in the Middle East. Airports and air bases in Missouri would be used to shuttle the advance guard of soldiers to Israel. The bulk of the army would head south by every means available to the Gulf Coast and travel across the Atlantic Ocean and Mediterranean Sea to Israel. It would take many trips across the ocean and several months to complete this request but in the end Israel was stronger and joyous at being made whole for the first time in 2,000 years.

After receiving the records from the 10 Tribes the Prophet presented them to a special group of seers and revelators who had been called by inspiration to translate ancient records. They had been performing this duty for months and had been using 'Seer Stones' or Urims and Thumims to ensure the records were translated correctly. They had already been busy translating ancient records that had been hidden in the Rocky Mountains for the past couple of months. The addition of the records from the 10 Tribes only increased their workload. This was considered a blessing and honor to perform this work.

It had been estimated it would take about two years to translate just the records found in the Rocky Mountains. There was a great deal of them, to be sure. Now with the records from the 10 Tribes needing to be translated from Adamic and Aramaic into English It would require either more time or more seers and revelators to accomplish this task within a few years. In the end, the Lord would provide what was necessary to complete His work more efficiently.

Even while the 10 Tribes' army was being shuttled to Israel as quickly as humanly possible, the work of translating the records from ancient America and the 10 Tribes continued. At this time there were a great number of events taking place in this nation and around the world. For now, I want to focus on this nation.

The survivors of the tribulations continued to reclaim this nation a town and a State at a time. The exception to this was the Lands of Desolation. They would one day be reclaimed but that would be in the future. In the inhabitable areas the large cites were avoided except to retrieve building materials. The re-establishment of large cities was not allowed. Many communities adopted the checker board layout for their communities. This is how it worked. Picture a checker board with red and black squares. Now make each of those squares a mile square. In the red squares you can build housing and schools with small corner shops. In the black squares you have farms, businesses, factories, and all other commercial ventures. This layout makes it almost impossible to create large cities and keeps the communities close knit.

The checkerboard layout was done on a voluntary basis State by State. Federal Government interference in this process was not allowed and would not be tolerated as it had been prior to the fall. The States were reasserting their sovereignty and free will just as the original Constitution had envisioned. Most of the States began placing in their own Constitutions the illegality of any personal or business income tax. They also made it illegal to assess any form of private property taxes. All revenue needed to operate the State was generated from a sales or transaction tax. Many States, in an effort to further restrict government, placed a cap of 8% on this sales tax. The States were taking the lead on many issues. What to do about the Federal Government was another story.

For the past several years the Federal Government had been a dictatorship in many ways. If we had elected an evil man as President prior to the fall, he may have set up a *Socialist* or *Communist* form of government. By this I mean a centrally controlled government which is the final authority on all matters within the nation. In the end he would have failed to maintain his hold on power but it would have been at the cost of a great deal of blood. A perfect example would be to look back at our 2nd American Civil War. This is what the *Rebels* were trying to implement by force on the American people.

Thankfully, prior to the fall, we had elected a man who was very Constitutionally Conservative and had a lot of Libertarian influences in his thought processes. After the fall, riots, and start of the 2nd Civil War he gathered all the members of Congress and the Supreme Court who supported the Constitution together and formed an advisory committee. The President had assumed dictatorial authority during these national emergencies, yet he did not want to rule as a tyrannical dictatorship. Every issue and concern was presented to them for discussion and debate. He would then have to make the final decision on some very difficult situations.

During the insurrection and Civil War the greatest and most difficult debate was over the use of nuclear weapons on our own cities and citizens. The committee was split over the justification and moral ramifications of such a horrific idea. In the end it was laid at the feet of the President to make the final decision and order the action. Looking back, the decision to end the uprising with such destructive force was the right decision to make. It ended the war in five months instead of several years and saved the lives of many Constitutional patriots. It was time for a Federal Government to be re-established. A Convention of the States or a Constitutional Convention was proposed to take place as soon as possible.

The people of each State were to select their delegates to the convention. This is where I got involved in the Democratic process. More than anything, I wanted to be a Delegate to a Constitutional Convention. I have never been so arrogant to compare myself to a Thomas Jefferson or a James Madison but I could see where their genius had been replaced by political ideology. I wanted to be given the chance to lock down the power and expanse of the Federal Government through the Constitutional process. When I was selected to represent my State, I was both excited for the opportunity and overwhelmed at the responsibility of the calling and my desire to help correct our past mistakes.

It was now January and five years had passed since the fall began. The Delegates all gathered in a community recreation center in Jackson County Missouri for the opening of our Constitutional Convention. It was not a luxurious building filled with creature comforts but it had plenty of tables, chairs, a sound system, and plenty of room for recording the entire procedure. It was critical for every person in the nation to witness this event and have a voice in their futures.

It had been previously voted on to have the Vice President of the United States be the Chairman of the convention. He was respected by the American people and he would be in charge of maintaining order and decorum. Other people who were not delegates were selected to be co-Chairman, Sergeant at Arms, Secretary, and Parliamentarian. The Vice President called the Convention to order and with this the first order of business could be proposed.

I had thought back many times on how I wished I could have been in Philadelphia in the summer of 1776. I would have witnessed the birth of the greatest nation the world has ever known. Now here I was some 250 years later and participating in the re-birth of our nation. It seemed surreal. Our Founding Fathers had something in common with our group of delegates; we both wanted liberty and to form a more perfect union. It was now time to get to work.

Between the time of being selected as a Delegate to the Convention and it being called to order, I had spent a great deal of time reading and re-reading the Constitution and the Federalist Papers. I had also re-read the writings and histories of our Founding Fathers. Not satisfied with my research, I read the writings of some of our most current Constitutional scholars. One of the most important books ever written on exactly what we were about to discuss was written by 'The Great One,' Mark Levin. It was called The 'Liberty Amendments.' Many of us would use this book to propose new Amendments during the Convention.

There were several serious issues I felt needed to be addressed. The issues of immigration, citizenship, taxation, and all forms of federal benefits needed to be proposed, discussed, debated, and voted on. With so many important issues to discuss, there was no shortage of citizens and reporters wanting to be in the room during the Convention. It was feared they could disrupt the proceedings. Transparency and a full disclosure of the Convention were paramount to the process. As stated earlier, a main media feed was sent out to the nation so all could see and/or hear what was transpiring. The recording of this would be highly significant for our posterity to understand why we did what we did. Distractions could lead to mistakes being made and we needed to get this right. No spectators and reporters were allowed in the room while the Convention was in session.

It was incumbent and/or obligatory on the Delegates to receive feedback and suggestions from the public. How do we do this without disrupting our critical work? The answer was simple. We would welcome questions and ideas from everyone but only in written form. There was a tremendous amount of notes to read. It was awesome to see the nation wanting to participate in this process and have their voices heard.

After calling the meeting to order, the Vice President announced one of the ministers he had invited to attend the opening of this Convention would offer a prayer on behalf of all Delegates and the nation. This particular minister was from one of the Southern Baptist Congregations in Oklahoma City, Oklahoma. When he arrived at the podium he took the microphone from its stand and knelt before the assembly, the nation, and the Lord. This inspired all of the Delegates to get out of our chairs and kneel with him. As a hush fell upon the room he began his prayer.

He said, "Almighty God, we come before Thee in the name of Thy Only Begotten Son who is Lord over all creations and the one true God of this nation to know Thy will concerning this new Constitution of this Promised Land. We are truly blessed to have survived Thy cleansing of this nation and the world. We confess at this time Thy judgments are just and true. We now find ourselves at a critical time in our nation. The inhabitants of this land, which is a Promised Land and a most favored, land above all others in the world had turned our backs on Thee and had embraced wickedness.

We stand before Thee with the desire to continue the work of our inspired Founding Fathers and re-form a more perfect union. We acknowledge Thee and Thy Beloved Son are the only perfect beings known unto man. We ask Thee to grant a small portion of Thy perfection to our cause. We seek to right our wrongs by restoring liberty to this nation and by way of example, to the nations and people of the world.

We covenant with Thee here and now that all we do in this Convention will be done with an eye single to Thy glory. We invite Thy Spirit and guidance into this room today and every day we meet as Delegates to this Convention. We ask of Thee to place the Eye of Providence upon this nation from this time forward and Thy voice of acceptance for the work we are engaged in to be sounded in our hearts as we do Thy will. These blessings we ask of Thee in the name of our Savior, Jesus Christ, Amen."

The Vice President or Chairman of the Convention rose to his feet and took the microphone from the Minister. He thanked him publicly for such a wonderful prayer and then he started the meeting with a motion of his own. He said, "Inasmuch as we are gathered here this day to correct our past mistakes, we should begin by starting where our Founding Fathers began. Therefore I propose we accept the original Constitution of the United States of America along with the first 10 Amendments as the highest law of the land. Do I have a second for this motion?" Voices rang out all over the room to second the motion. The proposal to vote on the measure was put forth and every member of the delegation voted to approve this first motion.

The Chairman thanked everyone for re-affirming our original Constitution. He said, "It was feared by some in our nation this Convention would be dangerous to our freedoms and liberties. You have proven to those who were concerned at this prospect their concerns were unfounded." He continued, "We are called here to create a new Constitution. We were not sent here to add a couple of Amendments to our Constitution and leave here not really having fixed anything. There are 17 additional Amendments deserving of our attention. We should go through each of them separately and re-affirm them or repeal them. We may even want to take parts or all of them and place them in a new Amendment. I propose we start with the 11th Amendment and give discussion to each of them as I have proposed. Do I have second on this motion?" Several Delegates voiced their support of this procedure. The vote was unanimous again to proceed as outlined by the Chairman.

The 11th Amendment was brought to the floor for debate. This Amendment does not allow the courts to hear or rule on a lawsuit by persons living in another State or country. This reaffirmed the doctrine of 'sovereign immunity.' Officials cannot be sued for exercising their sworn duties. After a short period of time and several speeches, it was agreed to re-affirm the 11th Amendment as it was written. This was done mainly due to it being one of the oldest Amendments in our Constitution. In 1795, while our Founding Fathers were still alive, it must have been important enough to use the Amendment process to right a wrong.

The only change to it would be the re-numbering of it. From this time forward it became the 12th Amendment. The reason for this numerical change was because when the Bill of Rights was proposed there were 12 Amendments contained in it. 10 of those Amendments were eventually ratified by 1791.

The 27th Amendment defines Congressional pay raises. It was moved to the 11th Amendment for the simple reason it was one of the original 12 Amendments proposed to our Constitution. It only took just over 200 years to ratify it. The importance of this Amendment should not be misconstrued. The move of it from 27 to 11 was only symbolic but it was clear there would be several realignments to our Constitution as the Convention proceeded.

The 12th Amendment which defines the election of the President and the Electoral College was left intact but it was moved to the 13th Amendment.

The new 14th Amendment would encapsulate the previous 13th, 14th, 15th, 19th, 24th, and 26th Amendments. It stated there would be no slavery or indentured servitude in this nation or territories. Citizenship is granted to those individuals who are born in the U.S. to one or two citizens of the U.S. Children born to legal residents in the U.S. or its territories have the option to declare their citizenship as U.S. citizens when they are 18 years of age. The right to vote shall be by only citizens of the U.S. The right to vote shall not be denied to any citizen who is 18 years of age or older based on their race, gender, religion, social status, or any other contrived reason. There shall not be any poll tax or fee to exercise this right. To ensure the integrity of all elections, all citizens voting must have a Federal Voter Identification Card with their picture on it. The cost of this card shall be borne by the Federal Government.

The new 15th Amendment would stand on its own. The previous 16th Amendment authorized the Federal Government to tax individuals and businesses on their income. It was declared within this Amendment that all income taxes are akin to State instituted slavery. The new 15th Amendment ended all income taxes on citizens and legal residents in the United States and its territories. All federal revenues can only be generated by way of a national sales tax. The Federal Government is forbidden to tax any real property within the U.S. and its territories.

Once the Delegates adopted the Constitution in its original form by a unanimous vote, there was no need to discuss the previous 17th Amendment which has to do with the direct election of U.S. Senators by popular vote by the citizens. The State Legislatures would once again select their two Senators to represent the individual States and protect them from an overreaching House of Representatives.

Two previous Amendments were not given any discussion. The 18th Amendment prohibited the consumption, transportation, and manufacturing of liquor within the U.S. and its territories. The 21st Amendment repealed the 18th. All such initiatives were left up to the States to decide and determine if they were warranted.

The new 16th Amendment sustains Presidential term limits as defined by the 22nd Amendment. It also includes term limits for members of Congress, all Federal Judges including Supreme Court of the United States Justices. The President would still be limited to two terms of four years each. All individuals are limited to a total of 12 years in Congress. All Federal Judges, including Supreme Court Justices are also limited to 12 years of service. The previous 25th Amendment was incorporated into the new 16th Amendment. It defines Presidential succession due to death, illness, or disability of the President.

The previous 23rd Amendment authorized electors for Washington D.C. This Amendment was not brought up for discussion due to there not being a National Capitol in this nation at this time.

Sharron asked an important question. She said, "How long did the process of reviewing and re-aligning the original Constitution take? Also, how long did the additional Amendments take to craft, debate, and vote on?"

I told her it took about a month to review our original Constitution and the 27 Amendments attached to it. The real work was in the crafting of the new Amendments. It took about three months to complete the work on this document. The general consensus of all the Delegates was we were not to repeat the mistakes of the past. Being there was an overwhelming number of Delegates who were members of the Independent American Party, the Libertarian Party, some from the Republican Party, and no Delegates from the now non-existing Democratic Party, the question was not how large can we make the Federal Government but how small can we keep it?

We all agreed the growth and never ending expansion of the federal leviathan should never be seen again. Every Delegate had their ideas on how to stop this from happening again. I was of the opinion we should use the greatest Constitutional thinkers of our time to help us accomplish this goal. To this end, I encouraged everyone to read Mark Levin's book titled 'The Liberty Amendments' and use his ideas as our guideline. Several other Delegates joined me and were able to insert several of 'The Great One's' ideas in some of the new Amendments.

The new 17th Amendment is a good example of how we used Mark Levin's writings to craft this Amendment. Chapter five of his book, 'The Liberty Amendments' was copied almost verbatim. We added a few clauses of our own to hopefully strengthen its contents. *This new Amendment basically says no expenditures from the Federal Treasury shall be made for any purpose or department not specifically listed in this Constitution.* This would include but not be limited to a national retirement system, a national healthcare system, a national welfare system, a national education system, or any other agency not specifically listed in this Constitution. There shall also not be any retirement system or healthcare system put in place or funded by the tax payer for any federal employee or elected officials. There shall be no Congressional 'pet projects' or 'pork barrel expenditures'. This Amendment also forbade the establishment of federal employee unions.

This returns employment conditions within the Federal Government to those prior to President John F. Kennedy. No longer will the American Tax payer be placed under the yoke of paying for benefits and retirement for our public servants. The age of professionalism and accountability has arrived. It will no longer take an act of Congress to terminate a bad employee. We have now returned the responsibility of retirement and healthcare to the individual.

The new 18th Amendment was inspired by chapter 7 of 'The Liberty Amendments.' It basically says there must be limits placed on Congress when it concerns the free market. The Commerce Clause of the original Constitution was abused by Congress to implement control over the economy and the courts upheld this belief. In 1791 the true meaning of the *{Interstate}* Commerce Clause was apparent and well understood by the citizenry. The term Congress can 'regulate the economy' did not mean it could control it. The term meant Congress was to keep trade regular and free from corruption. They were not to pick winners and losers within the economy. When Congress inserted itself into the markets it was usually on behalf of wealthy special interest groups. This form of corruption was usually followed by donations for re-election campaigns. Laws are to be made to keep the transactions in the economy transparent and honest.

The new 19th Amendment concerns private property rights. Private property should be considered sacred. Property owners should never be abused by any government whether it is federal, State, county, or local. In some rare cases it may become necessary for a government to exercise *eminent domain* on private property for a public project such as a highway, a dam, public transportation, or other projects that will benefit the 'public'. When this occurs, the property owner must be fairly compensated for his loss. By way of example, a government's desire to raise revenues by claiming *eminent domain* on a housing track so they can sell the land for commercial purposes in order increase property taxes is *prohibited.*

Also included in the 19th Amendment is the disposition of so called federal land. The Federal Government is forbidden from owning land other than what it acquires from the States for purposes such as military bases, federal courthouses, federal prisons, and federal office buildings. All land within the United States is placed under the stewardship of the State Governments. All former National Parks are now placed under the State Parks of their respective States. Any land the Federal Government needs for any of its purposes must be negotiated and swapped or traded for with the States. Because all public lands are under direct stewardship and control of their respective States, the States are now on equal footing before the Federal Government.

There was only one more Amendment added to our new Constitution. The 20th Amendment has to do with international agreements and trade. This final Amendment forbade America from joining any international body such as the United Nations. We are to remain sovereign and wholly focused on the welfare and prosperity of the American Citizen. American or multi-national corporations are not allowed to erode or violate American's rights and liberties. Congress and the President must always be focused on what is best for America and the citizenry.

It was now the first of April and all the Delegates were anxious to conclude the Convention and return to their homes. There was still a lot of work to be done to build up the communities and the States where they lived. The work of adding Amendment after Amendment could have gone on indefinitely but the major parts of the Constitution and the 20 Amendments were felt to have corrected the nation's course while staying true to the original intent of the original Constitution. Our work was finished. On April 6th, the Delegates voted to approve this new Constitution and send it to the States for ratification. The Constitutional Convention was called to a close immediately after the vote was taken. It was time to go home.

By the 15th of April every State Legislature had a copy of the proposed new Constitution in their possession. The proposed Constitution was sent out to every citizen for review and public comments. The acting Governors of the States called for a special session of the legislature to discuss and vote on the new Constitution. They called for the session to begin on June 20th and the vote to ratify this new document was scheduled for the 4th of July. This was not a coincidence.

Sharron chimed in and asked, "What did you do after the Constitutional Convention?" I told her I came back to my home State and worked tirelessly to encourage our legislature to ratify the new Constitution. As I traveled the State answering questions and soothing concerns about the new document, I had a sense the people in my State were pleased by the work we had performed over the past three months. Some people thought we could have gone further in protecting the citizens of the nation by adding more Amendments. They may have been correct but all the Delegates to the Convention felt they had accomplished the work they needed to do. It was now up to wise men and women in future generations to protect our liberties and expand freedom throughout the nation.

I had been asked by our Governor to be present when the legislature was in session to answer questions and promote the ratification of the Constitution. Up to this point, I had been away from home six months and it now looked as if It would be another two weeks before I could return home. If I was a betting man, I would have put a lot of money down on the new Constitution being ratified by our State Legislature. You could even say passage was a shoe in. I was in our State Capitol to be a cheerleader and an insurance policy for its passage.

My State and for that matter, the entire nation now followed a Constitutional/Libertarian philosophy which was quite a change from just a decade earlier. Ten years ago people asked what else the government could do for them. Today, people asked if our new Constitution was strong enough to limit the Federal Government from infringing on our rights. I believed it was. Time will tell if I am correct.

On July 2nd, many of the State Legislatures had a test vote on ratifying the new Constitution. There were a few votes in the legislatures against approval. This was not because they disagreed with the new document, but it was a vote to say they felt it could have been stronger in its protections. It was great to know there were people in this nation who trusted the governments of this nation even less than me. As Delegates we knew we could not please everyone with the work we were performing. I felt proud knowing if the government ever got out of control there were people out there ready to correct course with another Amendment. I believed the Republic was safe and in good hands.

In 48 hours our nation would have a new Constitution or we as Delegates would need to return to Missouri and try again. I had an exceptionally strong feeling or sense the three quarters of the States needed to ratify this new document would do so. In fact, I believed it would be more astonishing if any State did not ratify it. I was really hoping for a unanimous vote in the affirmative. The countdown continued to the 4th of July.

In order to show equality and to not give the appearance of a wave sweeping across the nation from east to west, all State Legislatures agreed to begin the ratification process at the very same moment regardless of where they were. At 9am in Hawaii it was 3pm on the East Coast and in every State Capitol the votes began. A roll call vote of every member of the State Legislatures was taken. Then the Constitutional officers such as the Governor, Lt. Governor, Secretary of State Treasurer, and other officers went forward and cast their votes.

Within an hour every State reported they had voted to ratify our new Constitution. It was unanimous. This would be remembered as one of the greatest 4th of July Celebrations in our nation's history. The Republic was restored, individual rights were protected, the States were sovereign, the Federal Government was placed in a very small cage, and freedom nearly lost was renewed. A National Day of Prayer and Celebration was called for. The festivities began in earnest. All I wanted to do was go home. Several hours later I walked in the door of my house determined to enjoy some time there. I would not be there for very long.

Before I left the State Capitol, the Governor asked me to be one of the Delegates to the State Constitutional Convention to begin in August. I took a deep breath and accepted his invitation. Why would I accept another assignment that would take me away from home again for an extended time period? It was a simple belief in me: when a government leader or a church officer asks for your help, you do it. For now, I was grateful to have a month at home before I departed to our State Capitol for an undetermined amount of time.

July vanished from the calendar and I found myself once again in our State Capitol the first week of August. The month at home did wonders to rejuvenate my mind and spirit. I was looking forward to participating in another Convention and helping to enshrine liberty in another Constitution. Once the meeting was called to order, the first item of business was a vote to accept the new National Constitution as the highest law of the land. It was a unanimous vote in favor of the proposal. Even though it was a symbolic gesture, it reaffirmed in our minds why we were here. The next item of business was for us to review our former State Constitution and determine if any parts of it were in conflict with the National Constitution. There were only a few conflicts found and they were highlighted for action in the near future.

There was some debate on one section within our State Constitution. Some Delegates felt there was a conflict with the National Constitution. Our State Constitution had both a personal and business income tax along with a property tax written into it. It was felt by some Delegates the10th Amendment of our National Constitution allowed States to do this within their States. This may or may not be true but we all felt if the Federal Government should be forced to function on revenues from a sales tax then our State should also be required to do so. My point of order on this subject was this: a government taxing your labor, regardless of the percentage is State endorsed slavery. With this being said, it was written into the State Constitution that all income taxes on individuals and businesses are prohibited. Also, all forms of taxes on personal property were prohibited. The State sales tax was capped at 8% just like the national sales tax.

Once we abolished State sponsored slavery in the form of all income and property taxes, it was time to limit the scope of spending. It was not uncommon for a State to spend 90% of their tax revenues to educate, medicate, and incarcerate their citizens. The State Legislatures would have to wrestle with these issues on a biannual basis every time they were in session. We wanted to give them assistance saying 'no' to the populace's demands by placing stop signs and dams into the State Constitution.

The next part of the Constitution was dedicated to education. It was decided there should be a public education for all citizens and legal residents from kindergarten through the 12th grade. The Legislature would have to determine the amount of money to be spent per pupil per year but our new document declared the amount was a voucher and the parents could use it to home school their children or use it at any other school whether it was a private, religious, or a public one. Competition for education dollars was injected into the education system for the first time in our history. We were not finished with education spending though.

We then moved on to fundamentally transform the college and university system. It was decided to end all State funding of those institutions. They would need to compete for their funding just like the primary education system. The real change for them was they would have to compete for private sector dollars. In a free market, a superior product will have customers lined up at your door. The same should be true concerning a superior college education. Now that colleges and universities were no longer part of the State government, they would determine their own collective bargaining status and tenure rules.

The next section we tackled concerned collective bargaining agreements for State employees. By Amendment it is prohibited for local, county, or State employees to form or be represented by a union. It is also prohibited for public employees to strike or create conditions such as work stoppages or slowdowns in order to negotiate better salary packages. The final part of this Amendment had to do with fringe benefits. The State is prohibited from providing health care, pensions, and any other form of benefit excluding a salary for its employees or retirees. The taxpayer would no longer be on the hook for public employees other than their salaries.

The final Amendment focused on the State's obligations to provide social or public safety nets. This Amendment made it clear that all tax dollars were to be considered sacred funds. The State should help to maintain life but it is prohibited from sustaining a lifestyle. A State welfare system is prohibited. All State prisons are to be humane but they are to operate with the least possible amount of tax dollars.

There is some latitude given to the legislature when crafting laws and spending bills but these Amendments will protect the taxpayers from abuse and reckless spending. Eternal vigilance is the greatest protector of liberty. Keeping most of government local or close to the citizen is the best form of government. Combining these two principles along with oversight and transparency ensures accountability over our elected officials.

It had only taken a month for us to review the previous Constitution, remove conflicting parts from it, and add new Amendments. As Delegates, we voted to accept this new document as our guiding law within the State. It was an overwhelming majority who supported this proposal. The new Constitution was sent on to the acting State Government officials for review only. It was placed on the ballot for the November elections. When I say elections I mean Federal Elections.

Our acting State and local officials would remain in place for another two years at a minimum. Our new State

Constitution would need to be voted on and approved two times by the voters in two general elections, two years apart before it would be our official Constitution. Once it was approved we could have an official election for State and local officials. It was a long drawn out process but everything needed to be done right this time.

After our vote, the Convention was adjourned and I headed home. The four hour drive went by quickly and soon I was in my little town of 2,000 residents ready for a break. Besides going to some rallies and speaking on behalf of our proposed new Constitution, I stayed close to home until election time. When November arrived and the election took place our new Constitution received a massive vote of approval. In two years there would be another vote and if there was another vote in favor of the new Constitution, our State could move forward with official operations and elections. Until then, they operated under the pre-authority and limits of the new Constitution to maintain consistency.

Sharron spoke up at this point and said, "Do you realize the history you have directly been a part of? Now I understand why the Federal Government wanted me to interview you." I told her she was very kind for saying those things but I never think about all the wonderful events and experiences I have had as being historical. I looked at them as someone needed to do this work and I was willing to answer the call. I felt others had done and sacrificed so much more. They were the real heroes from the fall until now. I thanked her again and continued my interview.

On January 3rd of the following year after we had ratified our new National Constitution, the 1st Congress of the United States went to work. Here is a list of what they accomplished in just one year. They eliminated the Federal Reserve System and Bank, placed America back on the gold standard, set the value of the American dollar against precious metals, loaned banks money at 2% interest A.P.R. so the banks could lend out that money at whatever rate the market would bear. They offered citizenship or legal residency to everyone in the 10 Tribes, instituted strict immigration laws, produced a balanced budget, re-aligned and reformed a small but powerful military, approved the purchase of land and funded construction for a new National Capitol in Missouri.

There was one more piece of legislation passed during this Congressional session.

In accordance with the Declaration of Independence which declares all *men/women/people* are granted by our Creator certain unalienable rights, such as life, liberty and the pursuit of happiness. Also the Constitution guarantees all people due process before their life may be taken by the State. To this end, Congress outlawed abortion, except in extreme circumstances. Life and the protection of life is of the utmost obligation of governments. Therefore the States are encouraged to institute an adoption program that is the least restrictive and least cost prohibitive for unplanned pregnancies. The States should encourage and promote the health and well being of both the mother and her unborn child.

It was one of the most amazing sessions of Congress in our nation's history. I viewed everything they accomplished as having strengthened the cause of liberty in the nation. I believed if they could roll back government like this in one year, what can they accomplish in the following year?

I think it would be appropriate at this time to discuss each of these Congressional accomplishments in greater detail. Let us begin with the elimination of the Federal Reserve System. Over a hundred years ago Congress authorized a group of bankers to oversee the monetary policy of this nation. This was not only in direct violation of the Constitution because it placed unelected people in charge of valuing our dollar. They gave these bankers a Federal title so people would think it was a branch of the government. It was not. Abuse and corruption have a potential to grow when any group is given power to make up its own rules concerning our money supply.

From this time forward, Congress would fulfill its duty and be the sole group of people to value the dollar. By placing America back on the gold standard, the Treasury Department was ordered to never have more paper currency circulating in the economy than there was gold, silver, platinum, and precious stones stored in the Treasury. They set the value of our currency against precious metals as this; an ounce of gold was set at $20 an ounce, Silver was set at $1 dollar an ounce, platinum was set at $25 an ounce, and the precious stones were appraised every six months to have an accurate value set on them against the dollar. This act of Congress made the dollar the most powerful and highest valued currency in the world.

Congress authorized the Treasury Department to loan out our currency to thoroughly vetted banks at a 2% annual percentage rate. This would bring a steady income into the Treasury along with stability to the loan industry. The banks would then loan out the currency at rates they set in competition with each other. The free market would decide what banks charge their consumers for loans. Also, all banks were required to insure all deposits by an independent insurance company. There would never be bank bailouts by the government again.

Congress also passed a 5% national sales tax on everything purchased in the U.S. and its territories. This, along with the 2% currency loans to the banks were the main sources of funding for the government. It does not sound like there would be enough revenues to fund the government but if prudence is used it would be more than enough. The best part of this form of government funding meant every person in America had 'skin' in the game. Class warfare based on taxes is now a thing of the past.

The 10 Tribes of Israel had been offered full citizenship or legal residency because they had earned these privileges due to their saving the Republic. After they defeated the Chinese Army and took up residency in Missouri, they had not sought any form of repayment or special treatment. They were following the Lord's Commandments to destroy our enemy and establish the New Jerusalem in Missouri. Many of these warriors accepted citizenship but others desired legal residency and wanted to eventually immigrate to their Land of Inheritance or Israel, and live there.

The immigration laws Congress crafted were very simple. You must apply for a visa or legal residency into this nation from your home country. You must prove you have skills that are needed in this country. You must promise you will be a useful member of society. You must learn both the English and Adamic languages as quickly as possible. These are the only languages used here. You must be self sufficient because there are no government programs for you to access. This nation is a land of rugged individualism. You have maximum liberty coupled with maximum responsibility.

If you come into this country illegally, you are guilty of a felony and you will be deported back to your home nation and you will never be allowed to visit or live in the U.S. again. Employers who hire illegal aliens will face a $20,000 fine and six months in prison per person, per event. We desire to have many people come here and dwell because our nation is nearly empty from the cleansing. We desire to vet every person who wishes to live here and accept only those who hold our same values. You must meld and assimilate into America; we will not assimilate to you.

After 20 plus years of Congress violating the law and their duty, this Congress approved a Federal Budget. It was a modest one, but it funded a small but powerful defense force, federal law enforcement including courts, the purchase of land in Missouri to build a National Capitol, and the funds to build all necessary building in our Capitol. We would build a new place for Congress to meet, a new White House, but the Supreme Court of the U.S. would be placed in the Capitol on the Senate side of the building.

Other official cabinet departments would eventually be built near the White House.

The final law passed in the first year of the First Congress was to outlaw abortion except in the most extreme of cases. The right of the unborn to partake of life, liberty, and the pursuit of happiness was paramount in this law. It was also declared in this law that no person in this nation shall be deprived of its life without due process of the law.

It had been an amazing first year of the first session from the First Congress of the US. We could focus on the success in Congress, but the real story was in the free market economy. With stability in our government and currency comes the willingness for people to take chances with their money. This is called Capitalism. The economy was starting to roar and the roar would get much, much louder.

As people spread out across the land they reclaimed the land and restored its potential to feed the nation and the world. The farmlands of the Great Plains were being planted and the future was bright for bumper crops and harvests. The oil and natural gas industries were being brought back on line to their full potential. Oil fields from North Dakota to Texas were pumping out and refining more and more energy for our nation and others. It would not take long for America to have the full electrical grid back up and running within a year or two. Life was getting back to better than normal.

The 10 Tribes were not exempt from this fervor of national renewal. Many of them did what they do best; they joined the U.S. Military. Others began to spread out into every corner of the land. They all had one trade that would be in high demand for many years to come; they could teach the Adamic Language to their fellow Americans and the world. Some would teach it to small groups while others established schools to pass on their knowledge.

It was hard to believe that a year had passed by since we had voted to ratify our new State Constitution and witnessed the achievements of our First Congress. We were now facing an immigration boom we had not seen since the early part of the 20th Century. Many tens of thousands of people were being approved to immigrate here. Once here, they went to work to achieve whatever American Dream they wished to pursue. Our nation was beginning to be replenished at a very rapid pace.

Speaking of our new immigration influx, it is important to understand why we desired a wave of new Americans. The cleansing of America had reduced our population by 95%. Other nations throughout the world had experienced the cleansing in similar percentages. But even with the wicked having been removed from every nation in the world, America was still the land of their dreams. This says a lot about our Land of Promise.

As the tens of thousands of immigrants arrived in this nation, they were sought after by employers to fill labor needs. Many parts of the economy were in need of labor such as construction, energy development, agriculture, transportation, manufacturing, service, and all other sectors of our economy. There was not a shortage of

work that needed to be performed; there was a shortage
of people to perform the work. Growth, restoration,
expansion, and the pursuit of happiness were taking place
all throughout America.

Let us jump ahead a year and look at what the First
Congress did in their second year of the first session.
They were not trying to outdo their accomplishments
of the first year. They spent the second year eliminating
old laws, crafting new laws, officially shutting down
former un-Constitutional and *un-authorized departments
and agencies*. The continued shrinking of the Federal
Government by permanently eliminating former Cabinet
Departments was wondrous to behold.

Sharron asked a very logical and important question. She
asked, "Since we are operating under a new Constitution
shouldn't we start making new laws based on the new
Constitution instead of focusing on old laws based on our
old Constitution?"

I replied, "In a perfect world the answer to your question
would be yes. Having said this, our new Congress thought
it best to first officially and permanently eliminated un-
authorized department and agencies from our former
government before making any new laws. By doing this,
they cleared the books of over half of the laws. If we take a
moment and think about what I just said, we will see our
nation was being judged and controlled by over half of
our laws that were *illegal or un-Constitutional*. How many
people were fined or imprisoned by illegal laws? It was
shameful even if there had only been one."

I continued, "I should list some of those departments and agencies Congress permanently eliminated. This will be a test on my long term memory. Let's see, there were *Agriculture, Energy, Environmental Protection, Education, Homeland Security, Health and Human Services, Housing and Urban Development, Food and Drug, Interior, Labor, N.A.S.A., Social Security, Medicare and Medicaid, Transportation, and the Veterans Administration*, and probably numerous others I am unable to recall right now. What a disgusting list of interference and abuse of federal authority. If we ever return to this type of government again, all we have gone through these past several years will have been in vain. "

And finally I affirm, "Playing the *Devil's Advocate* here, if we as a country ever decide to reinstitute any of these agencies it must be by *Constitutional Amendment*."

After the initial removal of agencies and laws had been completed, Congress moved on to other laws which were in need of serious attention. They removed the *Patriot Act, the National Defense Authorization Act*, and a hundred or so other laws that were masked with tyranny in the fine print, off the U.S. Code of Laws. They then removed all *Executive Orders* from the Federal Registry. By the time Congress finished their first term there were less than 200 laws still on the books. It would be the responsibility of subsequent Congress's to continue removing unnecessary laws from the books. They would also be tasked with crafting laws that were necessary and of a benefit to the entire nation. The hardest part of the work was complete. Eternal vigilance would be needed to secure liberty for all future generations of Americans.

One thing I forgot to mention was in November our State Constitution was ratified by over 90% of the citizens. We were now an official State with a Constitution and could elect officials and vest them with true authority instead of *acting authority*. I thought it was very promising for our State when those who voted against the ratification did so because they believed it did not go far enough in protecting individual liberties. They also felt it did not limit the powers and scope of the State Government. *I disagree with them on this issue*. Marrying the Federal and State Constitutions together builds a wall around the individual and his liberties. Nevertheless I was pleased to see people were looking for more liberty than they were for government handouts. What a beautiful change in attitude.

After five years had passed since the 2nd Civil War the new Federal Government believed it was time to reclaim the States around the Great Lakes and the Northeastern States of America. It was believed the radiation from the nuclear weapons used on those areas should have dissipated by now. It was also thought all the bodies from the 200 million dead in those areas would have decomposed and it should now be safe to go into those areas.

The military was tasked with sending troops in hazardous material suits into the worst of the areas and take readings on the soil and environment. This would be the final step before opening up those States to *emigration*. After several months of venturing into the most devastated lands in the union, it was concluded those lands were clean and ready for inhabitants. The real work of reclaiming those States and restoring the Republic to its former borders would soon begin.

Americans who had lived in those areas prior to the cleansing were given the opportunity to be the first people to re-inhabit their former States. They knew there would be a great deal of work to clean up vast swaths of land by burying the remains of the dead in mass graves. There was no shortage of people willing to emigrate into the Lands of Desolation. Those people who had previously lived there would be joined by tens of thousands. People from the 10 Tribes, people who had recently immigrated to the U.S. and thousands of Americans who had survived the cleansing along with a group of military defense forces with medical personnel who were all looking for challenge and a little adventure.

Large cities like Detroit which was destroyed by nuclear weapons were to be avoided except for needed building materials. The leap frog method of reclaiming America was now being employed again to finish the job of restoring the States to the Republic. It would take over three years to clean up the Great Lakes States and the Northeastern Corridor of States. One by one they were brought back into the Union and placed on equal footing with the other States. The one city given very little, to no attention was Washington D.C. The city had been totally destroyed by Russia and there was no point in visiting or restoring our former National Capitol.

It would take several more years to finish cleaning up America from the wars, plagues, and mayhem of the previous years. Every time a group of Americans pushed into a new area the process of restoring the lands continued. Ten years after the 2nd Civil War started, the cleanup of America was officially declared to be complete. The large cities are still avoided to this day. They are however, a great reminder to all of us of what happens when man turns his back on the Lord. There is no point in continuing to look back on our past. We are here in the present and the future is calling to us.

With that being said, and Sharron having no other questions, it was apparent the interview was over. She packed up her gear for the last time in my study and said her goodbye's to Linda and I. She went outside to her car, got in it and waved one last time as she drove away from our house.

It was not long after my final interview when I heard from Michael, David, and Wesley that they had been interviewed by Sharron. Sometime later I received the entire interview on a DVD and book. This included the interviews with everyone involved around me during the fall and cleansing. This book and DVD is now proudly displayed on my bookshelf. It seems to attest to me my life has never been boring.

I wonder what tomorrow will bring to my door.

EPILOGUE

History does not begin when we are born, or with our own personal memories or when we become self aware or conscious. Likewise, it doesn't end when we go to our eternal rest. History is everything that occurs looking back from tomorrow. The future is already known and written by our Creator and is only waiting patiently for us to play our role in it.

As the year 2020 arrives, the masks of the oppressive ideologies we have been discussing and examining, as well as the individuals and political parties who openly embraced the ideology of Karl Marx, in one form or another have been removed in this story. Embracing of *Progressivism, Liberalism, Socialism, Fascism, and Communism* twenty to forty years ago would have meant the end of any politician's career. Furthermore the ordinary citizen would have received deep condemnation while being scorned, ridiculed for embracing such ideologies.

The fall or collapse of America is not a mistake nor is it an unforeseen event. It was planned and implemented with exactness. The implementation of Marxist Ideologies in this nation suffered a few setbacks over the course of time.

These setbacks were at the hands of Presidents who pushed back and stood firm for liberty. Over the last century these politicians were the exception to the rule and once they were out of office the momentum towards *Socialism* accelerated.

There have been many books written as a warning on the impending collapse of America. They all have a common theme and similar storyline. I have now added my thoughts to this collective conscience. I felt it was important to highlight our nation's history in the first seven chapters. I did my best to point out what I believed to be important on how our nation unmoored itself from our Constitution. I did my best to explain why I believe many of our laws and even a few of our Constitutional Amendments added to our downfall.

In conclusion, I firmly believe every person living in this country is critical in fulfilling our nation's destiny. How we act when life and death choices are placed in front of us will determine our ability to survive the turbulent future. I believe those who experience these events will meet the challenge and have more awareness on their own role in history and the magnitude of the individual and their importance in those events. What we do and how we do it is of the utmost importance.

I hope and pray we will not shrink from the challenges and trials that will be placed in our pathway. We must endure to the end.

I hope you enjoyed this book and found it interesting, thought provoking, and worth the time you spent reading it. If so, pass it on and tell others about it and where they can obtain it.

Made in USA - Kendallville, IN
1188322_9780578571850
11.30.2020 1417